THE MIRE

PAINTING A MIRAGE

Samantha Rumbidzai Vazhure

First published in Great Britain in 2020 by:

Carnelian Heart Publishing Ltd
Suite A
82 James Carter Road
Mildenhall
Suffolk
IP28 7DE
UK

www.carnelianheartpublishing.co.uk

Copyright ©Samantha Rumbidzai Vazhure 2020

www.samantharumbidzai .co.uk

Paperback ISBN 978-1-8380480-4-4

Ebook ISBN 978-1-8380480-5-1

Editorial team:
Developmental editor – Daniel Mutendi
Copy editor – Andrea Leeth
Proofreader – Pamela Mumby

Cover design:
Main artwork – Applea
Background artwork – Charles Majange jnr.
Layout – Rebecca Covers

Typeset by Carnelian Heart Publishing Ltd
Layout and formatting by DanTs Media

About the author

Samantha was born in the district of Barking and Dagenham (London, United Kingdom) in 1981, to Zimbabwean parents who were studying in the United Kingdom and returned to Zimbabwe a couple of years after independence. Samantha's father is of Karanga origin and her late mother was Zezuru. Samantha spent her childhood in Masvingo, Zimbabwe where she completed her education at Victoria Primary School and Victoria High Boarding School respectively. She returned to the United Kingdom in 1999 after completing her A levels. She studied Law and Business Administration at the University of Kent in Canterbury and proceeded to study a Postgraduate Diploma in European Politics, Business and Law at the University of Surrey. Samantha works as a financial services professional. She is married to her childhood sweetheart, and together they have two children.

A note from the author

Painting a Mirage is a work of fiction. Many of the events in the story occur in real places, such as the towns and cities in Zimbabwe, the UK and the USA. These are places I have lived or been to, and they inspire my imagination to create realistic fiction stories. Similarly, I use some highlights of my own life to shape a more realistic story, but the details, such as characters and dialogue at such events are entirely fictional.

Other works by the author:

Zvadzugwa Musango – a collection of Shona poetry
Uprooted – a collection of poetry; *Zvadzugwa Musango* translated to English

Editors' notes

From the moment I stepped into the world created by Rumbidzai, I found it quite difficult to stay away from it. As we explored each chapter, and the conflict it presented, I was very curious to discover what was going on with each of the characters, and how they would develop. The cultural and religious themes that Rumbidzai seeks to illuminate work very well with the dysfunctional characters she has created for her novel. I got so attached to the intriguing characters in this story, to the point of feeling they owed me an explanation for their actions. Most characters in the book are enthralling, and I am abashed to admit that I fell in love with the most eccentric of them all, Baba! I look forward to the havoc that Baba promises to wreak in the sequels to Painting a Mirage.

~**Daniel Mutendi**, **Developmental editor**

There never seems to be a dull moment in the book as it feels like every page hits the reader with something unimaginable, unique, or astonishing. The book was a real eye-opener into the Shona culture. There were things I could totally relate with, and on the other hand, there were aspects of the culture that were completely mind-boggling. Vazhure somehow managed to intertwine an education of the Shona society with an engaging story of a young Zimbabwean girl, Ruva. The story takes the reader through the journey of Ruva's childhood living in a society where a woman's sole purpose in life is to get married, and to find a husband as soon as she is 'of age'.

~**Andrea Leech, Copy editor**

When I was asked to proofread this first book of three by Samantha, I did not know the extent of the emotions I would face as I turned the pages. The journey through this book is happy and sad and within its pages, we follow the struggle of a young girl Ruva. It's a journey which takes her to the very limit of her being. I found this book very difficult to put down, and I look forward to reading part two of this trilogy.

~ Pamela Mumby, Proofreader

Acknowledgments

My husband and children,
Thank you for being my biggest cheerleaders, for your unconditional love which encourages my creativity, and for putting up with me when I selfishly turn into a hermit and escape into the world of writing

My family and friends,
Thank you for your unending love and cultivation of my gift of writing through our shared experiences and hilarious conversations

My editorial team,
Daniel Mutendi, Andrea Leeth and Pamela Mumby – thank you for sharing your wealth of insights, and for your interminable patience

God,
My heavenly father who strengthens and guides me in all I do, whose divine expressions flow through my gift of writing

To the readers of my work…

'Our painful experiences aren't a liability – they're a gift. They give us perspective and meaning, an opportunity to find our unique purpose and our strength'
~ Edith Eger

Chapter 1

I did not hold a gun to my mother's head to make her speak. In fact, I do not recall ever asking her to divulge the state of her relationship with my father; but she did.

Mhamha had relocated to the UK from Zimbabwe to work as a nurse in order to pay my university tuition fees. She arrived during my second year of university and I was relieved to have Mhamha to myself. I had looked forward to Mhamha's undivided attention and vicariously shared her relief for escaping. I hoped my relationship with Mhamha would blossom into a more intimate mother-daughter relationship as we got to know each other better. We were now liberated women living in the absence of the fear, obligation and guilt that had plagued our earlier lives.

During my childhood, I had never felt close enough to Mhamha. I was always fully aware of the efforts Mhamha made to show that she loved me; the kisses, the hugs, the lectures, hearty meals, taking us to church every Sunday to ensure we developed into forthright upright individuals. Despite all Mhamha did, I never felt the bond I knew should have existed between us. I could never open up to Mhamha like other children did with their mothers. I was afraid of her affection and protection. I could not trust her.

Baba had come to visit us from Zimbabwe and his mobile phone was resting on a frosted-glass side table in Mhamha's lounge. A text message notification on his phone roused Mhamha's attention. Baba nonchalantly reached for his phone and suppressed a smile. He tensed up his jawline as he clenched his back teeth, then his right leg began to tremor in uncontrollable vigour. The ball of his foot laid firmly on the ground as his knee rapidly jerked up and down. It was his bouncing leg syndrome that prompted Mhamha to grab the mobile phone from Baba's hand and read the message aloud.

"I miss you daddy. Please don't forget to buy me a leather jacket and electric blanket." Mhamha parroted the message from Baba's *small house* with the vigour of a student who had been picked by a teacher to read out a comprehension passage to the whole class. The tension in the room was tangible, so we muted. We had been playing happy families in Mhamha's lounge, watching television, cracking jokes and reminiscing about the good old days.

"Who is sending you this message Davis? Hhmmm? Baba Ruva!" Mhamha's enquiry was uncharacteristic yet calm and stern, as if she was asking Baba a normal question. Her facial expression screamed with quiet pain, and I hoped I was in a bad dream I would soon awake from.

"*Iwe* Gamuchirai, you don't talk to me like that in front of the children, do you hear me?" Baba bellowed.

I had never heard my parents addressing each other by their first names. Next, the couple scrambled for Baba's mobile phone and squabbled as they ineptly removed themselves from the lounge, headed towards Mhamha's bedroom to argue about the message.

I had never seen my parents quarrelling. The only recollection I had about previous dissonance between them was the time Mhamha attempted suicide when I was around seven years old, at our childhood home. Mhamha had called me to her bedroom and started taking several Chloroquine tablets sitting up in bed, saying she had had enough. Then she instructed me to look after the family when she was gone.

"*Usare zvakanaka mwanangu,* take care my child," she bid me farewell then sunk into the blankets for her final sleep. I subsequently rushed to phone Baba at work, who in turn commissioned our family GP, Doctor Mbeva, to dash to our home to induce the expulsion of pills Mhamha had ingested. After the incident, no one ever shed light to me on what had happened, and life carried on as normal.

Tension colonised the atmosphere in the days that followed the text message incident, as we feigned normal respectful conduct with Mhamha who was clearly still upset, and Baba who was embarrassed because he got caught cheating, but was not sorry for what he had done. Baba seemed annoyed that Mhamha had exposed him, but he offered his usual punchlines and prolonged, loud boisterous laughs that made us doubt our perception of what had actually happened. I understood the situation painfully and distinctly remember that event marking the very first time I felt pure disgust for Baba, for being precisely the opposite of what he raised me to be – a good, compliant perfectionist. It was also the first time I felt disappointed by Mhamha who had raised me to be humble but forthright, truthful at all times and calling out misdemeanours of any sort.

I had indeed learnt these principles the hard way growing up. I as the eldest would have been beaten up thoroughly for my younger siblings' non-compliance, because I should have known better and should have stopped and reported their misbehaviour. I should have been the exemplary one, the perfect one who made no mistakes. Yet here we were, faced with the reality that Baba was not perfect after all, and that Mhamha had covered it up all our lives. Inevitably, I felt compelled to choose a side. Without consciously engaging a reasoning process, I naturally chose team Mhamha and mentally declared war on Baba.

I was around 22 years old when Mhamha first exposed my father, the hero she had raised us to know and admire. It was British summer time, and I patiently awaited the commencement of my masters' degree in September, while I rekindled romance with an old flame.

Mhamha had recently upgraded her living accommodation from a room she had rented in her younger sister's house to a three-bed terraced house in a densely populated area in Aldershot. She rented the new accommodation from a rude, elderly landlord of Pakistani origin who never repaired his property. Mr. Khan often turned up unannounced to check that his unkempt investment was not being vandalised by us. The interior walls of the house were covered in grotesque jade green textured wallpaper which reminded me of the colourful tie and dye kaftans worn by African women, except that kaftans were beautiful. A leafy oriental ochre design border broke the green wallpaper in half to create the most incongruous wall design. I blocked out that reality and pretended the walls were white to resist the compulsion to rip the wallpaper off. The senile floral maroon and canary carpet felt dirty no matter how much we vacuumed, so I never walked barefoot on it.

The house had been advertised as "furnished", but it came with two derelict brown velvet sofas in the lounge, one of which had a front right leg missing and was propped by a brick. There were double beds with stained mattresses in each bedroom. The beds had no headboards, an oddity I was not accustomed to. Quasi-functional obsolete dark wooden wardrobes were placed in each of the three bedrooms. They were ugly and tattered in a way that made me think ghouls hibernated in them and might break out at night to wake me from my slumber. Had the wardrobes been in a beautiful house, they may have qualified as "antiques in need of restoration".

I tried unsuccessfully to avoid imagining the tenants who might have lived in Mhamha's house before us. We avidly smeared bleach everywhere we could, and wiped surfaces with antibacterial spray to gain comfort that we would not catch unwanted surprises that might have been left by previous occupants. Mhamha insisted she would return to her home in Zimbabwe eventually, so she would not invest in furniture or anything that contributed to her comfort while she lived in the UK. I despised the physical appearance of Mhamha's imperfect home, which was nothing like our *bonne maison* in Zimbabwe. However, I could not bring myself to share my honest thoughts with her, because I knew the progress Mhamha had made on her own in the UK was a significant achievement.

I decided to sacrifice a little over £200 from the money I was saving for my masters' degree to buy a few modest accessories to make Mhamha's house more habitable.

Two beige soft faux fur throws with matching cushions to cover the hideous sofas, chrome and medium density fibreboard breakfast set for the kitchen. A coffee table with a matching nest of chrome and frosted glass side-tables for the lounge, one of which had been holding Baba's mobile phone when he received the contentious text message. I had also bought a plain metal Roman numerals kitchen wall clock that we hung up in the lounge. Whenever I travelled to Zimbabwe for holidays, I always brought back curios and crafts that I hung up and dotted around the rooms to make Mhamha's house feel more homely. Mhamha lived with me, the younger of my two brothers, Tongai and my sister Runako. The accommodation was sufficient for our needs, and I learned to accept that reality. There was also something very comforting and liberating about living imperfectly within a community that did not judge or have great expectations of us.

A year or so before Mhamha made the decision to emigrate to the UK, Baba's youngest brother, Babamunini Benjy, had taken his own life. He had been found hanging from the ceiling of the one-bedroom he rented in a shared house located in a high-density suburb of Masvingo. Such areas were commonly known as "ghetto location", or simply *rokeshen*. My uncle had behavioural challenges that nobody cared to acknowledge or resolve. He was depressed and had taken drugs for as long as I could remember, drank excessively, and lived a very wilful life, as did most men in my family, and many of the men within the society I grew up. Despite being a very intelligent boy, he was labelled as one who had managed to sabotage his progress in life and resisted everyone else's efforts to raise and mentor him into a respectable man. Amongst several dramas, he had been involved in arson at a rural mission boarding school to which he had been sent to help him focus on his education with less distractions. He had naturally been expelled from that school and got arrested.

In addition to that incident, there had been reports from the same school that Babamunini Benjy and his cronies were notorious for stealing pigs and goats from nearby homesteads, which they slaughtered and roasted in the wild to get relief from unpalatable boarding school food. Prior to that, he had also been expelled for drinking from a city boarding school, where he had been accepted because the head of the school was a relative. There had been numerous other incidents highlighting his emotional and mental instability; yet we had been conditioned to laugh and joke about it, and indeed talk about it as if it were nothing.

After my uncle was found dead, a bombardment of abuse and humiliation of Mhamha by my angry paternal aunts followed, as they publicly claimed that Mhamha was the cause of my uncle's death. We lived in Masvingo, a very small town where my parents were well-known and respected. My paternal aunts who lived in larger cities, had descended on our home and hurled profanities to Mhamha, in the presence of people who respected her and had come to pay their last respects to Babamunini Benjy. It was a widely held belief in Shona culture that when someone died, someone must be blamed for it regardless of the cause of death. Accidents, illnesses or even suicides were never considered valid causes of death. Instead, an unsuspecting, innocent, unfortunate individual was picked and the blame for death was placed on them – a heavy burden they would take to their grave, as I learnt the hard way through Mhamha's experience. Mhamha had apparently sold my uncle's soul to the spiritual realm in exchange for successful businesses, *kuchekeresa,* my aunts claimed. That was their story and they stuck with it.

The aunt who led this offence, Tete Gwinyai, had fallen out with Mhamha a few weeks before my uncle died. Someone had left money to be passed on to my aunt at one of our shops, and Mhamha had taken it as settlement for a long-standing debt owed to her by Tete Gwinyai. Being a gambling addict, she had habitually turned up at my parents' shops and intimidated staff, demanding money from the tills or groceries from the shelves, with no intention of ever paying back. She had an astounding sense of entitlement, which she imposed not only on all her siblings, but friends, relatives and anyone who knew her. Tete Gwinyai, the eldest of Baba's sisters, was also the most charming woman who had the gift of convincing people to repeatedly lend her large amounts of money, none of which she paid back. Growing up, I could never decide whether it was her beauty or brains that did the job. I thought she had both.

My parents studied in the UK in the seventies, after Baba received a Rhodes scholarship to study Politics, Philosophy and Economics at the University of Oxford. He had been awarded this privilege for achieving the best A level results in the country, he told us. Mhamha followed Baba to the UK and studied nursing in Peterborough. My parents had met on a train in Rhodesia, on their way to boarding school, in their early teenage years. Mhamha would travel to a mission school in the South West region of the country, passing through the Midlands, where Baba attended secondary boarding school. Their love blossomed quickly into a whirlwind romance promising a lifetime of bliss.

The liberation struggle in Rhodesia was in full swing during this time. My paternal grandfather, Sekuru, was a well to do businessman, community organiser and secret humanitarian who had been providing food and clothing to guerrillas fighting in the war. In the late seventies, Sekuru had been travelling back to his rural homestead in Chivi about 60km south of Fort Victoria, when he was stopped by Ian Smith's soldiers, searched and killed for being in possession of provisions for the liberation guerrillas. Sekuru was hit in the face with the back of an AK47, which broke most of his facial bones and damaged his brain. He called out for Baba on his deathbed, until he passed away. Sekuru had been planning to visit Baba in the UK, but Baba had discouraged and postponed the visit due to exam pressure. By this time, Baba had graduated from Oxford and was training to become a Chartered Accountant with one of the "big four" firms. The untimely death of his father left a chronic oozing lesion on his soul.

I was subsequently born in London in the early eighties, where my parents worked. I came at an inconvenient time, so Baba arranged for one of his sisters, Tete Gertrude to come and take me to Zimbabwe, where I would be raised by my paternal grandmother, Mbuya, in Chivi. Mhamha was neither consulted nor involved in these arrangements. Our separation tattooed an everlasting scar on our relationship. A detachment that birthed separation anxiety and a plethora of abandonment insecurities that would torment me for life.

When Baba completed his articles and qualified as an accountant, he returned home to take on the role of father to his eight siblings. Baba arrived in Zimbabwe at the age of 27 and received several executive career opportunities from reputable multinational firms based in Harare. Mbuya, however, had other plans. She decreed that Baba would carry on the family legacy by finding a job locally, simultaneously managing the family businesses, and helping her to raise the other eight. In return for that inconvenience, Mbuya bought him a brand-new Volkswagen Golf and provided a £20,000 cash deposit for a large property in Masvingo, whose mortgage my parents would service. This became our home, with vast farming land, a large five-bedroom main house with several reception rooms, a separate large three-bedroom grandparents' cottage several yards away, a secluded drab four-bedroom servants' quarters, a large swimming pool with nearby detached changing rooms, tennis court and immaculately manicured gardens.

Although my parents were already married when the properties were gifted to Baba, only his and Mbuya's names appeared on the title deeds to the property, including the businesses Mhamha later managed after sacrificing her nursing career. His financial partner was his mother. Baba worked briefly for a local accountancy firm before beginning a career as a senior official of the city council in Masvingo. During this time, Baba ensured all his siblings were educated in reputable institutions and played the role of father in their lives. He had been the one to interrogate their boarding school shopping lists, asking his teenage sisters patronising questions which always made them leave for boarding school heartbroken and in tears, "Why do you need tinned beef? Why lotion instead of petroleum jelly?"

Baba had also been the disciplinarian, inflicting a variety of methods to keep the herd in line. A *mboma*, hippo's tail whip, was one such tool he did not hesitate to unleash on troublemakers. Babamunini Benjy had on several occasions presented delinquencies that warranted the *mboma* treatment. One such instance was when he decided to take Baba's collectible classic Mercedes on a joyride out of town with his friends without Baba's permission. When my uncle returned, Baba fumed with rage and barked, *"Uri duzvi remunhu haikona?!* You're a piece of shit, aren't you?!"* then propelled several punches into my uncle's face, before finishing him off with the *mboma*. *Mboma* beatings seemed to silence my uncle only when the wounds were fresh, but the chastisement aggravated his behavioural issues once the physical pain wore off.

On quiet days, Baba would occasionally bring out the *mboma* and let us touch it and feel it, as a gentle reminder that non-compliance was not tolerated in our home. A gentle tap on the hand with the *mboma* tip left one's skin itching aberrantly. When challenged by inquisitive visitors why he needed it, Baba would declare that its main use was to hit snakes and other wild animals that might have trespassed into our house, then he would burst into a roar of contagious laughter. He claimed that one strike with the whip would break a full-size cobra or python in half. Depending on his mood, age of perpetrator and perhaps the severity of misbehaviour, gentler tools such as leather belts, mulberry tree branches and his own fists, were very much at his disposal.

Baba was also very charitable. He not only funded his siblings' education, but he extended his kindness to distant relatives. Anyone remotely related to us who had the potential to excel but could not afford to pay for their education was taken care of. Baba enjoyed feeding the masses and felt obliged to provide food and medicines to distant relatives who were not his responsibility.

Chapter 2

From a very young age, I sensed a growing fear and resentment by Baba's siblings towards him. Occasionally, they would descend on our home and after devouring five-star meals that Mhamha always managed to produce, the children were sent to bed. Arguments and tears followed, and sometimes we woke up to find that our aunts and uncles had driven back to their homes in other towns, drunk and upset. It was at such events that Mhamha was usually singled out and verbally terrorised by Baba's family. Baba neither defended Mhamha nor participated in torturing her, but instead he watched and stated he would not get involved. One such occasion was when Mbuya tried to impose a sanction on my parents, which Mhamha challenged. Mbuya had then quickly shifted the conversation to the fact that Baba loved her more than he loved Mhamha, so she would have the last word. The two argued persistently about who was loved more, while Baba absorbed the debate in silence, until Mbuya posed the question to him directly, "Tell us now Davis, once and for all, who do you love more, me or that wife of yours," to which Baba responded by leaving the room.

There were only two *varoora*, daughters in law, in Baba's family; Mhamha and one of my uncles' wife, Mainini Gemma. *Varoora* were very easy targets of emotional abuse because they were, culturally, viewed as inferior alien beings. Mainini Gemma, stopped turning up at family events when she had had enough, and was considered a rebel. No one confronted her absentia, however, and she seemed to earn herself some respect by not playing the games my family liked to play. Mhamha, on the other hand, religiously delivered kindness and first-class service to her persecutors. I never understood why Mhamha continued to care and look after people who clearly did not love her. Perhaps it was what she was taught to do, at those long after-church women's meetings she attended every Sunday while my siblings and I waited for her in the blazing sun after Sunday School.

There was no culture of authenticity, and pathological lying was a common family trait which was never rebuked, and so it was unconsciously encouraged. This unfortunately meant even those who told the truth were also not trusted but were often labelled insane. Mhamha despised these family features and was known for what they called "cash talk", which opened her up to further animosity. As if she suffered with Tourette's syndrome, she often shocked everyone by announcing the truth, usually in a short single sentence, when she felt tired of listening to fabricated accounts of events that had or had not happened. "*Inhema*! It's a lie!" was one of Mhamha's usual once and for all responses to predictable mendacities.

We were taught to forgive and love one another regardless of the repeated pain we inflicted on each other as a family through endless spectacles. Interestingly, love was taught without the mention of the word "love", or the accompanying actions to exhibit the feeling. Forgiveness translated to forgetting, and there was a default expectation to forget previous offences, and to keep one's guard down in readiness for subsequent violation. Our family loved drama and therefore cherished celebrations – weddings, graduations, birthday parties, Christmases, and funerals too. The order of these events was very expectable. Everyone turned up seemingly contented, then got drunk and left feeling very angry and unrecognisable. As I grew older, I learnt that family functions were extremely important to our family, because they presented an opportunity to reunite without apologising or addressing previous issues. Sometimes, those who got drunk and angry were simply airing their frustrations over unresolved issues. They became nasty and dished out offenses they would later deny, claiming no recollection of their behaviour.

Our family was well equipped with beautiful and handsome faces, academically smart, charismatic characters who loved to laugh and live large. There were, however, roles in the family that were assigned to selected individuals whose conduct was dictated. There were caretakers required to be compliant and do as they were told or suffer harsh consequences if they did not. There were others who got away with doing whatever they wanted, with no repercussions, and were usually rescued by the caretakers when things went pear shaped. The latter seemed to receive love and forgiveness no matter what they did. Double standards were the norm, and those affected by family hypocrisy were made to doubt their truths. In fact, they were quite often labelled "crazy" in order to discredit their grievances.

One of Baba's sisters, Tete Vimbai, was a beautiful, obedient, perfectionist. She had met her husband to be, Babamukuru Batanai, at a local mission boarding school. He had been a haughty, egotistical senior student who had transferred from another high school to my aunt's mission school. As a son of a successful businessman, he felt justified to beat other kids up and tortured those who did not comply with his irrational demands. With permed hair and tight-fitting pants, most girls worshipped the ground he walked on, but he was condescending to everyone except Tete Vimbai. He was despised by many and nicknamed the "Prince of Soul Glo" by my uncles, like Darryl Jenks in the movie 'Coming to

America'. Most onlookers had feared their union was a blatant mismatch that would not end well.

Like clockwork, Tete Vimbai had completed her GCE O-level, then went on to A-level to study subjects Baba had chosen for her, one of them being Economics which she did not enjoy and was not particularly good at. Naturally, she was made a school prefect. Despite being quite sharp, my aunt attained average grades as a result of studying subjects she was not especially competent in, then went on to complete a Secretarial course.

Tete Vimbai was subsequently employed at a local car dealership as the Personal Assistant to the owner of the business. At this time, she lived at the grandparents' cottage on our property, as did Baba's other siblings who had completed their education but were not ready to move out to live independently. I spent a lot of my spare time with my aunt during my primary school years, learning to be just like her. She loved sewing, and she would make me adorable little outfits that I would wear with love and pride. She would teach me to wear make-up, and I looked forward to wearing clothes she made me for mufti days at school. On one occasion, when I was around nine years old; I had worn a mini skirt and tank top Tete Vimbai had designed and made with make-up on. I felt beautiful in my yellow outfit with red polka dots. I returned home to find a disgusted look on Baba's face, who told me I looked like a whore, should stop dressing like one, and to wash the make-up off my face immediately.

Tete Vimbai and I spent a lot of time listening to American soul or rhythm and blues music. She would fuss over her weight and I would join her jogging sprees, although never quite understanding why such a beautiful woman would ever doubt her perfection. Babamukuru Batanai would turn up, and sometimes park his car outside our property, several yards down the road, to avoid any encounters with Baba. He would take us out for meals and buy me ice cream. Everything seemed perfect, except that Mbuya called Babamukuru Batanai "a snake in the grass". Babamukuru Batanai's father had been a regional salesman of household goods before establishing his own family business, and Mbuya knew him as a conniving colporteur. He was the "bigger snake!" Mbuya insisted.

Babamukuru Batanai married my aunt, made her resign from her job, and they moved to a leafy low-density suburb on the other side of town to start their new life. Tete Vimbai got pregnant and when she was ready to give birth, she moved back home briefly to have her child, a common cultural practice among the Shona, known as *masungiro*. This practice involved a man's relatives chaperoning their daughter in law back to her parents, with gifts such as livestock and money, so that her own relatives saw her through the childbirth and healing process, until she was ready to return home to resume her wifely duties. There were traditional beliefs that regarded this practice crucial. There was a need for the administration of traditional medicines that eased labour and avoided caesarean sections. These medicines were only allowed to be dispensed by the expectant mother's relatives, *kuvhura masuwo*. Another belief was that a blanket was meant to be placed over a doorstep, then trodden over by the expectant maternal grandparents to avoid their suffering from chronic backache. Many women also lost their lives during childbirth. *Masungiro* transferred that risk to the woman's family, so that the husband and his family were not held accountable if such a misfortune took place. My aunt had a healthy baby boy, James, who I loved dearly.

Within a few days of delivering her child, Tete Vimbai developed a peculiar illness. She first woke up with a patch of hair mysteriously shaven off the back of her head, leaving a bald patch. One day, not long after Tete Vimbai's hair had gone missing, after her morning bath, she sat at her dressing table to begin her daily facial cleansing ritual, then instantaneously lost her sight. She subsequently presented convulsions, her body tossing to hit the ceiling then falling back on the ground, then went stone cold, as if she had died. Mbuya was in Tete Vimbai's bedroom when this happened, as she was helping to mind the new-born baby. For several months, Tete Vimbai's symptoms included spasms, hallucinations and loss of speech. Medical doctors tested her for all possible illnesses related to her symptoms, but test results were negative, and they could neither explain nor diagnose her ailment. Doctors specifically ruled out Epilepsy because Tete Vimbai did not froth at the mouth, a symptom they deemed necessary for the diagnosis. A specialist intensive care medical team at a big hospital in Harare recommended Tete Vimbai be seen by traditional healers, as what she suffered from could not be fixed by Western medicine and was from their perspective *chivanhu,* that is, to do with blacks or witchcraft.

At this point, our family patriarchy was considering refunding Tete Vimbai's bride price or replacing her with a young healthy female relative, as would happen in similar circumstances in Shona culture. *Chigadzamapfihwa* was a form of marriage where a man was given a wife by his in-laws to replace his deceased wife, in order to look after the husband and his children. Similarly, *Chimutsamapfihwa* was a form of marriage where a man was given a wife by his in laws to replace a living wife who no longer wanted to have sexual relations with her husband, or who could no longer have children. In both cases of these arranged child marriages, the beneficiary selected a suitable girl of his choice, preferably one of bleeding age, a sister or niece of the wife to be replaced, who would be handed over with no questions asked. The patriarchy of the wife to be replaced had the discretion to apply these traditions to similar circumstances, as in Tete Vimbai's situation, where a wife was deemed useless to her husband.

Our family and Babamukuru Batanai's family took recommendations and agreed to jointly visit a reputable *n'anga*, a traditional healer. Upon arrival, the *n'anga* without being told the reason for the visit, apparently stared at my sick aunt's mother in law, Mai Godo, and asked her how dare she waste everyone's time, bringing them to a *n'anga* when she knew what she had done. In that moment, Babamukuru Batanai who was aware of his mother's reputation in witchery, got up and screeched, *"Mhai hamurevesi!* Mother, you can't be serious!"* then severely battered his mother, throwing fists into her face, kicking her in the stomach and spitting on her. Babamukuru Batanai was only restrained when everyone present had finally got over the shock of what had happened. The *n'anga* explained that certain magic potions and evil supernatural beings had been strategically placed in the grandparent's cottage at our home where my aunt lived, and at my aunt's mother in law's home. These items were to be removed by a specialist, in order to reinstate peace and health to our family. The *n'anga* warned them that the specialist had to be very strong spiritually, because they could lose their life on the job, if the supernatural beings overpowered them.

An exorcism pundit was identified, who agreed to travel back to Masvingo, via the Godo residence in Chivhu, where my aunt's hair was found in the ceiling, mixed with sand and strange looking beads. At our home in the ceiling directly above Tete Vimbai's bedroom at the grandparents' cottage, where she had initially lost sight and began convulsing, an army of wild black cats and strange beings that resembled featherless chickens with human-like faces were found living in a massive black hat. These beings had apparently been beating Tete Vimbai up, tossing her around and keeping her unwell. The exorcist successfully removed and burnt the beings with petrol. Tete Vimbai immediately got better, and could see again, but she had lost some of her memory and forgot she had had a child, so she refused to breastfeed him. Further trips to traditional healers who performed various healing rituals restored Tete Vimbai to normal health, but she was told she could no longer have children.

I remember how odd it felt speaking to my aunt again. There had been very restricted access to my aunt during her time of illness, so seeing her again and speaking to her felt strange. I wondered if she remembered me and everything we had done together over the years; she did, and I was relieved.

By the time Tete Vimbai recovered to normal health, Babamukuru Batanai had disowned his parents and siblings. Rumour had it that Babamukuru Batanai had impregnated a woman before marrying Tete Vimbai, denied responsibility and left the woman defiled. Mai Godo preferred the other woman, whose mother was also a well-known witch. It was believed that when Tete Vimbai got married and had James, the bitter mother of the woman who had been impregnated teamed up with Babamukuru Batanai's mother to bewitch Tete Vimbai, hoping to dislodge her from the marriage and kill her.

A few months after my aunt's recovery when I was around 13, I began to notice I was no longer allowed to visit Tete Vimbai at her house. Whenever I suggested going to visit her, I was always given an excuse to not go by the grownups. James was a little over two years old when our house phone rang, and hysterical screams followed. I had no idea who phoned, but our housegirl, Sisi Fungai, picked up the phone, listened attentively, then dropped the phone momentarily, displaying dramatic tremor-like movements, then announced in a stammer that Babamukuru Batanai had shot himself in the head and Tete Vimbai was nowhere to be found. Sisi Fungai had returned the phone to her ears and hysterically wailed into it, dancing around like she desperately needed to pass water.

Babamukuru Batanai had written a suicide note stating that he had to take his own life because of something Tete Mary and her boyfriend had told Tete Vimbai, then left directions to where to find Tete Vimbai. Babamukuru Batanai's father, VaGodo, and Mhamha had been the first to arrive at the scene of my uncle's shooting. They had been called by Tete Vimbai's housegirl after she had heard the gunshots fired by Babamukuru Batanai. It later transpired that Mhamha was the person who had called our landline to inform us of the shooting, but while she was on the phone, VaGodo had taken his son's suicide note and disappeared with it. At that point, Babamukuru Batanai was still alive, but he later died in an ambulance on the way to hospital.

Baba's youngest sister, Tete Mary, was often dragged into Tete Vimbai and Babamukuru Batanai's drama triangle and had blown the whistle several times to our family patriarchy that Tete Vimbai was depressed and falling apart, but she was told to mind her own business and labelled "crazy".

It transpired after Babamukuru Batanai disowned his family, that Mai Godo had been further enraged, then employed less aggressive methods to displace Tete Vimbai from her marriage to her son. Tete Vimbai began experiencing migraine headaches that were always coupled with visualisation of multicoloured auras that hindered whatever she was doing when the episodes attacked her. She could have been performing household chores or driving, or in bed with her husband, but she had to stop and wait until the episodes passed on. After a while, Babamukuru Batanai's older brother introduced him to a woman who would take care of his needs, as Tete Vimbai had proven useless as a wife. Babamukuru Batanai began emotionally abusing Tete Vimbai as his affair with the other woman got out of hand.

Tete Vimbai blew the whistle but was advised by our family patriarchy to suck it up, because that was what marriage was about. Her complaints would have been met by a common Shona cultural retort, *"Kurohwa warohwa? Kudya wadya? Kukwirwa wakwirwa?* Have you been beaten up? Have you eaten? Have you been bedded?" If a woman was not being beaten up and was being fed and slept with by her husband, it was generally considered that her toxic situation was not serious enough. The other woman had been contacting Tete Vimbai, revealing details about the affair, including lying to my aunt that she was expecting Babamunini Batanai's child.

Helpless and distraught, Tete Vimbai gave in to the fact that if Babamukuru Batanai could not love her alone, there was no point in remaining married. If there was no point in remaining married, then there was no point in living. As a devout Catholic, Tete Vimbai did not believe in divorce but received no marriage counselling. When she had had enough, she took her own life, and her son's.

A few days later, Tete Vimbai and James were found dead, decomposing in her car at a farm out of town, in a secluded location. It had taken our family and the police longer than usual to find them, because Babamukuru Batanai's suicide note could not be found, and VaGodo denied retrieving it from the shooting scene. Eventually, a military helicopter was dispatched to search for the missing duo. Tete Vimbai had fed James rat poison and taken some herself. Her post-mortem revealed she was a few months pregnant.

Tete Vimbai left long suicide letters to various members of our family explaining why she had taken her own life, but I was around 13 at the time, considered too young, so was never given the opportunity to read them. In a letter to Mbuya, Tete Vimbai had said to her mother, "That snake you warned me about finally bit me." I overheard grownups saying Tete Vimbai had tried fasting alongside novenas. It was obvious to me even as a child, that none of the help she had been offered by the grownups had worked for her.

What followed was a series of events I could not relate to. People gathering, speculating on the reasons behind the suicides, crying uncontrollably, and a funeral. I had never been to a funeral, let alone a funeral for three people in one sitting.

On the day, I felt blue like the sky that hovered above us. It was a blazing hot day and the atmosphere reeked of rotting bodies. An odour akin to the troubling whiff of a putrefying rodent hidden in unfamiliar nooks and crannies of a residence to which one was acquainted. Except we helplessly faced the fetid bodies of souls whom we knew and loved deeply. Tete Vimbai and James had started turning green and grey on some parts of their bodies.

Family members took turns to consistently spray air freshener around the coffins, in an effort to neutralise the stench. House flies were very much part of the gathering, travelling freely between the rotting dead bodies, pit latrine toilets, our sad wet faces and food cooking in massive rusty open top drums. The shocking death of my aunt's family headlined national newspapers for a few days, and the vice president of the country attended the funeral. When he stood beside the graves and began his funeral oratory, reiterating the rumours surrounding the deaths, Tete Gwinyai stood up suddenly and charged towards the vice president. Screaming that she had had enough of his nonsense, Tete Gwinyai pounced on the frail politician and began to beat him down. By the time his bodyguards came to his rescue, the vice president had been clobbered into silence by Tete Gwinyai.

Tete Vimbai's death at the age of 25 was undoubtedly one of the most traumatic experiences of my life. She, her husband and son were buried at Babamukuru Batanai's rural homestead in the middle of nowhere.

After Tete Vimbai's funeral, our family only returned to the burial site once, one year later to mark the first anniversary of the treble death, then never again. Numerous family squabbles to repatriate Tete Vimbai's body to our family graveyard took place for many years thereafter, but our family patriarchy who believed Tete Vimbai had been selfish in taking her own life, and that a married woman should be buried at her husband's homestead anyway, won the debates.

Tete Mary was rebuked by the whole family for talking too much and gossiping to Tete Vimbai about

Babamukuru Batanai's other woman. She was blamed by the whole family and community for her own sister's death.

Chapter

3

It was around the time of Tete Vimbai's death that I developed an unhealthy need for male attention. I had already had a couple of boyfriends at school, but I needed the attention of an older man. I found myself befriending older girls, and before I knew it, a certain older sixth form girl who was having an affair with a Science teacher in the school introduced me to a male friend of hers who said he was 21. I was not yet 14 when I started dating the older boy, Peter. He had repeatedly failed his A level exams and was preparing for another re-take. Peter seemed infatuated by me, religiously studied my movements around town, and knew details about my life that most people did not. Peter had a younger sister, another older girl at my school, who consistently delivered little notes to me from him on a daily basis. I knew I did not love him. He was someone who would have to remain hidden as he was undoubtedly "beneath me", a term that was commonly used to describe men of a presumed inferior status by my family. Once he got comfortable enough, Peter began talking about sex.

I needed love and attention, not sex. I knew sex was a sacred act that should not be taken lightly, but Peter made a lot of effort to make it sound worthwhile. I knew from my Sunday school teachings that sex out of wedlock was a sin, and that at the age of 14, it was also a crime. However, I had no one reliable to talk to about the pressure I was going through, so I said "no" and asked Peter to never talk about it again.

Love, sex or anything of the sort, were not topics that were ever spoken about at home. I distinctly remember feeling too embarrassed to tell Mhamha that I had started menstruating. Mhamha had bought me some sanitary pads, that were part of the initial boarding school shopping list, which I had returned home with each school holiday; until one day "pads" appeared on my new term boarding school shopping list. My period came when I was 13, a rather pleasant surprise which confirmed I was normal and would have children of my own one day. I had gone for a toilet break with a friend during a boarding house gardening session and had screamed at the sight of blood on my underwear, despite knowing why the blood had appeared.

My friend Chipiwa, who had escorted me to the bathroom looked at me with a gentle smile and said, "Awww…You're a woman now." Sanitary pads did magically appear amongst my boarding school provisions, term after term thereafter, and life carried on as normal.

My relationship with Peter was unhealthy. As it progressed, he became controlling and manipulative towards me. He started pressuring me to spend time alone with him, but I would frustrate him by agreeing to meet with him then not turning up. I often instinctively felt the meetings were not worth my while and would simply not show up, despite the efforts Peter had gone to prepare for them. On one occasion, when I had promised to turn up, Peter had apparently cycled a twenty-kilometre round trip to Wimpy, a local fast-food restaurant, where he had bought me a burger and chips. I did not turn up and he was furious. I felt guilty after that instance, and to make up for all the times I had not turned up, I succumbed to spending time with him at his friend's house.

We found ourselves in a tiny rented single room with shared facilities, in a *rokeshen*, very close to Baba's prestigious grocery food and drink retail businesses. When I arrived by taxi, I was surprised to find that our meeting would take place in a dimly lit room with a very high miniature window. It resembled our servants' quarters, where I liked to socialise with our workers during their days off work. I would usually stay outside because our workers hardly spent time inside themselves.

Peter and I sat on a single bed propped by bricks, adorned by a threadbare floral maroon and cream crimplene bedspread, in a room that felt like a prison cell.

"You look a bit tense Ruva." Peter said as he enticed me to drink some cheap whiskey he had bought from Baba's bottle store. I reluctantly tasted the drink which he had mixed with ice cold coca cola in a light green metal teacup. The room was torrid and dusty, and I felt thirsty as we spoke, then drank more.

"May I have some water please," I asked Peter eventually, when I began to feel befuddled.

"I wouldn't recommend the drinking water from here; it's not safe for the likes of you Ruva. It's dirty and suitable only for us *rokeshen* people who are used to it. Your drink should cool you down babe, have a bit more."

Within a short space of time, I had consumed half a bottle of the whiskey. Peter told me how beautiful and sexy I looked, and I giggled a lot, not because of what he was saying, but the unfamiliar sensation of being drunk seemed to make me laugh impulsively. My head spun faster, and that being the first time I had ever consumed alcohol, I passed out.

I was unaware of how long I had been unconscious when I woke up to the pain of Peter on top of me. He was huffing, puffing and sweating, as he slowly tore through my stubborn hymen. "No!" was all I managed to say as I tried to control my gagging reflex. The experience was mind-numbingly painful, unrelatable, disappointing; a feeling I could only compare to forced insertion of an oversized ember into my vagina. A detestable tribulation that cultivated my fear of intimacy. As I tried to push him off me, I asked Peter what he was doing. He told me I had agreed to it, so I was uncertain I was being raped. Tears streamed from my eyes as I told him to stop, then he whispered he was nearly done, *"Ndaakutopedza!"*

Too weak to escape, and confused by Peter's strangely unfamiliar persona, I endured the violation to the end, then felt him pulling out and wrapping his used condom in a newspaper. He had not bothered to undress me, and I worried that my creased dress he had lifted out of the way would draw unnecessary attention to me when I got home. Still naked, Peter walked to a corner in the room where an old cardboard box sat. He opened it to retrieve an ironed maroon men's shirt. As if he was doing me a favour, he handed me the shirt and said, "Here, use this to wipe off the blood," which I did quietly. I put my knickers back on and tried to disregard my upset vagina.

I was disgusted by Peter, and a deep resentment for him saturated my being as he walked me to the taxi that would take me back home. When he said, "Goodbye Ruva," I looked away and knew I would never see him again. *What have I done?* was the thought that ate through me as the taxi drove me home. My head throbbed; I could smell rubber and blood on myself and felt nauseous due to the hangover. I tried to replay my date in an attempt to figure out how it had ended so badly, but I could not make sense of it. Although I did not remember agreeing to have sex, I resolved that it had to be my fault because I should not have been alone with Peter in the first place. With that conclusion, I lost trust in myself.

Despite feeling confused and riddled with shame, I impulsively turned the negative event into a positive experience. Perhaps it was my coping mechanism, but I did not want anyone to pick up on my negative emotions. Mhamha's younger sister, Mainini Joy, lived with us at the time, and I told her a lot of my secrets to seek her validation. When I told her with feigned excitement that I had had sex for the first time, she appeared shocked and disappointed in me.

"What have you done? You are far too young to have sex!" she exclaimed then proceeded to give me a lecture that I had made a very big mistake, inevitably exacerbating the shame I felt. I had wanted to tell her the truth, that I may have been raped, but I could not.

The next day, Mhamha had found out about the rape. She, Mainini Joy and I congregated in my bedroom where Mhamha explained that a local resident had seen me going into Peter's friend's house and had informed Mhamha. As we lived in a small town, this explanation seemed rational and plausible. I suspected Mainini Joy may have sold me out, but it was pointless to dwell on how my mother had actually found out. She knew and there was nothing I could do to change that reality. Mhamha was irate and wanted to know minute details of what had happened, including whether Peter had used protection to rape me. When she found that the risk of dealing with an unwanted pregnancy was minimal, Mhamha stated her intention to report Peter to the police and get the story to the local newspapers. I felt shame knowing that Mhamha knew I had had sex and could not imagine the whole town, the whole country, everyone who knew me, knowing that I had had sex. In fact, Mhamha used the word "rape" in a way that made me feel like I had been defiled. A way that made it certain that no man would ever love me or take me seriously or consider making me a wife.

Like a rotting fruit on a market stall, that was once sweet and fresh, but now imperfect with signs of rotting, I felt useless. A fruit subject to momentary fondling and inevitable return to its owner by dissatisfied potential buyers. I had not realised until that moment how desperately I wanted to get married. Marriage was an escape that would allow me to live my own life as I willed it.

I found myself begging Mhamha to do nothing about the rape and trying to convince her of Peter's innocence.

"I begged him for sex." I found myself confessing. It was apparent that Mhamha took my admission personally as failure on her part, and she took direct responsibility for my failure to keep my legs closed.

Mhamha did not usually beat us up, and when she did, the beatings were moderate and forgettable. On this day, however, when the interrogation was complete, Mhamha descended on me like a dragon, lashing me with several mulberry bush branches she had carefully selected for my waywardness. Mhamha thrashed and flayed my body with all her energy until the branches turned into rope. Rope beautifully transformed into fresh cordage, with wonderful texture and a distinctly fresh botanical smell; it could have braided several magnificent floppy baskets.

Our housegirl eventually burst into the room yelling.

"*Mhamha chimuregai! Zvakwana kani, chimuregai mhani! Rovai ini horaiti!* Please stop Mhamha! That's enough! Beat me instead!" Sisi Fungai pleaded on my behalf as she forcefully removed the ropey mulberry branches from Mhamha's hand, then dragged me out of the room.

I did not cry, but could barely walk due to overwhelming pain, after the beating. My skin throbbed from the corporal punishment I felt I deserved, and a burning sensation resulting from the forceful sex endured the previous day tormented me. Despite being a warm afternoon, I wore my long-sleeved trouser cotton flannel pyjama set to cover up my bruises.

My siblings wanted to know what I had done to deserve such an unusual beating from Mhamha, but they got no answers. The shaming facial gestures and mocking laughs we usually inflicted upon each other following receipt of corporal punishments were not presented that day, which made me feel more ashamed. I suffered in silence.

When Baba returned home from work, my siblings sped to report to him that I had been beaten by Mhamha but would not give reasons why. *"Ruva arohwa naMhamha asi haasi kutaura kuti arohwerwei!"* Baba did not seem surprised by the reports and announced he had had enough of my lack of interest in education and my growing appetite for men. Baba went on to belch that I was turning into a whore like his sisters. With a tone that implied he had finally found an opportunity to relieve his growing frustration with my behaviour, he ordered me to collect several mulberry bush branches that were commensurate with my behaviour, so that he could "teach me a lesson" to strengthen Mhamha's message.

Baba said nothing about the rape. In fact, the rape was never spoken about after Mhamha was done with me. It was quite possible that Baba was unaware of the rape, because first, such an abomination would have been serious enough to get Mhamha in trouble for failing at her job of raising me properly. Second, it was not uncommon for transgressors to be beaten up simply because they had been beaten up by somebody else earlier. The second beater always felt justified to provide a second helping of chastisement for misbehaviour that had warranted a beating in the first place.

I did as I was told and collected several mulberry branches, which Baba thought were inadequate, so he charged to the orchard to pick more branches. I was then dragged into my parent's bedroom by Baba, flung onto the floor like a heavy rug, then received a shower of lashings from all directions like torrential rain on a windy day. I felt physical and emotional pain I had never felt before, whip after whip, strike after strike, on wounds already inflicted. Like a bag of dried maize cobs, I took the pounding. Like a defiant dog that had entered the house and stolen a prime cut of meat, I took the battering. Like a snake that had taken a wrong turn during its afternoon stroll and ended up trespassing a veranda, I endured the assault. I wanted to look at Baba's face to search for an expression of love, but I was afraid. Afraid that I would not find it and afraid of what I might have seen in place of it.

The generosity of Baba's buffeting was coupled with admonitions that made his message to my soul profound.

"*Si! Ya! Na! Ne! Chi! Hu! Re!* Stop! Acting! Like! A! Dirty! Little! Whore!*" Baba yelped, one flog after the other. The pain in his voice convinced me that he too suffered from the lashings, perhaps even more than I who was receiving them.

Feeling powerless and ashamed, I wept stationary and decumbent. After a while, although the thumps kept coming, I stopped feeling the pain. My body felt numb, and for a moment I wondered if this was what Jesus had felt during his persecution, before crucifixion. I may have climbed out of my body because I could see it being pelted by Baba. I fleetingly wondered if I would die that day, then decided I would not. I returned to my body and gathered the little energy left in my core, then found myself rising from the floor. I leapt onto my parents' Queen-size bed, and in that moment of delirium, I stretched out my arms like a performing artist enjoying the climax of their performance. I released a long gush of urine onto my parents' bed and screamed "Noooooo!" then Baba stopped.

A few days later, I returned to boarding school, swollen all over, bruised, limping, unable to explain or describe to my schoolmates what had happened to me. Some deep bruises on my right knee became septic and developed into four boils which could not be ignored. I limped to the sickbay one afternoon for treatment by the boarding school matron.

"What happened to you *mwanangu?*" she asked, shaking her head knowingly.

"I don't know matron. They are just boils that need to be squeezed," was my cold response. When the pus was drained out, I felt immense relief and the wounds began to dry out.

I never heard from Peter or saw him again. I did not attempt to contact him. There was no need to. There was no trust, no protection, no love. After much pondering, I wrote to my parents, acknowledging their lack of love for me and informing them that I would not return to their house when the school term ended. I intended to check myself into a local hostel for homeless children. My wider family found my vicious letter humorously daring and nicknamed it "the cup final". Upon receipt of the cup final, Mhamha came to visit me in boarding school and told me that she and Baba did love me. This may have been the first time Mhamha told me that she loved me. I did not know how to take the words. They were words I thought were only used by men to women they intended to have sex with. Mhamha explained that Baba cried when he read my letter. Baba apparently wanted me to understand that there was no formula to parenting and that my parents were learning and developing their parental role on me as their first child. Without understanding the meaning of Baba's explanation, I forgave my parents.

Following the trauma of being raped and being punished for it, I put my head down at school and focused on the business of being compliant. During my third form in high school, I was selected to be a boarding house monitor. This two-year function involved working alongside an older school prefect to maintain order in the boarding house. The responsibility implied mentorship for future leadership in the school. My new role was followed by extracurricular memberships to the school magazine club, where I contributed and edited articles; the UNESCO club, where I learned to volunteer in the local community; the Drama club, where I got the opportunity to express my emotions. By the age of 16, I had become a role model, mentor and pillar of support for many in my school and local community. The responsibilities empowered me to focus on positivity and my potential to soar. It was around this time that I decided to join the Hockey club. I had never played hockey and was not particularly good at it, but I had become infatuated by a boy called Morris, who I intimately thought of as "Baby".

Baby was an excellent hockey player. He was a clever nerdy boy who had no reason to ever speak to or look at me. Well, he would have looked at me because all the boys did. They all thought I was beautiful and treated me like a celebrity. Perhaps it was because I had entered and won a few beauty pageants in my school. However, after the rape, I began to loathe beauty because I thought it was what had led to the attack. In fact, I felt defiled and stopped believing I was beautiful after I had been raped. I also began to believe that Baba had been right all along, so I stopped dressing and looking like a whore. *A dirty little whore.*

Before the rape, I had entered beauty contests in my school because my youngest aunt, Tete Mary, who was like an older sister to me, had won several beauty titles in Masvingo and nationally. Although my childhood chubbiness had dissipated, I still did not have the height and petiteness of a real model. Perhaps I had won beauty titles at my school simply because I was a relative of a real beauty queen. Comparisons between siblings and close relatives within our family were normal. Younger siblings were pressured to emulate and follow the footsteps of older siblings, so I had at that point found myself unconsciously following the footsteps of Tete Mary. In addition to this, I had already been inspired by Tete Vimbai, Tete Primrose and Mhamha, who had identified their husbands in their early to mid-teenage years and were praised for that achievement.

I was indifferent to the superficial labels, status, or how I looked and simply wanted to be loved unconditionally. I did not want to be loved by a man simply because I came from an important family, for being physically attractive, as a reward for being compliant, or for being great at something. I was exhausted by male attention which I knew was too easy to succumb to and would inevitably end in pain. At that tender age, I had seen enough drama to know there was more to life and relationships than being worshiped for looks and status. I did not need to date boys for money like other girls of my age, some of whom fell in love with local taxi drivers. The predators had suddenly mushroomed in Masvingo, ferrying young naïve girls in brand new Nissan Sunnys and luring them into adolescent pregnancies and polygamous child marriages.

In addition to the modest pocket money I received from my parents, I avidly wrote letters to my aunts and uncles, and they regularly enclosed significant sums of money in their responses to me, so I always had my own money. Yet, I still had the need for male love, so I decided to look for it in what I thought was the right person, for the right reasons. Marriage was the end game dictated by society, and so I began playing it as soon as I could.

I did not want a rich, famous man, or any man that remotely reminded me of Baba. Morris was a calm, down to earth, aloof schoolboy with potential, and that was perfect for me. Together, we would build our perfect life and live happily ever after.

Chapter 4

Most people who knew our family well thought my aunts and uncles were charming inveterate cheats and compulsive liars, who lived two-faced lives and could not be trusted. Mhamha concurred and reiterated this view, all the time.

"Those people know no boundaries!" Mhamha would say in passing, sounding exhausted by Baba's family. I had no idea what boundaries were. Because I had been raised like Mbuya's child, my aunts and uncles felt like my siblings and Mbuya like my mother. I loved them unconditionally and could not understand the need for "boundaries". Mhamha felt like my other mother. I spent most of my primary school holidays visiting Mbuya, with my biological brothers, Tizai and Tongai, together with our cousins,

Tsvakai, John and sometimes their younger siblings. My sister, Runako had been born when I was seven years old and was too young to join us, so she stayed home.

Growing up, my aunts, uncles and their cousins treated me like their youngest sister and this treatment ranged from giving me constructive and destructive advice, to subtle bullying from the younger ones. Obscure bullying tactics ranged from tricking me into eating fresh hot pepper, which they made me think was tomato; or playing aggressive games like *fombo* so that an opportunity for physical attack was created. *Fombo* involved placing a little stick at the top centre of a small heap of sand, then each player was required to scoop off a substantial amount of sand, until the stick fell. Whoever made the stick fall would be chased by the other players, and beaten down, until they tapped a chosen tree in the garden. I was a chubby child and could not run very fast. The others would cleverly ladle away considerable heaps of sand, leaving just enough allowance to ensure the stick would fall when I scooped the sand next. The chosen tree was always too far, so I would always drop the stick and endure assault until I wet myself.

They drilled into my head that Mhamha was not good enough for Baba. They seemed to think she was inferior, and that Baba could have done better by marrying one of the local more beautiful girls. It was common for them to throw hurtful statements at me.

"Can you imagine how beautiful you would look if your father had married Pattie and had had children with her. She had lighter skin and a better body shape than your mother's."

They had several nicknames for Mhamha, which I was aware of but never used myself. My aunts and uncles also had the ability to sabotage a lot of Mhamha's efforts to raise me into a responsible grounded woman. Through them, I learnt to trust no one, including Mhamha. They were my brothers and sisters after all, whereas Mhamha was just my other mother.

My high school holidays were sometimes spent in Harare visiting my aunts. At that age, I no longer appreciated going to Chivi to spend entire school holidays with Mbuya. Tete Gwinyai was divorced and lived with her youngest sister Tete Mary, who was seven years older than me. Tete Gwinyai had the most erratic mood swings, which ranged from inexpressible tantrums, to the warmest expressions of love and generosity. Tete Gwinyai was known for engaging in fist fights and beating people up. She could go from shouting about the most trivial matters, or thoroughly beating up her kids, to dialling a pizza delivery for the masses present at her home within a very short timeframe. Sometimes there were more than 15 of us visiting Tete Gwinyai at the same time. Her younger siblings and cousins, or nephews and nieces.

Fast food was a big deal for us because we only had one fast food and no pizza restaurants in Masvingo at the time. In fact, I was only exposed to a lot of new and foreign lifestyle concepts when I visited Harare, and I found them interesting. Baba took us to dine at the Great Zimbabwe hotel once in a while and interesting events that we laughed about for years to come unfolded there. Sometimes Tizai and Tongai would feast on bread rolls with ketchup whilst waiting for the main course, despite being discouraged to do so, and were too full to eat the food they had ordered when it arrived. Babamunini Benjy and Tete Mary who had spent a significant part of their childhood in Chivi requested *"mupunga nebhekoni"*, rice and bacon, or *"sadza nechidzva chehuku"*, *sadza* with a chicken drumstick, when they were encouraged to order whatever they wanted to eat at the five-star restaurant.

Baba would chuckle at such requests; he often served a rather prolonged raspy cackle that sounded like an animal whose throat was being cut open and its breath had begun to escape through its exposed trachea. When the night was young and he had not consumed much alcohol, Baba sometimes suppressed his heartier laughter. He would then suggest that my uncle and aunt try the buffet options rather than making up their own *a la carte* menu.

As he became tipsy, Baba proceeded to tell us about his induction to fine dining in the centuries-old halls at the University of Oxford in the 70s, where he had attended three course meals dressed in his graduation gown before graduating, because he was guaranteed to graduate, he said.

He mingled with some of the world's most important people at Oxford, he said. Baba had grown up in Chivi, then attended the strictest Catholic boarding schools in Zimbabwe where he recited endless prayers in Latin from primary to secondary school. He now proudly enumerated his foreign Oxford experiences in a pretentious gruff voice and elegant English accent we could not relate to, then burst into his more familiar prolonged boisterous laughter. We laughed along with him, not because we thought his stories were funny, but because we feared and adored him, and not joining him would have exacerbated the awkwardness of his hysterical laughter.

We found the fast-food experience less pretentious and less complicated than the hotel dining experiences and more exciting simply because it was inaccessible to us. When Tete Gwinyai wanted her house to herself to entertain her guests privately, she got her drivers to take us all in several cars to Westgate shopping mall and ensure we each had enough money to buy what we wanted, watch a movie at the cinema and have a meal before being ferried back to her home. That would have never happened back home. There were no shopping malls or cinemas in Masvingo anyway. Our cousins in Harare often laughed at us for living in an undeveloped town that had no traffic lights or skyscrapers.

Sometimes Tete Gwinyai sent all the girls to get their hair braided at a high-end hair salon, and sometimes she would hire hairdressers to come and braid our hair at her home. Sometimes we all went for full body massages, manicures and pedicures, and she paid for it all. Tete Gwinyai lived a very flamboyant lifestyle and had a bartender and two housegirls. She wore designer wear, a concept I first learnt from her in the mid-90s. She would swing into her lounge and proudly announce that she had just insured her Fendi or Versace sunglasses, or her latest diamond jewellery, then erupt into prolonged contagious laughter. I had heard the names of her designer wear mentioned by American rappers on television, but I had no appreciation of how valuable it was. Insuring trinkets seemed like a strange practice to me, as I did not know anyone else who did it.

Tete Gwinyai's home was adorned by the most exquisite furnishings and her en-suite bedroom was a heavenly sanctuary. Her oversized bed had several colour co-ordinated decorative bed pillows. In fact, half her bed was covered by silk and cotton cushions; some with edging or crotchet laces and ribbons, some with gathered or pleated frills, some with deep chesterfield-style buttons or pearls. It looked royal and enchanting, but I still could not help wondering why she needed so many. All the cushion covers and bedding were changed at least three times per week by one of her housegirls, Gogaz. Sometimes she allowed me to soak in her jacuzzi bathtub with exotic bath oils and foam bath. She had bath bombs and salts in varying colours and grain sizes, and a vast array of bathing gadgets I never saw back home. When Tete Gwinyai allowed me to bath in her jacuzzi, she walked in on me and reminded me to shave my armpits and private parts. An introduction to a man would always take place thereafter. The arranging of precarious relationships was Tete Gwinyai's speciality, and they were usually with married or disease-riddled men.

Tete Gwinyai was a well-known businesswoman who ran fashion boutiques, bars, dealt stolen cars and was a casino addict. Her businesses seemed to be as turbulent as her mood swings. She had access to many men and often expected Tete Mary and I to participate in her manipulative tactics to get deals done in her favour. Like a pimpstress, Tete Gwinyai expected Tete Mary to keep her male business associates distracted in any way necessary. As an avid beauty pageant contestant who had consistently maintained her slender figure, many men found Tete Mary very attractive. I was usually used as a dangling baby carrot, because I was never around long enough to be captured and devoured, as I had to return to Masvingo for school.

One school holiday when I was around 15, I heard Tete Gwinyai speaking to a man called Geoff on the phone about me.

"Huya uone chikeke chiri pano, Come and see a little cake I have here."

When he arrived, I was surprised to find that he looked older than Peter. I had not thought about sex since the beatings by my parents, but his age made me think he might expect it. Geoff invited me to sit in his car that was parked in Tete Gwinyai's driveway. He was the son of a wealthy politician and ran a garage in downtown Harare. He was a car mechanic commissioned to fix Tete Gwinyai's stolen cars, but she hoped to get the jobs done at heavily discounted rates, or for free, if I complied.

He stared at me lustfully with his hand firmly placed on my thigh and remarked, "I've heard so much about you baby. You're beautiful Ruva, and I want to make you my wife. I've already spoken to your aunts about this and they gave me their blessings!" I was confused by the conversation and did not speak much. *How could a man who barely knew me want to marry me?* I thought to myself. I had heard that people in Harare lived a fast life, so I rationalised that Geoff's speech was normal in that context. All the men who came to Tete Gwinyai's home walked, drove and talked fast.

The following day, Geoff returned to spend more time with me, and he brought with him a bouquet of red roses and a box of chocolates. I was flattered by this gesture and began warming up to him. As the days progressed, Geoff phoned and came to visit me daily, showing signs of agitation if ever he found that I left Tete Gwinyai's house. I sometimes visited my older maternal cousin Moira, who lived with her husband Alan. I thought Geoff's annoyance with my absences meant he valued me, so I slowly began to trust Geoff and was falling in love with him. I felt attracted to the less glamorous side of him, like his greasy overalls. We had begun kissing in his car one late Friday afternoon, when his mobile phone rang. He addressed the woman who had called him as "sweetie" and arranged the picking up of a child from nursery. Before he hung up, he told her that he loved her.

I was more perplexed by the call than I had been by Geoff's express intention to marry me. Sensing my agitation, Geoff squeezed my thigh and said, "That was Karen, my wife. You kind of look like her actually, except that you're much younger and fresh. I love you too much to lie to you, so I'm going to be honest with you right from the beginning. I'm married and I love my wife, but I love you too. I'm going to have to leave you sweetie because Karen can't pick Junior up from nursery today." I was traumatised by Geoff's audacity. "What, you have a wife and a kid!" was all I managed to say, and he laughed off my concern ever so gently, in a manner that made me question whether I was overreacting.

Afraid of Tete Gwinyai's wrath, I continued to see Geoff while I was in Harare, and I endured more of his conversations with Karen in my presence. I felt immeasurable jealousy that made me certain I could never share a man. When he eventually asked if I was a virgin, I knew exactly what he was after. I generally avoided difficult conversations, so I could not tell Geoff to his face that I was not interested in a relationship with him. I avoided the question and made myself scarce to him when I returned to Masvingo, and the relationship died naturally.

During another school holiday, a wealthy man who owned a car dealership showed interest in me. Thomas was an unmarried well-known womaniser who had moved in with his wealthy uncle in Masvingo during his early twenties. He had had a rural upbringing, had been mentored to run businesses by his uncle, and now owned a mansion and ran successful businesses in Harare. I had returned to Tete Gwinyai's house from a day out and found Tete Gwinyai perched on a stool behind her solid oak home bar. Thomas and his friends had been enjoying her expensive whisky on the rocks whilst networking and negotiating car deals with my aunt.

As soon as I walked in, she announced, "*Heeeeee wako uyo! Chikeke!* That one is yours! Your piece of cake!" to Thomas who grinned in delight and announced that he would take me out that very evening. Tete Gwinyai instructed me to go and bath immediately, in her room, where she followed me and initiated the shaving ritual.

Thomas was in his mid-30s and looked grotesque. He was the sort of man who, no matter how much he cleaned up, and no matter how much money he owned, would always be uncouth. No matter how hard I tried, I found nothing about him attractive. He looked unwell and confidently spoke broken English. I wished he just spoke in Shona, because there was no real need for him to converse in English, especially because he found it so challenging. As we drove out through Tete Gwinayi's electric gates in his Mercedes, Thomas spoke nonstop with the excitement of a little boy who had just scored his first goal. One of the men who had also been sitting at the bar, Thomas's cousin whose name I never caught, was in the backseat, and we would drop him off somewhere before proceeding to our meal. "So, when did you came?" Thomas asked.

When I told him how long I had been in Harare and when I was going back to Masvingo, he exclaimed, "*Eish* going back so soon? I likes you a lot hey! Are you free after dinner? Maybe we can go to my cabin after?"

We stopped at a garage, where Thomas wanted to make an impromptu purchase. As soon as he stepped out, his cousin whispered loudly, "Whatever you do, don't sleep with him! Thomas has AIDS and he's on a rampage, spreading it to young beautiful girls like yourself. Earlier this week, he returned from India where his blood was drained and replaced; I know this because I was holding the fort while he was away. I wouldn't wish what he's doing on anyone, so I felt I needed to warn you. But please don't tell him or anyone else, because I'll lose my job!" Just then, I noticed Thomas stuffing the merchandise he had bought into his pocket as he quickly walked back to the car.

I was shocked by the warning, but I thanked Thomas's cousin for the caution, then we dropped him off at a flat in town. After our dinner at an expensive Thai restaurant, we proceeded to Thomas's mansion where we sat on a sofa in the lounge and attempted to conversate. I was usually easy going and could strike a conversation with anyone, but knowing what I knew from his cousin, I struggled to relax or open up to Thomas. I was almost 16 then, so perhaps our massive age gap did not help the situation. Before I could hint that I wanted to be returned to Tete Gwinyai's home, Thomas began squeezing my thighs and asked, "They are so hard, *kasi* you exercise?"

"Yes, I play hockey. That's why I'm firm," I replied matter-of-factly.

"*Waaaal*, that's amazing! The older women are jellies! I wish they could see this and learn from you. Can I kiss you?" he asked, with a permanent grin plastered across his face.

Before I could respond, Thomas had begun suffocating me with a stale smooch. As he smothered his inflamed lips on mine, he stuck his tongue down my throat, then put his right hand in his pocket and simultaneously unleashed condoms which he threw onto the coffee table in front of the sofa. His grip on my thigh tightened, and he squeezed one of my breasts in the unkindest way, it felt like a teacher's pinch. Shocked by what was about to happen, afraid that I might be raped again, or that if I did get raped, Thomas might remove the condom during intercourse and infect me with HIV, I burst into tears! I wailed in a remarkably quasi-loud discordant manner akin to the cries of the more distant relatives of the deceased at a funeral. Although my reaction surprised Thomas, it seemed to amuse him.

"Are you virgin or something?"

"Yes!" I lied

"*Waaaal,* that's so sweet. Maybe we do this another time hey?" he said, still grinning, and breathing heavily. He got up to stuff the condoms back into his pocket in such a dramatic way, standing so close to my face, as if to parade his erect penis imprinted on his soft denim chinos. As if he hoped I would be enticed to change my mind. How could I give in? Mhamha had given me endless lectures about AIDS, I would not let her down now. Besides, the beating after the rape was still very fresh in my mind. It would have taken a lot more than the sight of a temperamental phallus to turn me on, even if I had not been warned about Thomas's HIV status. I continued to sob, avoiding eye contact with him.

My reaction seemed to excite him further, but my suspicion was that he made an unusual effort to restrain himself, because my family knew him. And on that note, I dodged the bullet. Thomas took me back to Tete Gwinyai's house, and when we arrived at the gate, he said he would not come in. Instead, he opened his glove compartment to retrieve a giant brick of brand new 20-dollar bank notes, tied together tightly by rubber bands. I never counted the money, but there were undoubtedly thousands of dollars, quite an obscene amount of money for a mid-teen girl in the mid-90s in Zimbabwe. When he handed the money to me, I was unsure what the cash was for, so I asked, "Do you want me to pass this on to Tete Gwinyai?" Thomas chuckled and said, "It's for you sweetie. Isn't we're getting to know each other better? That one is for you. Buy yourself some sweets. Once you know me well, I'll teach you grown up things." I felt awkward accepting the money, so I thanked him for it and handed it all to Tete Mary when I got into the house. Thereafter, I feigned illness or pretended to be on my period, whenever Thomas came around. After investing several more outings and expensive gifts with no joy, he eventually gave up on me, probably because he had so many other women at his disposal who he did not have to work so hard for.

Sometimes, Tete Gwinyai walked into Tete Mary's room where we spent hours chatting, and announce, *"Gezai vasikana muende kushop kunomira seri kwe counter, hanzi ma punter haasi kutenga nhasi.* Spruce up girls and go parade behind the counter at the bar, apparently the punters are not buying enough alcohol tonight." We were conditioned to never say "no", so we complied.

I did not dare to disclose my Harare holiday experiences to Mhamha. Going to Harare was a welcome alternative to the permanent state of fear we lived in at home, and I could not afford to sabotage that temporary relief.

Tete Gertrude owned a school and was married to an eccentric man who imposed so many rules on his family, so the visits to her home were scarce and uneventful. We often spent time with Tete Gertrude at her school office. My other aunt Tete Primrose relocated regularly due to her husband's profession which required his family to shift locations.

Baba also had several female cousins who he had raised like his sisters. They were restless souls who often got heavily involved in the affairs of Baba's family and business. Interestingly, as if they did not deliberately throw me in lions' lairs just like Tete Gwinyai, my aunts occasionally threw at me statements like, "You are unlikely to amount to anything. Someone will impregnate you before you complete your GCSEs and you'll be doomed to the life of a trophy wife to some abuser, if you're lucky enough to get married." As I grew older, I developed the discernment to know what not to believe and to distance myself from risky social engagements. Their views also fuelled in me a desire to prove them wrong, so I intensified my perfectionism and mindfully began to work harder at school.

Before the age of 17, I was neither ambitious nor competitive. I was comfortable and felt adequate being ordinary. My focus was always to stay away from activities that warranted beatings, and to do the bare minimum to keep myself out of trouble from my parents. I hated most sporting activities because I believed they exposed my body, which I was ashamed of. As a child, I had had to be consistently mindful to not dress like a whore; and at school I was consistently made fun of for being fat. Athletics involved wearing short shorts, which revealed too much skin, including the darker patches caused by chaffing on my inner upper thighs. Short shorts also did not protect my thighs from the friction that caused the chaffing.

From a very young age, I sabotaged swimming lessons by "forgetting" my swimsuit at home. In the beginning, schoolteachers tried to punish me for this, but they gave up in the end. On one occasion, when I was around seven years old, a female teacher made me take part in a swimming lesson stark naked, because she thought that might encourage me to "remember" my swimsuit going forward. I was laughed at by all the boys and girls in my class, and my hatred for swimming was birthed that day. That hatred later developed into a phobia when I nearly drowned in our own swimming pool at home.

Baba's siblings had visited with their children and had gone to socialise at the grandparents' cottage which was several yards away from the main house, where our swimming pool was located. Tete Gertrude's eldest daughter Tsvakai and I were very close. I had wanted to prove to Tsvakai that I was not afraid of swimming, so against Baba's orders to never go into the pool unattended, I changed into my swimsuit and dived into the deep end of the pool. I could not swim, and Tsvakai who could swim, did not want to break a rule by jumping into the pool to save me. As I was drowning, Tsvakai ran as fast as she could to the grandparent's cottage to alert the parents of the incident, "Sekuru Davis! Mbuya Gamu! Maiguru Gwinyai! Mhaaa! Come quick! Ruva is drowning!"

Baba came sprinting to the rescue, pulled me out of the water and performed some first aid. As soon as I had coughed chlorinated water out of my chest and showed signs of recovery, Baba frantically searched for a branch in nearby bushes to beat me up. When I saw him coming for me brandishing the branch, I leapt up, still dripping wet and ran for dear life. We ran less than two laps around our swimming pool, before he caught up with me, because I felt weak from the near-death ordeal I had just experienced. I received a good flogging and the phobia for swimming set in that day.

Hockey became the only sport I felt comfortable playing. Other than the fact I had a crush on Baby who was good at it, the hockey uniform was less exposing. It was acceptable at my school to wear cycling pants underneath short hockey skirts as long as the colours matched.

I did not particularly like academic learning either. Baba ran an incentive to reward 50 dollars to anyone whose class position was five and above. 50 dollars was considered a lot of money in Zimbabwe those days; when a bottle of Coca Cola cost two dollars. The offer was open to my siblings and I, extending to cousins and the wider family. I had been in a top class throughout primary school but was never in the top five position in those classes because the competition was stiff, and I did not have the energy to compete. In those days, I hated bumping into vaguely familiar faces who were either relatives or family friends that did not shy away from asking the dreaded school holiday question.

"*Wakaita nhamba ani?* What was your class position?" This was a common cultural practice, where all grown-ups felt they were communally raising a child and could ask them what I felt were intrusive questions. One's response to the class position question determined their worth until the next school holiday. When I did not want to disclose my class position, I confidently affirmed to the enquirer that our school reports had not yet arrived. If I was in the company of an adult who already knew my class position, they would respond on my behalf.

"*Unotamba uyu,* she's too playful!"

"*Idofo iri,* she's a failure!"

And if I had done well that term, "*Une njere sedza bambo uyu,* she has her father's brains this one!" These labels, usually projections of other people's fears and shame, became engraved in one's young mind and would linger there into their adulthood.

Before my teenage years, Baba encouraged us to take on acting and performing at the local drama circle, where he was chairman for several years. I enjoyed these times as they developed my personality and life skills. The few white people in our small town hung out in these places and we were exposed to them. We never got interesting parts in pantomimes, partly because we did not have the confidence to be as dramatic as the white kids. Baba always got good parts and it was always a pleasure to watch him acting, despite not fully understanding the meaning of his performances. I particularly remember his exceptional performance as Squealer in George Orwell's Animal Farm, acting alongside his brother, Babamunini Tafara who was Snowball, and Baba's best friend who was Napoleon in the play. Baba performed comedy as Mr. Bean at a talent show once, with Mhamha silently acting beside him as his prop. He also delivered a superb rendition of Louis Armstrong's "What a wonderful world" at a few local talent-shows.

Baba encouraged me to take piano lessons, which he paid for privately until the husband of my music teacher got arrested for sodomising little boys. I loved music and took part in many talent-shows, where my siblings, my cousin Chenai and I would rap and dance. Chenai was the daughter of one of Mhamha's younger sisters, Mainini Rosey. Chenai lived with us for a few years because her mother had a job that required international travel.

One of my favourite performances was MC Lyte's "Keep on keeping on", where Baba played his keyboard as I rapped and danced on stage. People who knew us were envious of how great and united our family was. I knew a lot of people who would have traded places with me any day. These activities stopped when I went to boarding school.

Very occasionally, Baba taught us memorable life skills like drawing a human face symmetrically. Such experiences were memorable, not because there was anything spectacular about them. They were unforgettable because they very rarely happened.

Chapter
5

When I joined high school, the school gave us the option to choose our classes based on our primary school exam results. I signed myself into one of the lowest performing classes and fabricated poor primary school results, which the school did not bother to verify. In that class, I was always in the top two and enjoyed Baba's 50-dollar incentive for a while. Plus, it was a welcome break from tormenting judgement of my intellect from opinionated outsiders. However, it was not long before I was singled out by teachers as having too much potential to be in the class I had assigned myself. I was "promoted" to the second best out of six classes, where I surprisingly still managed to stay in the top five class position. I was a creative child who enjoyed music and the arts. Food and Nutrition was my favourite subject, which I excelled in. I hated Mathematics but loved playing Chess. Apparently, Maths was not our family subject. We grew up on this mantra, so a seed to hate the subject was sown at a very young age.

I did not expect to pass GCSE Maths because no one expected me or encouraged me to do so. It was therefore shocking when my GCSE results indicated I had passed eight subjects, including Maths! During the two school terms preceding my final GCSE exams, Baba repeatedly promised that if I failed Maths, he would make me repeat the Maths exam as many times as necessary at my old school, until I passed it. This surprised me because no effort had ever been made by my parents previously to help me get over my phobia and resentment for the subject. Baba had for the first time arranged a Maths teacher from my school to come to our home and teach me the full GCSE Maths syllabus during the final school holiday leading up to my GCSE exams as a last resort.

The Maths teacher was lovely, but I felt intimidated by her, mostly because she was a Maths teacher and also because she was mixed-race and did not speak Shona. Any non-black people who did not speak the local languages were considered superior. I therefore felt pressured to take Maths very seriously to make the Maths teacher feel she had not wasted her precious time on me. I also feared the prospect of turning up at my school in civilian clothes months later to retake the Maths exam, queuing up at the gymnasium where exams were taken, familiar faces in A level school uniforms walking past, waving subtly, feeling sorry for me and not stopping for a chat. For three months preceding my final Maths exam, I focussed on studying the subject solely, notwithstanding the risk of compromising and failing all my other subjects, but the effort was worth it. Against all odds, I did very well in my GCSE exams and proceeded to A level.

For the first time in my life, I had to think about what I wanted to be when I grew up. Having enjoyed Food and Nutrition, I told Baba that I wanted to study Food Sciences at A level, with a view to managing a big holiday resort or becoming a Nutritionist after high school. Baba stated that Nutritionists were not significant because he had never heard of them; and that women who worked at hotels were *mahure,* whores. He declared I would study Arts subjects with a view to becoming a lawyer, because there was no lawyer in the family, and one was needed to offer free legal advice. Baba also believed I had a better chance of gaining the highest scores in those subjects, so that I would go to Oxford University, like him. Baba jokingly stated that I now had the potential to fetch him a good sum of money one day.

At A level, I studied Shona, Divinity and Literature in English. I had excellent Shona and Divinity teachers and an unconscious incompetent teacher for Literature in English; he had been transferred to my "group A" high school from a rural mission secondary school as a promotion.

It was decided that despite Mhamha's disapproval of my paternal aunts' influence on me, I would go and stay with them in Harare during school holidays so that I received extra tuition in Literature in English. Mhamha's brother, Sekuru Tonderai, was a lecturer in the Linguistics department at the University of Zimbabwe at the time. I met with him daily during the school holidays to assimilate as much knowledge as I could in that short space of time, and it paid off. I was surprised to find that I loved the Arts subjects that the school had chosen for my A level study. My fifth and sixth form years were undoubtedly the best years of my life.

I do not remember having many meaningful conversations with Baba before I commenced my A level studies. I had clearly proven the potential to become important one day like him when I passed my GCSEs and had earned his attention by doing well in school. Although I had been a talkative and confident pre-schooler, I had grown into a quiet school-aged child, and avoided speaking to him, in case I stepped out of line and earned a beating. Even when invited to open up, I could not speak, because I had seen my aunts and uncles being reprimanded when they succumbed to the same invitation. I generally could not express my emotions and suffered internally, so I was labelled "moody" by the whole family and I learnt to live with that tag. I acquired the skills to interact and express myself more freely as an adolescent in boarding school, where I felt less judged, especially when I earned positions of responsibility within the school. It was around the time I began my A level studies that Baba resigned from permanent employment in the city council to pursue politics and was elected member of parliament.

Baba was a high-profile charismatic man with many slogans and statements that lacked emotional intelligence. He always had the last word and laughed a lot. He had a unique ability to end even the most upsetting conversations with a roar of somewhat contagious laughter, which made one question their own reality. One always wondered whether they were justified in feeling hurt or were being ultra-sensitive? He was the sort of person who made people feel privileged to be in his company. People loved him though. The sophisticated, educated man who society put on a pedestal because he had his act together. Baba travelled a lot and sometimes took Mhamha with him on business trips. He brought us small gifts from these trips, and we looked forward to them.

People also feared Baba. Fear in their eyes was plain to see when they spoke to him, even when he laughed hysterically like a free-spirited gentle soul. Baba had an erratic and unpredictable mood. Everyone generally knew to not start any conversations with him unless invited to, or unless he started them himself. Baba operated unsociable hours, generally being awake drinking every night and asleep during the day. Unexpected visitors who turned up unannounced in the morning to see Baba caused our family deep stress. No one really wanted to take on the job of knocking at Baba's door to alert him of the visitors. His responses were always predictable and often ruined one's entire day. A simple *"Pfutsek! Get lost!"* was enough to destroy one's tiny heart.

Baba's younger siblings feared him. I feared him too. On evenings he chose to be home early, he watched the television in silence, and my siblings and I sat close by, hoping for a bonding conversation to ensue, but that very seldom happened. If we dared to speak, Baba would tell us to "shut up". Sometimes, Tizai and Tongai out of boredom, picked a fight or started a farting competition which they called *surirabhundu,* stink ant, that turned our lounge into miasmic Tophet, which Baba ended abruptly by lifting both boys by a single ear and either chucking them outside the house in the dark, or in their bedrooms and switching off their lights. This was a common punishment that made us all terrified of the dark as children. If they dared to scream or kick the door in a panic, they first got a warning *"Ndinokumamisa!* I will make you shit!" If the warning was ignored, they were silenced by a thorough trouncing. On other days, if he thought one was being inconveniently moody, he bellowed the most heart-rending remarks.

"Usangoita sewaminya duzvi iwe! Stop acting like you have swallowed shit!"

When I wore clothes Baba thought were inappropriate, he found the most hurtful and degrading words to make his feelings known.

"Enda unokurura izvo upfeke kwazvo, uri kuita segongi! Go and put on something more decent, you look like a prostitute in that!"

One of the most memorable statements by him was during a graduation ceremony for the University of Zimbabwe, which was broadcast on ZBC1. He had forced me to watch the ceremony with him then casually announced at the end of the program.

"Ndikafa ndisina kuinda kuneyako graduation *ndinopfuka!* If I die before attending your graduation, I will come back to haunt you as a ghost." That was probably the only thing he needed to say to guarantee my graduation. I was terrified of ghosts! Thereafter, Baba reiterated that he had done better than his own father in life, so he expected me to do better than him. As far as he was concerned, first born children were obliged to do better than their fathers, then look after the rest of the family. Parentification was a common family and cultural trait we all accepted as normal. It had been imposed on Baba to look after his eight siblings, and he now hoped to pass the baton stick to me.

Baba was a larger than life character who was relaxed and frivolous with money, compared to Mhamha who was content with frugality and being ordinary. He and Mhamha drove BMW 7 Series that were the envy of Masvingo. Baba loved pleasing the senses and people close to him were conditioned to facilitate his great expectations. Every single day, no matter what time he arrived home, Mhamha would wake up from the sofa where she would have been nodding off waiting for him to produce an elaborate freshly made meal. Most times, he did not eat what we ate, because he could not stomach it. When mediocre meals were served, such as *sadza* with dried *matemba* white bait, served with greens, he would at best nibble crumbs of the food then push his plate away. Baba thought the likes of *matemba*, *ndumba* sugar beans, minced beef and sour milk were inferior accompaniments to any starch and did not touch them. If my siblings and I were around when Baba refused to eat "garbage", we gladly volunteered to take his dishes to the kitchen and devoured the leftovers within seconds. It was therefore in Mhamha's best interests to always prepare delectable two or three course meals to avoid the awkwardness and wasted energy felt when Baba did not eat his food.

Amongst his favourites were fresh mushroom soup as a starter, fried seasoned whole rainbow trout, or jumbo king prawns, served with home-made peeled thin cut potato chips and coleslaw for mains. I hated to imagine the trouble Mhamha went to make her luscious meals a reality. Acquiring fresh king prawns in a small town within a landlocked country was no joke. The main course was always followed by freshly chopped fruit or berries and ice-cream or a warm home-made pudding served with freshly made custard sauce or pouring cream. Baba always proudly announced at family gatherings, including my parents' wedding anniversaries, that Mhamha's cooking was the deciding factor that led to their marriage, and we all laughed with him each time he made this confession. He sometimes proceeded to recite his exquisite Oxford dining experiences and hinted that after such an induction to fine dining, he expected nothing less.

What was more impressive than the meals she prepared for Baba, was the fact that Mhamha never went to bed until Baba returned home. Sometimes Baba arrived home during early morning hours, but despite having to wake up early the next day to do school runs and stock orders for several businesses, Mhamha consistently delivered quality service. As a child, I never wondered whether Mhamha actually enjoyed doing these things she was so good at and was sometimes praised for. I took it for granted that she did. Mhamha did not have a social life. With the exception of a couple of colleagues she had worked with previously and bumped into once in a very blue moon, she did not have time for friends. Mhamha did not like the idea of me having friends either. Every time I mentioned a friend, especially one with local parents, Mhamha seemed to know something scandalous the parents of the friend had done and discouraged association with them. She knew married mothers of my friends who had had affairs with married men, or who were said to be involved in witchery. Mhamha encouraged me to be content with playing with my cousin, Chenai.

Mhamha's custom of discouraging my friendships improved slightly during my later years in boarding school when I diversified my circle of acquaintances by befriending girls from out of town whose parents Mhamha did not know. Mhamha did not mind a couple of girlfriends from my neighbourhood. She knew they were as secluded and protected as I was, so would likely cause me no harm. Mhamha was highly intuitive and could probably sense that the few friendships I had experienced were unhealthy.

Generally, the friends I made liked to get me into trouble through gossiping and lying. I could never understand why, but I knew that most people envied my position of privilege. Their perceived view was that I had it all, and when Mhamha came to visit me at boarding school with a box full of breakages from our grocery store, they thought I was the luckiest person in boarding school. But when I ate the stale crisps and biscuits that had softened due to being ripped open by mice or otherwise, I did not think I was privileged. When I heard others talking about the intimate relationships with their parents that I did not have, I did not feel privileged. I forged more intimate relationships with my aunts and uncles instead, by writing to them regularly, and the pocket money they sent me in their replies would finance my fresh tuck and other luxuries, like cheap perfume.

I attended the Methodist church with Mhamha and my siblings every Sunday. The church was located in the *rokeshen*, where we owned grocery stores and a bar. It was not very far from the one room where Peter had raped me.

The *rokeshen* church services were long and tedious. I often wondered why we did not attend the more concise and predictable service at the branch in the town centre. When I queried this, Mhamha clarified her preference to listen to the Word in Shona, whereas the town branch worshipped in English and that did not touch her soul. Mhamha was a descendent of a former wandering herbalist, who had welcomed missionaries and facilitated conversion to Christianity and subsequent establishment of the Epworth Mission in Zimbabwe. Her family were deeply humble, religious people, closely affiliated to the Methodist church.

Mhamha was to an extent a celebrity in her church and the reality of this situation dictated that Mhamha attended several focus group meetings after the main church service. Men and women met separately to discuss religious issues that affected the respective groups, but the meetings were in actuality political battle grounds that evidently sapped Mhamha's energy. She was at one point challenged to stop bar trading, as running a business that merchandised alcohol was not compatible with genuine Christian practice. In her usual "cash talk" style, she had rubbished this challenge and still turned up at church to face other confrontations. My siblings and I attended Sunday school after the main church service, then impatiently waited for Mhamha to finish the meetings. Baba was Catholic, but he never attended church. He would stay in bed every Sunday and declare that he spoke to God directly while we were out.

At some point during our school-age years, the older of my two brothers, Tizai, decided he would no longer attend church. He started by feigning constipation every Sunday morning, and Mhamha tried several techniques to overcome this hurdle, but it did not work. Mhamha even attempted her tried and tested method of inserting a piece of solid soap into my brother's anus to encourage bowel movement. This was an ordeal all of us experienced when we suffered constipation. On some occasions, if Mhamha had the time, she combined the soap method with the safety pin method, where she would make one lie horizontally across her lap, face down, then pick and coerce the stubborn faeces with the back of a large safety pin, until the passage was relieved. When Tizai's consistent constipation launched, soap was inserted into his back passage every Sunday morning and nothing came out. We eventually left him behind sitting on the toilet, only to find him well again after church. Mhamha ultimately gave up on waking him up to go to church on Sunday.

Unimpressed by Mhamha's efforts, my younger siblings reported Tizai's delinquency to Baba, hoping he would force Tizai to resume church attendance. Baba's indolent attempt to resolve the matter comprised a perfunctory question, *"Ko unoregerei kuinda kusvondo nevamwe iwe?* Why have you stopped going to church with the others boy?"* Tizai's mumbled response to Baba marked the end of that conversation, and just like that, he was vindicated.

When I began my A level studies, with Divinity as one of my subjects, I gained the confidence to convince Mhamha to allow me to attend the Methodist church service in town.

"Attending the English church service will aid my Divinity study." I explained.

"I also know a few schoolmates who attend the town centre branch, so we can have Divinity group discussions after church, while I wait for you to finish your meetings in the *rokeshen.*" Mhamha honoured my request and I was granted my first taste of liberty.

The Church taught me to be obedient, and I understood obedience. The reality of my life gave me no choice. Church taught me to judge not. I did not understand the practical implications of that directive. The reality of my life was that everything was either good or bad, even if it had nothing to do with me. Church also taught me to love neighbours and enemies, but never myself. The love for oneself was assumed through scriptures ambiguously delivered, which neglected to elaborate how one was to love themselves. This turned me into a judgmental perfectionist with no self-compassion. By then, I had also learnt through Baba's intermittent attention, that I had to work very hard for love, because it was scarce.

Although Baby and I knew each other from the age of 13, we began dating during our A level study at the age of 17. He studied Maths, Physics and Chemistry and still played hockey. By then, I had been made the captain of the Girls Hockey First team. Both of us were school senior prefects. I had been appointed boarding house head girl and president of the UNESCO club, School Magazine club and Drama club. Although I was very busy with unending extracurricular responsibilities and the burden of studying, I always made time for Baby. From when we started off as friends, through what felt like a long courtship, to when we became an official couple, I would drop whatever I was doing just to be with Baby. I had become petite and more confident in my being. We were not ashamed to walk around the school holding hands and kiss behind the school tuck shop and other outbuildings. We were often startled by the school groundsman during lengthy snogs. He would magically appear like a mobile scarecrow and shoo us like birds that had landed on a crop field.

Baby and I were not uncomfortable talking about humiliating aspects of our childhood. We would share our common bed-wetting experiences into the early years of primary school, including how I was shamed daily by younger siblings who had stopped bedwetting earlier than me; how they would sing *"Chitaitai chinotunda"* the peeing firefly song. Baby also shared how he had received thorough daily whippings for the inconvenience he caused his stay at home mother who hand-washed his smelly bedding.

We fell in love and were obsessed with each other. We saw and wrote letters to each other daily and could not imagine life without the other. Despite my small-town reputation of being "the sexy rich man's daughter that every man wanted a taste of", Baby respected me and loved me for who I was. We spent hours on end looking deeply into each other's eyes to search for the truth. We sat in empty classrooms most afternoons, Baby kissing, massaging and studying my hands like a fortune teller. When Baby touched me, I was convinced I felt his palm lines which promised the precise future I hoped for. Despite not understanding what love was then, I had no doubt that we sincerely felt deeply for each other. Most importantly, I did not have to work hard for Baby's love. Little gestures I made meant the world to him.

Baby's family moved a lot due to the nature of his father's work. This was why he was in boarding school then, and why he had been in boarding school from a very young age. One day, during a school holiday, I spontaneously decided to visit Baby. His family lived in Karoi at the time, and I was in Harare for the purpose of getting extra tuition from Sekuru Tonderai. I was staying with Tete Gwinyai who had several drivers and cars. One of the drivers was a distant relative of ours, and we got along. I asked Mukoma Lamek to take me to a bus terminus very early in the morning so that I would catch a bus that passed through Karoi on its way to Kariba. This mission was a top secret that Tete Gwinyai would never have approved of, because her view was women were never to bend over backwards for men, especially those of a lower social status.

All went according to plan and I arrived in Karoi around 10am. Upon arrival, I walked around town hunting for a telephone booth, so that I could call Baby, entice him to walk into town and surprise him with my presence. Unfortunately, all telephone booths in Karoi were broken, so my plan B was to ask local people where Baby's family lived. As I walked towards the nearest fuel station to start asking for directions to Baby's home, I saw Baby walking across the road with a friend of his, Kumbirai. He spotted me immediately, because he said there were no girls as fine as I was in Karoi, so I had made him look. Baby was ecstatic to see me and was genuinely amazed by my audacity. We spent all day talking, holding hands, looking into each other's eyes, until I had to think of heading back to Harare. We embraced tightly then kissed briefly. I was lucky enough to catch the last chicken bus from Kariba, which turned up full at 4pm, but I scrambled on and would stand all the way to Harare.

I did not feel the pain of standing on the bus despite being tossed about when the driver suddenly swerved at high speed to avoid animals on the road, because I reminisced about the very satisfying day trip I had had. The bus was unusually smoky and had a crooked chassis which was bent towards the left, and its body bent towards the right, making it look like an invention that had gone horribly wrong. When I was not daydreaming about Baby, I occasionally worried the bus might blow up any moment, but it arrived in Harare just after 8pm. Mukoma Lamek, who had kept my secret safe, and Tete Gwinyai, who had been clueless of my whereabouts, had both been worried about me. So, when I returned to Tete Gwinyai's home, I forged a story about having spent the day at a local shopping mall pampering myself and watching movies.

Baby had a way of making me open and honest with him, and I trusted him with my life. I told Baby very early on in the relationship about the rape, and the news broke his heart. That afternoon, we had been sitting behind our school gym where a lot of couples liked to hang out. He took my left hand and would not let it go as he empathised with me. "Look at me Ruva," he said to me gently. "What that guy did to you was evil. I will never let another man hurt you like that again, ever! I promise. Don't worry about the past; you are beautiful, inside and out, don't you ever forget that." Although we spoke about the rape once, Baby's words that day unleashed an eagle spirit that had been lying dormant inside me. With Baby's love, I began to feel beautiful, lovable and empowered. He healed my fear of intimacy, and we became attached. Perhaps too attached because nothing else mattered to me as he did.

As I fell deeper for Baby, I slowly detached myself from my aunts who thought he was beneath me. I still wrote to them occasionally and told them about how serious our relationship was. Baby was aware of what my family thought of him. Tete Mary had once paid me an impromptu visit at my boarding school and demanded to see Baby, who she interrogated, intimidated and warned to not mess me about. Baby seemed aloof to the visit. Thereafter my aunts joked and laughed about how the experience had been the perfect induction into our family drama.

Baby respected my boundaries and never crossed any lines – a feature that had been missing in my life that I was thirsty for. He was ever so punctual for our meetings and never made me wait. We sat together on the bus during trips to hockey tournaments. Baby would buy me fast food and other goodies with the little pocket money I knew was being sacrificed, and he insisted on spoiling me. Baby often told me that I reminded him of his mother, with whom he was very close.

One day, we were caught in heavy rain after our lessons and decided to stay out and get drenched. Baby loved the look of my erect nipples imprinted on my wet school shirt. We desperately wanted each other but never took things further. As school prefects, complying with rules was something Baby and I took very seriously. It had been a romantic afternoon and he had smothered me with love and attention all day. We looked into each other's eyes one last time before returning to our respective boarding houses, and he declared he wanted to marry me and make me the mother of his children. Delighted by Baby's proposal, I smiled and confirmed, "I would love that."

Chapter
6

The economic downturn and political upheaval in Zimbabwe at the time impacted my parents and indeed, all families in the country. I had been protected from most of this disruption by the confines of boarding school. Everyone had been struggling financially in Zimbabwe, so mobile phones and access to the internet were luxuries I had no care for. We had had no access to newspapers in boarding school either, so I was neither attuned to nor interested in current affairs. I left for the UK a month after completing my A level final exams. I looked skinny, having lost a lot of weight due to exam pressure and a deteriorating boarding school diet. I had a British passport by birth, so I returned to reside in the UK. My parents who had made that choice, assumed I would be accepted into a

UK university as a local student, by virtue of my citizenship. They saved up £1000 which they gifted me in an envelope full of travellers' cheques on the day I left. I was to find a job as soon as I arrived in the UK to start earning a living.

A few days before I left Zimbabwe, I visited Mbuya in Chivi for an emotional send off. Mainini Joy and Tete Mary were also present and would travel with me to the UK. Mbuya who was in her mid-60s was unwell and slowly losing her memory; nothing surprising for a woman her age in a country where the life-expectancy was low. I felt hurt and helpless to see her in that state. A goat and several chickens were slaughtered in our honour, and a few speeches were made to strengthen us ahead of our looming journey, which Baba famously dubbed "the Exodus".

On our day of departure to the UK, I was heartbroken. I hugged Baba for the first time in my life, and I felt like I had received an award. Hugs and kisses from Mhamha and her mother, Gogo, soothed my soul as they told me they loved me. Mhamha usually kissed my right cheek and Gogo always kissed both.

I was leaving behind Baby, the love of my life. What would I do without my family and siblings? My future in the UK was impossible to imagine, and I was consumed with fear of the unknown. Being an 18-year-old girl who had been protected by the walls of boarding school during my adolescence, I had never been on my own or worked other than in my parents' businesses. I was now travelling to the

UK to escape the harsh reality of the Zimbabwean economy and politics. The fact that I may not have wanted to leave home would not have been entertained, so it was never spoken about. I felt the only opportunity I had to become more intimate with Mhamha had vanished. I desperately wanted to tell her I had fallen in love with Morris, and that despite the rape, I would put things right by getting a good education, getting married, having children, and becoming an exemplary woman she would be proud of. The pain in my heart would not allow me to find the right words for her, so I did not speak. Endless tears spoke for me instead.

On arrival, Mainini Joy would enter the UK as a visitor with the intention to remain illegally thereafter. Tete Mary would catch a connecting flight from the UK to the United States to start a new life there. When we landed in the UK, Mhamha's other younger sister, Mainini Portia, who already lived in the UK picked us up from the airport. Baba's sister, Tete Gertrude, was also in the UK at the time, escaping the pain of her tedious divorce. She had left her school in the capable hands of her long-serving staff. Her daughter Tsvakai was now living in the United States.

Tete Gertrude had been castigated by our family patriarchy for wanting to leave her very difficult husband. She was called all sorts of names and suffered the inevitable wrath of going against the patriarchy's expectations. The treatment of Tete Gertrude made me believe that divorce was the worst transgression one could ever commit in our family.

I could not relate to what Tete Gertrude might have been going through, but I perfectly understood that her soul-searching holiday would do her some good. I found it strange, however, that I had never heard Tete Gwinyai, who had on several occasions openly infringed the boundaries of her marriage, being reprimanded for leaving her husband many years before Tete Gertrude's divorce.

We all travelled to Mainini Portia's flat in Finsbury Park, where she dropped us off and said she had to work. It was New Year's Eve 1999 into 2000 so she did not want to miss the good rate of night shift pay, and she would be in touch a few days later. We felt relieved that year 2000 came and the world did not end. It turned out to be just another ordinary day added to the list of false apocalypses. More importantly, the Millennium Bug did not materialise as predicted. Although I did not have enough interest in technology to appreciate the gravity of the Y2K glitch, I knew it would be extensive enough to affect me in one way or the other.

We drove from Heathrow Airport to Finsbury Park via central London, and I was shocked by my first impressions of the UK. I had imagined in my mind that London would be adorned by multicoloured glass skyscrapers beneath a blue sky, but the domineering grey landscape was depressing. Historic grey buildings beneath a humid grey sky greeted me like a lucid nightmare. I did not have an appreciation of graffiti on walls near railways; the artwork looked untidy and stood out like a child who turned up in mufti on a normal school day. I had not expected to see such disorder in a first world civilisation.

I had never seen so many white people in one place, everywhere. For the first time in my life, I became conscious of my blackness and felt like a minority. It was bitterly cold. The weather shook me to my core as I slowly took in my new world and swallowed the disappointment. There were no old soulful cars in sight, except a few that had been deliberately maintained to a high standard and only their number plates betrayed them. We eventually arrived in the borough of Highbury and Islington, and I began to notice more foreigners as the buildings became denser. I was delighted to identify a few familiar features I had seen on British television programs – black cabs, red London buses and telephone booths. I truly was in London, I thought in feigned excitement which I hoped would convince me that everything would be okay. A feeling similar to what I felt the day I told Mainini Joy that I had had sex for the first time.

When we arrived at Mainini Portia's dingy council flat, we drank cups of tea in severely stained chipped coffee mugs. I looked around her tiny kitchen for Vim, a Zimbabwean scouring powder we used to remove stains from crockery and kitchen utensils, but there was none. Such solvable imperfections had not been tolerable where I had come from. I would have scrubbed the mugs with the same vigour I had used to squeeze pus out of stubborn acne, but there was nothing to be done. A few days later, Mainini Portia invited Mainini Joy and I to the nursing home she managed in Surrey. She let us work on trial and if we proved we could do the work, we would be offered permanent employment. Mainini Joy had no choice, so she excelled and was offered a job. I on the other hand struggled with touching, seeing and smelling gross bodily fluids oozing out of sick elderly foul-mouthed people who shouted profanities to the carers looking after them. I continuously belched and spewed for the short amount of time I was at the nursing home, then was dismissed with no pay the following day.

Feeling relieved, I returned on my own to Mainini Portia's flat in Finsbury Park, getting lost along the way, having not been taught how to use the London Underground system. I often wrongly assumed that catching a train traveling the opposite direction on a parallel platform would take me back to a previous stop. It also took me a while to learn to read the London Underground Map. An uncle of mine, Babamunini Tom, also lived in the one bed flat – the husband to Mainini Rosey, and stepfather to Chenai who had lived with us because her mother travelled internationally. Babamunini Tom slept in the lounge and did not speak much. He was a functional alcoholic who left for work very early, before I woke up and returned late at night when I was already in bed.

Weeks of trial and error unfolded, where I looked for jobs in the wrong places and learned life in the UK the hard way. On icy cold mornings, I walked in central London underdressed, ringing doorbells at Bed & Breakfast accommodation that had a "vacant" sign on their doors because I misinterpreted the signs to mean there was work available. One day, I felt lucky to come across a five-star hotel that allowed me to start work immediately as a chambermaid. My colleagues in that job barely spoke a word of English. They were mostly angry-sounding Eastern Europeans who seemed too impatient to coach a slow moving, dozy African girl who struggled to grasp the concept of target-based bedmaking. I was dismissed as incompetent on the second day of work, unpaid, because I had failed to meet the goal of single-handedly cleaning 30 hotel rooms to the expected standard within a day.

I had no curriculum vitae, did not know what one ought to have looked like, and had never needed to have one. Everyone I knew at this point was living in the UK illegally, so all advice I received about how to go about anything was illegal. No one knew how to apply for a valid national insurance number, so I made one up, in the format used by illegal immigrants when applying for jobs illegally. While I waited for the right job to turn up, I occasionally met with Tete Gertrude and visited her friends and acquaintances. She introduced me to sisters of an ex-girlfriend of one of my uncles, Babamunini Farai, who had died of AIDS.

Babamunini Farai was one of Baba's brothers who never married, but had several children by different women, who he sometimes acknowledged and sometimes did not. My uncle was an alpha male who was loved by everyone, except broken-hearted women or male rivals who threatened his throne. I, as well as my siblings and cousins were mesmerised by him. He was handsome and outspoken, ran a few businesses and drove BMWs like Baba. As the family mascot, his role provided comic relief when tensions were high, using his jester persona to diffuse family conflict as and when necessary. He consistently cracked jokes, pulled pranks and lied a lot, so it was never easy to tell when he was being serious about anything. Like Baba and his other brothers, Babamunini Farai displayed the bouncing leg syndrome, or continuously opening and closing his knees during a man spread, as if plagued by impatience, except that he did it even during the most light-hearted moments. On countless occasions, Babamunini Farai would call our landline at my childhood home, instruct us to bath and get ready because he was going to take us somewhere special. We always trusted him and complied, and he would not turn up, yet we still believed him again and again when he repeated the prank.

Babamunini Farai drank excessively, gambled and womanised compulsively. He was notorious for often throwing tantrums when he got drunk at family gatherings, challenging the unfair distribution of Sekuru's wealth and how Baba was the wrong person to manage it. He would often point out that Baba's younger siblings did not have a sense of purpose or belonging and lacked the right leadership to nurture them into the successful characters Sekuru had intended them to be. Baba rubbished his rants, often shutting him up with *"Pfutsek!* Take responsibility for your own life *mhani!"* Babamunini Farai would leave our home distraught, revving his car noisily in the driveway first, then speeding off into the night, and life would carry on as normal thereafter.

The women in Babamunini Farai's life were the most adorable people I had ever met. They were all so eager to please my uncle and his wider family. As children, we always looked forward to their visits, which were sadly designed to make the women feel like they were getting a step closer to marriage with my uncle. Some of the women looked so alike, I once mistook one for the other, telling her how I had enjoyed spending time with her only a few days back, and the woman insisted she had not seen me in months. When challenged by Mhamha about his player habits and the risks they caused to his health, my uncle would laugh in response, explaining he immersed himself in a bath full of bleach and other disinfectants after each sexual encounter, so he was safe.

When my uncle finally got sick, he suffered from terminal liver cirrhosis and died at the age of 32. I was 16 years old and writing my GCSE exams when he died. I was utterly heartbroken, then asked Mhamha why Babamunini Farai could not get a liver transplant like other people. No one in my family had referred to my uncle's illness as AIDS, and Mhamha seemed annoyed by my ignorance as she handed me some cash talk. "Can you not see that your uncle died of AIDS? Could you not see how his skin had darkened, how his hair was wavy as if it was permed, how much he had lost weight? You see this is what worries me about you Ruva! If you cannot recognise a man with AIDS how will you survive in this world? You better remain celibate if your eyes can't see!" I cried inconsolably.

My uncle's girlfriend's sisters, Janet and Jean were free-spirited individuals who simply had no direction in life. Every single time I visited them, I would receive several text messages with shopping lists of groceries to bring along, which I complied with. The intel about my parents giving me £1000 to take to the UK was public knowledge and everyone wanted to benefit from it. It was unheard of among the circles I hung around, that one would come to the UK with "such a large amount of money", with no "specific purpose". To me, it was just money. Perhaps it was because the currency was foreign to me, but I did not have an appreciation of its value. It was neither too little nor too much.

I later learned that people who could have helped me or directed me to the right places simply did not because they felt I had money so could sort myself out. Janet and Jean got me into a lot of unnecessary trouble. There was a gentleman who hung around their house, Michael, who portrayed more intelligence and direction than everyone else. He said he would show me where to apply for work, open a bank account and "permeate the system". One day, I was travelling with Michael on the London underground, when he asked me how I was related to Janet and Jean. I explained that their older sister Stembile had been my late uncle's girlfriend. Michael went on to ask how my uncle had died. Without giving the question much thought, I naively responded that Babamunini Farai had died of AIDS. I sensed Michael's mood switching instantly and a bead of sweat broke on his brow. "So those girls want to kill me!" he exclaimed. Michael later explained that he had been childhood friends with Stembile, but they had recently got in touch and were considering dating. He explained that Stembile did not look healthy, so he had avoided rushing into a relationship with her. He thanked me for being honest with him.

Michael subsequently asked me to hand over all my money to him for safekeeping and I gave him £800. After I gave him my money, Michael told me that he fancied me and wanted us to date. When I told him about Baby, he invited me to be his friend with benefits instead. He had never seen "so much beauty and brains loaded into such a small package", he had told me. When I rejected his advances, Michael subsequently vanished then changed his mobile number. I did not dare tell my parents that the money they had given me had disappeared with Michael. Around the time of Michael's disappearance, I got a job serving on a till at a fast-food restaurant at London Victoria railway station. I was delighted to finally have a job that did not make me feel sick. However, the restaurant manager thought I looked depressed and often stood behind customers during busy times, sign-languaging me to smile.

Everyone I knew in the circle of Zimbabweans made fun of the fact that I had left the comfort of my parents' home to come to work in a fast-food restaurant in the UK. None of them understood why the daughter of a "well-to-do politician" would choose to "come and struggle" in the UK. I did not understand it either, but what I knew certainly was that I had not chosen to be in the situation I found myself.

"Ha! Ungauya kuUK kuzokanga machips shuwa! Ha! You relocated to the UK to fry chips, honestly!"

None of them believed my story, that I would go to university in September that year. It was simply unheard of among the people I knew. A few weeks later, my A level results were published, and I had performed exceedingly well, being the best Arts student in my year at my school. I attained two As and a B and although I failed to get into Oxford to read Jurisprudence to Baba's disappointment, I received an unconditional offer to study Law and Economics at the University of Kent, albeit with an unexpected complication.

Due to not having resided in the UK for at least three years prior to my application, I had been classified an international student and had to pay international university tuition fees. I offered my parents the option to defer the place in order to buy time to save up for tuition fees, but they insisted I left London immediately, go to Kent and find a job while I waited for the university year to start in September. I left Finsbury Park without ever visiting the Park itself.

According to my paternal aunts, Baba was very proud of my academic achievement. They began addressing me as *mwana wadaddy*, "child of my father", and would tell me how proudly Baba spoke of me. I wanted to believe them, but my intuition insisted there was something wrong with that claim – such a special message could only bear weight if delivered by its source. However, I embraced my reality and began soaking in the rays of Baba's love. He had begun having meaningful conversation with me when I passed my GCSEs, and for achieving excellent grades for A level I was now nicknamed "his child". The promotion felt surreal, and I would do whatever it took to maintain my new status.

Baba specifically instructed me to board a train to Canterbury, then buy a newspaper at the railway station on arrival and look in the classified section of the paper for rooms to rent. I did as he instructed and found myself in the beautifully serene city of Canterbury in Kent. When I moved into my room in a shared house, I had used up the little money I had left to pay the deposit and first month's rent in advance and was left penniless. Whilst I waited for my final pay from the fast-food restaurant, which I received weekly, I lived on a rich fruitcake Mhamha had baked and packed for me in a large recycled metal biscuit container. The cake had matured beautifully by then; and for a whole week, I ate the cake for breakfast, lunch and supper, with black sugar-free tea.

I got a job at a fruit machine casino in Canterbury where I worked from around April until September, while I waited for the university year to commence. I worked with a very friendly all-women team and became very close to one of my colleagues, a well-educated Syrian refugee called Reem. She was my first proper friend in the UK, who created my first email account. Reem was unhappily married to an English man, a "control freak" who was working towards a doctorate at the university of Kent. She would talk about her sad marriage all day long when we worked on the same shift, and I listened to her stories tirelessly with compassion.

Reem always had escape plans that never materialised. She was beautiful, appeared happy, and she wore her brunette hair in a short bob haircut, which she flicked confidently before she lapsed into deep thought every now and again. I could always sense the pain in her heart just by looking at her face, even when she smiled. Perhaps the prospect of getting permanent residence through the marriage kept her going. Her perseverance certainly seemed to serve a higher purpose, because I often wondered how someone capable of escaping the Syrian war could not escape a bitter marriage to an English geek.

I resigned from the casino a few days before I moved to the university campus, as my lecture timetable could not accommodate the shift work at the casino. In the months that followed, I occasionally visited Janet and Jean in London. They always had a plan or a party to go to. They all found it hilarious that I had a serious boyfriend in Zimbabwe who I thought would marry me one day.

Michael eventually reappeared and promised to pay back my money in instalments. It transpired that he had a child who lived in Zimbabwe and attended Tete Gertrude's school. When I mentioned to Tete Gertrude in confidence about Michael disappearing with my money, she had threatened to expel his child from her school. I later discovered that Michael had actually been sleeping with Stembile, and my revelation about the cause of Babamunini Farai's death had confirmed his suspicions. Taking my money had been his own way of shooting the messenger.

September came and my parents had miraculously managed to raise some of my tuition fees. I paid the first tuition fee instalment and commenced my course. Baba had selected Law and Economics for my studies, and my course director had summoned me following a quick perusal of my academic certificates. I had a "C" in O level mathematics and had studied Arts subject at A level, so he wanted to have a candid discussion about whether Economics was the best choice for me. I explained to him that the course selection had been Baba's and that he would never agree to change the course. "How about we switch the course to Law and Business Administration, and you don't tell Baba about it? Otherwise you face three years of suffering that you'll never get back. Your life, your decision." There was something about the way the course director spoke that empowered me. I knew I would never enjoy Economics and would probably fail and disappoint Baba anyway, so I swiftly replaced Economics with Business Administration, without consulting him first. It seemed like a sensible compromise, as I would still major in Law for Baba. I felt liberated to make such an important decision without his input.

When Baba eventually found about this change, he was disappointed and it was too late to revert, but I did not care. I settled into university and for the first time in a long time, I felt a hint of calm, but the next few years would be the most challenging, financially and emotionally, for the whole family. My parents were to focus on raising my tuition fees while I worked for my accommodation and living costs. Mhamha owned a hair salon in Zimbabwe, where I had learned to braid hair. This proved to be a useful skill as I earned a decent income from braiding hair for most of the black girls on campus.

As I began earning my own money, I learnt to make more decisions without consulting anyone first, which made me feel freed. I began to buy my own clothes and to dress as I pleased without feeling like a whore. Everyone around me dressed like one but no one seemed to care! As time progressed, I slowly began to feel like a grown up. I hand-wrote to Mhamha and my siblings frequently, and it was always delightful to receive their responses. My siblings always sent me their wish lists, which I felt obliged to fulfil as my absence from home was costing them the little luxuries they might have enjoyed if I had stayed in Zimbabwe. I would always send them cheap trendy fashion wear and CDs from the UK even when I had very little cash to spare, in the same way my aunts and uncles had sent me cash in their replies to my letters when I was in boarding school. Tizai always asked for my latest pictures, so I bought a small camera which I used to avidly take photographs of myself to send home. Sometimes I wore a bit of makeup for photographs to show that I had grown up since I had left home, and that would be a talking point on our calls with Mhamha teasing that I had truly grown into a fine woman.

When I wrote to Mhamha I always apologised for "all the trouble I had caused her" back home. When I made these apologies, I was specifically apologising for getting raped, but I could never say those words, and I always wondered whether Mhamha knew what I really meant. She replied and told me how proud she was of the woman I had become, and to stop being so hard on myself. In one of her letters, which I thought of as my redemption, she explained that, "Whatever experiences you went through growing up, I was only trying to mould you in a shape that I felt and liked, not in a shape you liked yourself. Mothering is always difficult, but I don't think bringing you up was such a disaster." The Redemption was my classic tearjerker, which I kept safely with all my other letters. Mhamha always ended her letters by telling me to "pray, be good and think good always, because that makes you a good person" and that she loved me. Her words gave me the strength to be gentle and kind, even in situations where I ought to have not.

On one occasion, Mhamha surprised me by enclosing a letter to the Queen with a response to my letter. "That's one of my desperate attempts to get help. Maybe the Queen might forward it to the right organisation that might offer help or simply regard it as nonsense, but I like to try and watch for results. Please address an envelope and send it to Buckingham Palace." Despite feeling sceptical about Mhamha's attempt to get financial help to pay for my tuition from the Queen, I sent the letter anyway. I never got a response. The economic situation in Zimbabwe only got worse and I felt extremely guilty for putting my parents through the challenges they faced, to fund a course I did not enjoy or care for. A course I had to do to make Baba happy.

I also wrote to my cousin Chenai, and my friend Fadzai who had dated Morris's friend Tanaka from high school. Their responses always brought me joy.

Baby remained in Zimbabwe to study Chemical Engineering at the National University of Science and Technology. We remained in touch, writing to each other regularly by post and very infrequently by email. Baby would have needed money to pay internet cafes in order to access emails. I called him often to begin with, then less regularly as the financial burden of doing so grew on my part. There was no expectation for him to reciprocate the calls, because he did not work. When I had spare cash, I bought him CDs of his favourite soul and rap music. I missed Baby deeply and remained committed to the relationship. All my spare time was spent in part time jobs to raise money for food, accommodation, clothing and calling Baby. By the end of my first year in the UK, I felt incredibly homesick so my parents and I collectively paid for a flight to Zimbabwe where I would spend Christmas.

I informed Baby that I was coming home, and we were both excited to see each other again. Our conversations became raunchier as December approached, because we knew the time to consummate our relationship was imminent. When Baby and I reunited, the spark of our love had diminished. Distance had taken its toll on our relationship. I had become self-assured and he felt intimidated by me. The detachment between us was evident.

In a desperate attempt to re-spark the fire we had once felt for each other, we decided to journey from Bulawayo where Baby now lived, to Harare by train – a trip that lasted nearly 16 hours. The journey was tedious and mundane, with drunkards on board, extremely dirty toilets and the train stopping intermittently for very long periods of time in the middle of nowhere. We had fortunately bought food and drinks to take on the trip, but we eventually got tired of eating, and of talking, and of each other. When we arrived in Harare, we did not make further attempts to resuscitate our dying relationship. I focused on spending time with my family until I returned to the UK and lost touch with Baby thereafter. There was no formal break up or closure between us.

I visited Mbuya, whose health had deteriorated. She could barely remember me, and I knew that was the last time I would see her alive.

Chapter 7

Towards the end of my first year at university, Mbuya died at the age of 65. She had suffered from dementia, arthritis, type-2 diabetes, and had gone blind. Mbuya was morbidly obese for as long as I could remember. Most of my paternal family was morbidly obese and proud of it. Being overweight in our society was seen as a sign of wealth, good health and success, and it was simply part of who we were. Food was undoubtedly a family comforter.

Mbuya had been a teacher, then a local businesswoman and master farmer who produced hundreds of bags of maize for the Zimbabwe Grain Marketing Board each year, all of which were very high accomplishments for a black African woman in her time. Mbuya might not have known this, but she was a revolutionary for women empowerment. While she advocated equality by supporting female politicians, of which she had a few girl friends in high places, Mbuya's impatience with men was obvious.

During her life, I became aware of some incidents that made me question Mbuya's sanity. One of Mbuya's shops had been burgled and the male burglar had been caught. A seer of some kind claimed to have been led to the burglar, so Mbuya demanded to see the accused. Being a big woman with limited mobility, Mbuya had surprisingly managed to get up and personally sprinkle dried hot pepper in the accused's eyes. The man roared in pain and squirmed, pleading innocence, but Mbuya did not stop until the thief admitted he had stolen from her shop and would return all the stolen goods to Mbuya, which he did.

On other occasions, Mbuya would emasculate her male workers by uttering profanities and calling them names, in front of their wives and children, when she felt such treatment was necessary. Mbuya had the gift of language that she used unashamedly to put people down, particularly men. She did not hesitate to respond to skiving excuses from male workers with vulgarities, *"Rumhata!* asshole!"

Sacrileges, *"Zvikumbo zvinenge mudonzvo waSatani!* Legs that resemble the devil's walking stick!"

Reprimands, *"Huma semushuku unovava!* Forehead that resembles a wild loquat tree that bears sour fruit!"

"Shure kunonhuwa nhamo! An ass that reeks of poverty!"

I could never reconcile Mbuya's imperious disposition at home with the near-meek religious persona she displayed as a respected church deaconess.

Mbuya employed somewhat gangster tendencies, such as keeping an axe in her bedroom. She maintained a protocol whereby anyone who arrived at her home after a certain time would tap on her bedroom window first, using a specific tapping code.

"Who is it?" she asked first.

"Who are you with?" she queried next.

"Why are you here?" was usually her final question.

When Mbuya was satisfied with the responses, she requested her visitor to stand back from her window, to allow her to peep through the curtains whilst pointing a lit torch at them, to satisfy herself that their responses were genuine. She would then pick up her axe and proceed to open the door for her visitor. She did not discriminate when applying her strict protocol, so even her own children and siblings were familiar with it. I often wondered if Mbuya's over the top decorum was a tactic she had learnt to implement to protect herself from Ian Smith's soldiers during the liberation war. The practice did wear off eventually as she got older.

Mbuya was mesmerised by clever people and was particularly obsessed with people who had high-set ears. She openly declared that they were far superior and more intelligent than everyone else, inadvertently offending those with low-set ears. Mbuya did not hesitate announcing other people's perceived stupidity even when it was not called for. She also believed that people with large foreheads had bigger brains and were cleverer.

Mbuya had her obvious favourites and I was lucky to be one of them. She never laid her hand on or scolded me. Mbuya adored me and my childhood outspokenness. She ensured I tasted everything from her secret food stash that she did not share with anyone else. Mbuya could demolish a whole Crimson Sweet watermelon and pass on the watermelon juice to me to drink, while her other grandchildren watched. She sometimes unleashed a mouldy, smelly whole cooked chicken from somewhere and expect me to help her eat it. Throwing food away was never an option for her, yet there was no refrigerator or electricity at Mbuya's rural home, until many years later. Her role as my protector and vicious defender was obvious. When I arrived from the UK as a baby, Mbuya had apparently not announced my arrival, even to her own sister, who found out anyway and mourned for being overlooked. Mbuya had feared I would be bewitched and killed by jealous family and neighbours, so I was kept in a locked house under constant watch.

During one school holiday, when I was around eight years old, my aunts, uncles, cousins and I had gone to one of Mbuya's massive fields to farm the land, as was routine. Tete Mary, Tizai and I were given the responsibility to herd Mbuya's cattle. Tizai and I had got bored of watching the grazing ruminants and decided to play inside a nearby dry riverbed. Tete Mary must have been lost in thought trying to catch termites to snack on, so did not overhear our conversation. Tizai suggested that the concave shape of the meandering river meant if we were to walk on the riverbed in opposite directions, the river would eventually connect and so would we. Without giving the idea much thought, I agreed to the adventure, turned my back and began the journey down the riverbed. My brother did the same but quickly felt tired and bored then returned to the others. I continued to walk within the confines of rocky and sometimes crumbly walls of a drought stricken tributary for a protracted distance, and what felt like many hours. As I walked in the river, the walls became higher and darker, and I began losing my orientation. I felt like I was surrounded by gargantuan abstract figurines, towering above me like human beings would to an ant. A cloud of fear overwhelmed me as I walked further along the riverbed. I sensed imminent danger when I heard growling sounds, then noticed where they were coming from. A pack of at least eight black wild dogs with red eyes were lying down, lifting their heads and wagging their tails in excitement. It was certainly a breed I was not familiar with.

I was raised to fear dogs. To me, dogs were not pets but protectors of humans that lived outside to guard the home from intruders. I was afraid of sweet little dogs that would ordinarily pass for harmless pets. I had also seen dogs starved all day to increase their rancorousness overnight and was terrified of them. It did not matter to me how big, small, adorable or vicious a dog looked; they were all dangerous animals as far as I was concerned. What I saw that day were wild animals ready to kill. They could have been rabid! As I walked on confidently, as if I had not seen the dogs, I withdrew eye contact, felt an adrenaline rush permeating my bloodstream then sped past the scene before anything transpired. Consumed by trepidation, I may have had an out of body experience where my soul ran past the animals and my body followed at its own pace. The animals might not have been hungry. Perhaps I was just lucky. I never understood why the dogs did not run after me. I sprinted on river sand for what felt like a couple of kilometres in continuous meditative prayer, then stopped when my heart felt like it was ceasing. I was a chubby little girl who did not usually run. When I came to shallower river walls, I decided to climb out of the dry riverbed and look for water. I emerged at the edge of somebody's field, feeling dirty, clammy and exhausted, and knew intuitively there would be a homestead close by.

I walked through a dry maize field until I arrived at what looked like a deserted home. The cyan sky was clear, the atmosphere scorching, still and silent, like a ghost town. I rationalised the home could not have been deserted, because through a mirage, I observed the arid yard which had evidently been swept earlier. The russet landscape felt authentic, yielding two very tall Aloe Excelsas and a mature *mukwakwa* tree, the only vegetation on the homestead that stood assuredly despite the absence of rain for several months. Familiar twig-broom patterns were gorgeously imprinted on the ground. The sweeping task had been done with precision and care, exactly how Mbuya would have expected the girls to do it. I never understood why it was so important for girls to wake up daily at the crack of dawn to sweep the dust, for the purpose of decorating the yard with wavy patterns imprinted by twigs used for the task. A laborious practice I later learnt contributed to soil erosion, which I despised like many others.

I decided to call out before leaving to search for the next homestead. *"Tisvikewo! Vepano! Kokokooo!* Helloooo! Is anybody home! Knock knock!".* A petite black cat surfaced from one of the unpainted mud huts on the homestead and stalked towards me. Black cats belonged to witches and represented a bad omen, so I slowly backed away in preparation to sprint for dear life. I froze as a Methuselous figure emerged from the same mud hut, leaning wholeheartedly on a dry slim tree branch for support, walking towards me slowly, squinting and scanning my face for familiarity. As the fragile grey-haired female centenarian approached me, I could smell the cow dung that would have been used to brace the spines of such elderly individuals.

"Ndiwe ani? Who are you?"

"My name is Ruva," I uttered with a trembling, furtive voice. The elderly woman's face relaxed as she announced she knew me, the child who had been posted from Britain and had been cushioned under her grandmother's loving wings. The brittle woman managed to shake gently as she ululated in excitement.

"*Ulululululululuuuuu! Yirirriririrrirririririririiii! Ruva cheBhiriteni!*" (ululating sounds - little Ruva from Britain!). She called me *murungu wangu,* my white person.

"*Ndini Mbuya Shuro. Uchandiziva?* I am grandma Shuro. Do you remember me?" She introduced herself then offered an agomphious grin. I shook my head and hesitantly smiled back at her.

"*Makadini?* How are you?" I asked.

"*Ndiripo muzukuru wemuzukuru wangu!* I am well, grandchild of my grandchild!" Customarily it was essential for children to ask all elders if they were well, even when they could not care less. Mbuya Shuro could have been anyone, in a community where everyone seemed to be related through totems-in-common or otherwise. She asked if I was hungry. I confirmed I was, then the elderly woman invited me into the kitchen from where she had appeared.

The kitchen was a round hut made of mud and a roof thatched with dried straw. I felt relieved that the woman knew me. I had never met the elderly woman before so to me, she was still a stranger. She could have been a witch – she owned a black cat. Mbuya had always taught me to never accept food offered by strangers as I would be poisoned or bewitched. Under normal circumstances, I would have complied with this rule, but after the ordeal I had just experienced, I was famished. I also had a serious intolerance for hunger. I rationalised the mitigating factors and accepted the risks as I followed the elderly woman into the mud hut. She knew me and where I was from. She knew I was born in Britain and sent back to Baba's homestead to live with Mbuya. The woman was clearly excited to see me. She even called me her *murungu!* In order to cover my back, I decided to perfunctorily decline the offer, stating that Mbuya said *"Ukakwata unoroiwa!* If you eat at strangers' homes, you will be bewitched!"

In fact, Mbuya was known to decline food and drink when visiting neighbours and family suspected of witchery, and would openly state, "Well your witchery is well known in these parts and I'm not ready to die yet. Perhaps if you taste it first, then I might have some after you."

The elderly woman dismissed the excuse, letting out a subtle giggle that implied she knew we both did not really believe Mbuya. I would be fine, I resolved, as I sat cross-legged on the earthen floor like an obedient child, eagerly awaiting the food. At the centre of the hut was a gently burning small fire. Above the fire was a low hanging wire string full of dangling organic delicacies, stretching from wall to wall. Among the smoked delicacies were maize cobs, pumpkin leaves and degutted mice. Next to the fire was a clay pot with leftover *sadza*. The elderly woman grabbed a couple of bruised yellow metal Kango plates and asked me to wash my hands in readiness for our meal. I washed my hands in a stained plastic dish, which contained water that had clearly been used several times before. The elderly woman washed her hands too then reached for a few mice, which she threw on a wire rack above the small fire.

As I watched the roasting rodents, I felt my stomach juices flowing. The black cat leisurely entered the hut, sat next to the elderly woman, then sprung onto a cold mouse she tossed towards it. I had never tried this trendy source of protein that was often enjoyed by a lot of people in rural areas. In no time, the elderly woman and I enjoyed the *sadza* and mice. She spoke incessantly and asked about a lot of my relatives' health. Without waiting for my answers, she switched from one topic to the next, sometimes responding to her own questions. I did not care, I felt safe.

After our meal, the old woman offered to walk me back to Mbuya's field. She knew a shortcut which would get us to the field in less than an hour, so we embarked on the journey back. Upon arrival, Mbuya was delighted to see me safe, "Thank God you're back Ruva! Are you okay?" Mbuya thanked the elderly woman for bringing me back. The elderly woman announced she had fed me mice and declared she had not bewitched me, to set the record straight. Mbuya glanced at me with an inspecting eye Her British granddaughter had been fed mice! *Was she really okay?* After the elderly woman left, I narrated the story of how I got lost and ended up at the elderly woman's homestead. Mbuya who was immobile due to obesity and arthritic pain, leapt onto her feet, hissing in anger, viciously breaking a thick branch off the tree that had provided her cool shade. Tete Mary, who had been looking after my brother and I near the river sensed danger and immediately got up to run for her life.

"*Batai munhu!* Catch that person!" Mbuya shrieked. In predictable malicious glee, all the sprinters in the family were delighted to oblige. The chase was short-lived. Babamunini Benjy dived onto Tete Mary from the back like a sumo wrestler, then rested on top of her, pressing her face down, until the other pursuers arrived to offer him assistance.

Tete Mary was dragged in the dust, across the field like a wounded wild animal headed for unavoidable slaughter, towards Mbuya. Her futile efforts to scratch the ground in resistance only broke her nails and bruised her delicate palms. I saw the look of fear in her moist red eyes, then the inevitable happened. Mbuya thrashed her daughter with the branch until it broke into countless pieces. As Mbuya battered Tete Mary repeatedly, she shouted in a teary voice.

"*Handirovi iwe mwanangu, asi ndiri kuranga vupenzi huri mauri!* I am not beating you my child, but I am chastising the idiocy in you!" This was something Mbuya would say when delivering a particularly thorough trouncing, a statement that implied her children were obsessed by some dark force she felt obliged to overcome.

I sat there watching helplessly, and the guilt that engulfed my soul as I witnessed my aunt being punished for an offence she was not responsible for would live with me forever. Later that night, my aunt approached me to try and say she was sorry. I ran away from her because I thought she would kill me. For many years after that day, I noticed with immense guilt the big scar on my aunt's lower abdomen, whenever she changed clothes in my presence, and I remembered with much remorse why it was there.

I was baptised in the Dutch Reformed Church of Zimbabwe, the church to which Mbuya was a member. I only attended that church with Mbuya during school holidays, when I visited her rural home. Mbuya proudly showed me off in her church, as her British granddaughter who could recite countless Bible verses in Shona. Sometimes she caught me unaware when her church friends visited her home.

Mbuya randomly exclaimed, *"Vaefeso 6 vhesi 1!"* (Ephesians 6 vs 1), to which I enthusiastically responded *"Imi vana teererai vabereki venyu munashe, nekuti ndizvo zvakarurama!"*

"Mateyo 7 vhesi 7!" (Matthew 7 vs 7), to which I readily responded, *"Kumbira uchapuwa, tsvaka uchawana, gogodza uchazarurigwa!"*

"Johwani 14 vhesi 1?" (John 14 vs 1), to which I excitedly responded, *"Moyo yenyu ngairege kumanikidzwa; tendai kuna Mwari, mutendevo kwandiri."*

Sometimes Mbuya and I would sit together in comfortable silence, when everyone else had gone to bed, until we got bored, then broke into song:

"Kuteerera,
ndiyo badzi nzira,
yekufara naJesu,
kuteerera!"

"Trust and obey,
for there's no other way,
to be happy in Jesus,
but to trust and obey!"

The news arrived a few days before the beginning of my first-year final exams. It was a quiet spring Monday morning, and I had had a very late-night studying in my room at the student village on the university campus. Around 9am, I was woken by a very loud knock and heard my name being called.

"Ruva! *Iwe* Ruva *iwe*!"

If I did not respond quickly enough, he would throw little stones on my window to grab my attention; a habit I loathed deeply. Nigel was a Zimbabwean friend I had met on campus a few months earlier. He was a final year Law student, who had given himself the responsibility to look after me, like an older brother. He knew who I was, and I suspected he was kind to me because he felt privileged to be known by me. I dragged myself out of bed and went to open the door.

As I let him in with a deliberate frown on my face, I heard a text message coming through and I cursed under my breath. *Why won't people leave me alone?*

I returned to my room and sat on my bed, then opened the text message from Tizai. It read, "Mbuya is dead."

Our domineering matriarch was gone! I was heartbroken and inconsolable. I did not have any credit on my pay-as-you-go mobile phone to call home. I had no money either. This had become my reality and I was comfortable with it. Nigel went out to buy me an international calling card worth £20. I called home, sobbing, and spoke to my parents and other relatives. Nigel asked if I had eaten, and whether there was any food in my house he could cook for me. I may have had a few outdated value store brand potatoes, fatty minced beef and frozen vegetables from Netto supermarket.

Nigel, who had a well to do sister funding his studies, offered to take me back to his flat where he would look after me during this difficult time. We walked back to his cosy flat off campus, where he cohabited with a Ugandan girlfriend, Karen who was away on holiday at the time. Evidence of her existence was all over the apartment. I stayed in the flat trying to study for my exams while Nigel went to shop for groceries at Sainsbury's supermarket. I had never shopped at Sainsbury's and did not even know where in town it was located.

Nigel turned up with fresh organic vegetables, fresh fruit juice, freshly baked granary bread, branded cereal, branded snacks, prawns, chicken breast fillet, fish I had never eaten before – it could have been salmon or sea bass. He cooked for me three times a day and slept on the couch while I curled up in his huge warm bed with crisp white ironed cotton sheets, where I cried myself to sleep. Since arriving in the UK, I had not eaten such healthy food or experienced generosity and hospitality of this magnitude. I could not relate to such kindness from a man who did not expect sex in return, so I thanked Nigel for his generosity but remained guarded. Nigel continued to buy me international calling cards as and when I needed them.

I phoned home at regular intervals to get updates on funeral arrangements, as I wanted to attend Mbuya's funeral. I had spoken to my course tutor about my grandmother's passing and they had suggested that I took compassionate leave with a view to write my exams as re-takes in the summer. My family collectively advised that it was not worth missing my final exams for Mbuya's funeral. My presence at her funeral would not bring her back. Plus, there was no money. Calling Zimbabwe to listen to funeral hymns over the phone, imagining myself hugging and kissing Mbuya's corpse goodbye, were some of the things that got me through the ache of missing her funeral.

Tete Mary was going to travel back home for her mother's funeral. She told me that someone would send me money. I was to buy a flight ticket soon after my exams and travel to Nebraska, where I would spend summer with my cousin Tsvakai and Tete Mary, when she returned from Mbuya's funeral. A man did transfer the money into my bank account and off I went to Omaha for the summer holidays.

Following the passing away of Mbuya on a Monday, Tete Mary boarded her flight on a Wednesday, and she arrived in Zimbabwe on a Friday to find to her horror that they had buried her mother before she arrived. Everyone had begged Baba to delay the burial to Friday, and he had said he would think about it. The church elders from Tete Mary's church, who had paid for her flight, also spoke to Baba to express how important it was for my aunt to attend Mbuya's funeral. It was decided she would be buried on the Wednesday. Tete Mary was picked up from the airport by a friend, who drove her to our rural homestead, which was around a four-hour drive from Harare.

Due to insurmountable grief, Tete Mary jumped from the moving vehicle that was winding down the dirt road, about a kilometre away from our homestead, and sprinted in hysterical frenzy towards the family graveyard. She arrived at Mbuya's graveside, where the diggers had left their tools nearby as was customary, then began digging up her mother's grave. She was immediately restrained, then she lay on top of the grave instead, hugging the heap of soil and crying her heart out for over an hour. Baba told Tete Mary that he did not think going ahead with the funeral in her absence would affect her that way. He consequently allowed Tete Mary to organise Mbuya's memorial service before returning to the United States, as compensation.

It was at Mbuya's memorial service that Mhamha delivered one of her most unforgettable cash talk speeches. Predictable Christian oratory encouraging the bereaved to be hopeful had prevailed that day in the usual fashion.

"Do not despair, for you will meet again in heaven."

Mhamha, as the older *muroora*, was asked to say a speech at the memorial service to which she obliged, first with gentle words of remembrance then a shocker to sign off.

"This woman might be going to heaven, but I doubt any of her children will ever see her again, because none of them are going to heaven! Her children will see each other in hell, because as we all know, that is where they belong. You! Children of this woman," Mhamha exclaimed, pointing to where Baba and his siblings sat aloof, "If ever you want to see your mother again, you must drastically change your behaviours and repent!" Only subtle murmurs of disapproval were heard when Mhamha finalised her speech.

Mhamha, who had experienced much tension with Mbuya over many years, had become very close with her in the end. Mhamha had vigilantly taken on gruesome tasks like cleaning up after Mbuya's incontinence, responsibilities Mbuya's own daughters had avoided. She faithfully looked after Mbuya on her deathbed until she passed on in our childhood home.

Tete Mary remained in Zimbabwe for a few weeks before returning to Omaha. Mbuya's belongings were distributed, and notwithstanding the provisions of her will, I was given a headscarf, woollen hat and a saltshaker. Disregard of wills was a common family trait. Whoever was present when belongings were distributed fought over the most valuable assets of the deceased, and whoever was absent got a token, or nothing.

Chapter
8

At the end of the summer holidays, Tete Mary and Tsvakai were very sad to see me go back to the UK. Both of them and their friends, who I had grown to like very much, tried to convince me to defer my university studies and stay in the United States to work and raise funds for my university tuition fees. Tete Mary and her friends had facilitated my application for work at a call centre where they all worked as students and I got the job, despite the absence of a valid work permit. I had mingled with black Americans through my work experience and learnt more about their culture. They all seemed mesmerised by Africans and wanted to visit Africa. Some ignorant ones wondered how we had learnt English so quickly.

"Ummmm, so did you like have to learrrn English on your flight here or something?" they would say in their melodious accent, genuinely wondering how supposedly primitive people who lived amongst lions had made their way to the best place to be in the world.

I had begun putting on weight but felt at ease in the United States where every other person around me seemed morbidly obese and out of shape. I was surprised by how uninhibited American men were, compared to the shy English men who never asked women out on dates unless they were sure they would score. The confidence of American men reminded me of Zimbabwean men who tried their luck with any woman, even if the chances of a positive response was remote. American men also liked "thick bitches", which I felt was rather disrespectful towards women, especially as one that had only dated with the intention to get married. When I was not working at the call centre, I braided the hair of work colleagues and the Zimbabwean community I was introduced to by Tete Mary. I was introduced to a Zimbabwean woman, Nancy, who was already braiding hair and had a huge clientele. She asked me to help with braiding her clients when she was busy, and we became good friends.

My parents did not agree to postponement of my studies, so I returned to the UK to begin my second year of university. When I was not studying, I was attending lectures. When I was not attending lectures, I was working. When I could not make ends meet financially, I missed lectures to work. I was registered with several temporary employment agencies and was not too selective with the jobs I picked, as long as they were not foul.

I was enticed by one healthcare recruitment agency to spend a day with a disabled patient who was paralysed from the waist down. They allegedly "just needed company with very light assistance" as the patient was on a catheter and did not need toilet assistance. The hourly rate was favourable, and they would pay for my taxi to get to the client, so I agreed to do the job. Upon arrival, I found a white woman heavily bejewelled with gold and gemstone trinkets and adorned with intricate tattoos, sitting in an expensive-looking motorised wheelchair. As I inspected the rather long muscular arm that held the door for me, an unexpectedly hoarse voice escaped their protruding Adam's apple and said, "You're alright darling? Come in love!" I could not hide my shock as I reluctantly stepped into what felt like a lair to which she returned an insolent pout and an amplified single eye roll. Their sluggish blink emphasised the thick 2cm long eyelash extensions that sat on shiny blue eyelids. I had never seen a cross dresser in my life. *A stunning phenomenon*, I thought. Men could dress, act and live like women and it was ok. A much-needed education about liberty considering my upbringing in Zimbabwe, where homophobia and zero tolerance for sexual eccentricity was very much alive.

Once I took my coat off and feigned to feel at home, I hit the ground running. They wanted me to paint their long nails and do their make-up. I did not ordinarily wear makeup myself and left the wearisome effort to special occasions only, so I was not an expert at it, which they found frustrating. They had hundreds of different coloured wigs in varying lengths and shapes, some straight, some wavy, some curly; which they asked me to place on their bald head and take pictures of them. The patient sometimes broke into teary hysterical frenzy, explaining that they used to be "normal", but they worked in a factory where health and safety were not prioritised, and was injured in an accident that damaged their spine and bound them to a wheelchair for life. They could no longer face the world, so confined themselves to their house filled with gadgets and all the worldly things they could ever wish for.

I was not sure what to do because I had not been trained to deal with an emotionally unstable patient and was mindful of potential boundaries imposed by regulation or otherwise. I was not sure whether giving them a hug would have been deemed crossing professional boundaries or not, so I looked at them and said I was sorry. They said they were ok because they had been compensated with more money than they could have earned in their lifetime, and they never had to work again. Their predicament filled me with sadness. After playing dressing-up in their bedroom for several hours, the patient instructed me to go upstairs and find a particular camera they wanted to use. I was to walk through two massive reception rooms before reaching the staircase that would lead me to the camera.

As I walked through the dark silent space with all life completely shut out by thick blackout curtains, I felt I was being watched. I could not see where I was going, so I stretched out my arms to feel any obstacles before bumping into them. I could hear my own amplified breathing, then I was startled by a voice that randomly exclaimed "Hello gorgeous!" but I could not see who said it. Before I could figure out who was speaking to me, another voice further along the room said, "Shut up you silly bitch!'

The conversation seemed to arouse further movement in the room, then more voices, joined by high-pitched trills, screeches and weird vocalisations.

There was no visible television, *was I dreaming*? Consumed by a fear of darkness, I increased my pace in a disoriented manner, then bumped into cold metal cage bars, which turned on motion sensor lighting, dimly illuminating the room to reveal a pandemonium of parrots on the left-hand side of the room, bickering away at each other. There must have been at least twenty of them. I had only ever seen parrots on television and had never considered that such animals actually existed in real life. In utter shock, I sprung to the other side of the room where I jolted into a cage harbouring a parliament of large owls. A few of them shifted slightly to recalibrate their comfortable sitting position, swivelling their heads from left to right. One of them, an enormous horned fowl with yellow piercing eyes eyeballed me with a stare that made me scream and run back to the patient's bedroom. I found them laughing their head off – they had been watching me on camera!

I was afraid of birds because I had been attacked by a fowl when I was around six years old, during a school holiday when I had gone to visit Mbuya in Chivi. She had asked me to go and pick freshly laid eggs from her chicken run, a routine that had taken me a while to get accustomed to. That morning, the chicken must have discerned my feigned confidence as I walked in and nervously picked the warm eggs, placed them on a small reed basket and briskly walked out. It must have got fed up with laying eggs that were taken away from it unceasingly. I had sensed imminent danger as the chicken fattened itself then paced in circles with its wings spread out in readiness to take flight. Before I could escape, the bird abruptly took off and landed on my shoulders, then launched a pecking frenzy on my head; but it was too late to break free unscathed. All the while screeching, its wings flapped onto my face to disorient me as I ran out of the chicken run with the eggs intact in my little basket.

There was no one in sight to rescue me, and even if there was, they would have laughed at the spectacle first before trying to help. In the end, I resolved the eggs were not worth it, so I dropped the basket and ran for dear life. The chicken flew off my head as soon as I dropped its eggs, and I never went back into the chicken run. My phobia for all birds was born that day. Owls on the other hand brought a completely different dimension of fear to my being. The birds were widely linked to evil, death, misfortune and many other superstitions during my upbringing in Zimbabwe. So, I simply did not want to be anywhere near them.

My shift at the disabled cross-dresser's house was long, tedious and unrelatable. Although I had felt deep empathy for my client, almost everything I experienced with them that day was incongruous with my body, mind and spirit, and I felt exhausted. I realised the sort of work I had access to was not to be enjoyed. I loathed jobs that bewildered my senses in any way, so I practiced my liberty to avoid them going forward. I indefinitely ruled out any primary healthcare work thereafter. When my shift ended that day, I walked to the nearest bus stop to catch a bus into Canterbury. Recruitment agencies were very good at getting staff to work in remote locations when they were desperate, but they very seldom arranged for workers' transport back home.

It was a spring evening, and the wind blew into my face with an assuring cleanse. It made me feel free. It would soon be dark and there was no one else in sight. Seagulls flapped their wings in the peachy sky above me, squawking tenaciously in a comforting way that made me feel less alone. A 20-minute stroll took me to the bus stop, where I inspected the bus timetable with hope. I had just missed a bus and would have to wait for an hour for the last bus to Canterbury.

"*Nhai Mwari!* Dear God!" I thought. The bus stop was in the middle of nowhere, somewhere between Reculver and Marshside. There was nowhere to sit or anywhere to go to kill time. My pay-as-you-go mobile phone had no money on it, so I could not phone anyone to pass the time. Luckily, it was a dry evening, so I stood there and lost myself in deep thought.

Growing up was emotionally tough, I mused, but I was in a much better place now. I did not realise it at the time but leaving Zimbabwe had been the perfect solution to my bondage. I had the freewill to shape my life the way I wanted going forward. My mind replayed the usual traumatic events I had been through, as it did often to preoccupy itself. At that age, I observed and thought a lot but rarely introspected.

A throbbing pain in my stagnant ankles awoke me from my thoughts. I realised the next bus would arrive in 10 minutes, then waited patiently. Very few cars had sped past me during my wait, but when I heard the deliberately slow roar of a bus gliding up the winding road, I knew my suffering for the day was nearly over. When the bus was in full view, I began waving it down in an exaggerated manner to ensure the bus driver saw me. As the bus approached the stop, it maintained its speed, and the grey-haired white man behind its steering wheel looked me in the eye and drove past the bus stop. I paused for a moment in disbelief, clenched my teeth to avoid an inevitable watery blink, then swallowed a hard, painful nothingness.

I had heard of such bus drivers. If they saw passengers of colour in the absence of white people waiting at bus stops, they felt justified to drive past these people who were taking their jobs and benefits. But I was a British citizen, born in Dagenham and in fact an Essex lass! Was I not entitled to benefit from the country of my birth? What had been a meditation of hope immediately switched to a self-patronising stream of consciousness. Questioning the blackness of my skin, and whether it might have been a karmic contract I signed to learn some life lessons, I loathed my God-given predicament. Why was my skin considered inferior? I had not chosen it! What was the meaning of this? I stood there feeling helpless, tears now freely trickling down my face. The temperature of the wind was dropping, and the pale pink sky was barely visible. I began walking to Canterbury, a 10 mile walk I was not sure I could accomplish. 15 minutes into my eerie walk, my mobile phone rang!

Belinda was a friend I had been introduced to by Nigel before he completed his final year at the law school. She was a mental health student nurse, and her husband was an engineering research associate at the University of Kent, who later completed his PhD there. The Canterbury couple were very kind to me and checked on me every now and again. They invited me to join them during weekends and when they had gatherings at their home. I became very good friends with Belinda, whose hair I braided in exchange for free meals and company. She introduced me to a wider community of Zimbabwean women in Canterbury whose hair I braided, attended their social gatherings and felt at home.

"Uri kupi iwe, huya udye sadza! Where are you? Come and join us for *sadza*!" said the voice on the phone. When I told Belinda what had happened, she drove to where I was and took me back to her house for an evening of warmth and laughter.

"Inotambika shaz! These things happen my friend!" she said, trying to lighten the mood. *"Aaahh,* that's what these old white bus drivers do Ruva, they are racists! But it doesn't matter, ha ha ha ha!" she chirped away in her usual jovial disposition. *"Chitora* licence *iwe!* Get a driving licence girl!" she suggested, knowing fully that I did not have the time, willpower and financial capacity to do so.

Thereafter, I found myself working 12 to 14-hour shifts of hard physical labour at farms, factories, and in bakeries, or catering as a waitress at events. In those jobs, I endured being looked down upon by egotistical managers who were clueless about treating other human beings with respect. To them, I was just a desperate black girl looking to earn money for her next meal. I did not bother mentioning that I was a student at the local School of Law. There were many times I pondered if these managers would have treated me differently if they knew who I was. I wondered if the greatness of my family name back home would have vindicated me or exacerbated their harsh treatment. I concluded that I was neither defined by who my family was nor what I was studying, so my background was not worth mentioning. The menial jobs did not define me either. I had never chosen my socio-economic status, yet I had been loathed by many for it when I was growing up. I had always hated privilege for that reason, and this was my opportunity to prove to myself that I did not need it.

I frequently grappled with the idea of privilege in my mind. Whereas I was deemed privileged in Masvingo, nobody really knew my family outside that sphere of influence. In fact, the Masvingo elite loved to be treated like royalty, even when they had done nothing extraordinary to warrant that reception. Their need to be adored, combined with a condescending attitude towards others, as well as a heightened sense of entitlement, was most times cringeworthy. I knew the progeny of several members of the Masvingo elite who had left Zimbabwe to trial life in South Africa, the United States, Australia, and eventually the UK in quick succession, but decided to return home only after a few months away, because they could not stomach an ordinary existence.

The UK elite were not half as pompous as Zimbabweans who had amassed a little bit of wealth. This was especially clear to me now that I had left home and was able to objectively liken my former community with their societal equivalents. By trying to compare apples with apples, it became crystal clear in my mind, that privilege was subjective, and that our identities were nuanced and intersectional.

I often doubted the socio-economic status my family had been awarded back home, and my new lifestyle in the UK fuelled those doubts. I sometimes wondered whether their desperation for clout was a complex resulting from feelings of inferiority associated with growing up in a marginalised society.

The educated members of the Masvingo elite felt especially superior, and I often thought of how Mbuya had retorted in their faces, "You're educated but uncivilised!" to wake them up from their delusion. A few of them, respected politicians, had often visited Mbuya ahead of elections to lobby her to influence local voters in their favour. On such days, the politicians drove to her home at dawn and spent all day sitting next to Mbuya on a reed mat, shelling maize cobs and peanuts, intimately discussing her personal life first, before moving on to discuss politics. Onlookers were intrigued by such important visits, but Mbuya saw right through the drama, made her own mind up without undue influence and did not hesitate to put the entitled politicians in their place.

In the UK, I had often heard many Zimbabweans declaring a profound statement, "*UK ndimaenzanise!* UK the equaliser!" which for Zimbabweans meant their socio-economic status back home was irrelevant in the UK. They said this because all Zimbabweans suddenly had access to basic resources in the UK, which was unheard of in Zimbabwe. I remember meeting Patience, a woman from Masvingo who had worked for Mhamha once. I met her in London and when I asked her how life was going, she said, "Well, I can now eat apples and sausages like you did back home Ruva. And when I'm sick, I can now be seen by a real doctor, just like you did back home. So, life is good!" Her response compounded my realisation of the relativity of privilege, and that in my case, it had been based on my access to basic human resources in a marginalised society where accessibility to those resources was scarce.

I did not realise this at the time, but the view of the UK being "an equaliser" was partly true, albeit a largely ignorant statement that needed qualification. First, immigrants were not entirely equal. Some were legal and some illegal, and that difference in immigration status made the former more privileged than the latter. Second, although everyone had access to basic resources in the UK, those resources were graded. The quality appraisal of food, for instance, resulted in its scaling between economy and premium brands in supermarkets, or the distinction between organic and genetically modified products. We did not all eat the same apples, or the same sausages. The quality of products we had access to depended on our level of income, and that income depended massively on our immigration status. On occasion, I privately made an Orwellian joke in my head, that *all apples were equal, but some apples were more equal than others*!

It was this lack of clarity that caused most foreigners to become too excited by cheap food and overindulge, resulting in obesity and eventually the development of chronic illnesses and disability.

The UK equalised foreigners, not only by bringing them down to a level playing field through access to basic resources, but by making them all feel inferior, unless they significantly transcended the lower social classes. Most first-generation Africans fit into the bottom three of the seven socio-economic classes in the UK: the precariat, traditional working class and emergent service workers. They had to subsequently jump through onerous hoops to graduate into the upper four socio-economic classes: technical middle class, new affluent workers, established middle class, and the elite. The chances of those Africans becoming established middle class or elite were negligible, and most foreigners who had escaped the bottom three social classes sometimes sacrificed all their earnings to send their children to private schools with the hope to propel them into the upper two classes. That was the obscure future I was headed for, and I had no idea how my life would pan out.

There was something I loved about being on a "level playing field" with everybody else. It was a comforting feeling of pride and contentment that came with knowing my hard work and talents warranted success. If ever I became successful in a meritocracy that the UK was, I would not be guilt-tripped by onlookers attributing my success to privilege; because even those from less-privileged backgrounds had access to free education and other resources, could work hard too and be rewarded for it. I intended to exert maximum effort to climb the ladder that led to better apples and sausages, and when I got there, I hoped to play my part to equalise the power.

When I was not working, I listened to recorded Law and Business lectures I had missed during the day. Somewhere between attempting to memorise legal precedents to quote in essays and exams, and trying to understand foreign legal concepts, I would fall asleep and return to work the next day. I also braided hair to top up my income.

A distant cousin of mine, Nicholas, who I kept in touch with called me one day with strange news. He had received a letter from Peter. Nicolas and Peter had attended the same mission boarding school in Zimbabwe and were friends, something I only found out when I had relocated to the UK. Peter was in prison serving a 14-year jail sentence for two counts of statutory rape.

"I was very surprised to receive a letter from Peter. *Eish,* I don't know how he's going to survive that length of time locked up in Chikurubi. He's been in there for a few years already by the sounds of it, and he seems like a completely changed person, quoting the Bible and everything. Anyway, towards the end of the letter he asks me to tell you he's sorry. What did he do to you?" Nicholas would not have known about the rape.

"He cheated on me, that's why we broke up," I said.

The memory of the rape broke my heart, and the thought that Peter had done it to two other girls, or maybe more, filled me with rage. Feeling completely helpless, I consoled myself by concluding that Peter's conscience would punish him for what he did to me.

A few weeks into the semester, Baba informed me he was travelling to Stuttgart on a business trip. I arranged to fly to Germany to meet him and was very excited. I had missed Baba. I flew to Stuttgart only a few days after 9/11 and was rather worried about my safety. The time with Baba in Stuttgart was pleasant. We wined, dined, and window shopped when he was not in meetings. Baba even told me how proud he was of the woman I had become and added that had it not been for his beatings, I would not have turned out the way I had. I concurred and laughed in synchronicity with him. I had bought my family lots of gifts from the United States, which I took to Germany for Baba to take back home. I had bought Babamunini Benjy some designer clothing which he had asked for while I was in Omaha.

I had enjoyed visiting Germany, until I experienced a nerve-racking altercation with a ticket inspector on a train on my way to the airport. Assuming I could buy my ticket on the train as one could in the UK, I jumped on the train and relaxed. When the ticket inspector turned up, he spoke no English and was not interested in my explanation. Due to misunderstanding each other, he must have thought I was a ticket dodger and manhandled me off the train at the next stop. Despite feeling perturbed by the ordeal, I managed to jump onto a taxi that whisked me to the airport to ensure I did not miss my flight.

A few days after the trip to Germany, I was studying in the library on campus one evening when I missed a call from Tizai. I would have normally waited until I finished studying to call him back, but something made me walk out of the library to call Tizai back immediately. The voice on the other end of the line announced that Babamunini Benjy was dead. He had hung himself, and this only four months after Mbuya's death.

"But why? He is just 26 years old!" I cried into the phone.

The whole family acknowledged that Babamunini Benjy had not coped very well with Mbuya's death. I was told my uncle had uncharacteristically wailed hysterically, holding onto Mbuya's casket at her funeral, as if he intuitively felt his end was nigh because his protector was gone. He was Mbuya's last, and despite his countless delinquencies, she had cushioned and protected him as most mothers would have done. Mbuya overfed and spoilt my uncle, who incessantly complained that no one cared for him.

The last time I had seen him in Chivi during the preceding Christmas, he had looked swollen with inflammation and obesity. I had laughed with him about the irony of the latest mural graffiti he had personally inscribed on his bedroom wall, which read, *Them belly full while we starve!* A message undoubtedly directed at Baba, who could not care less about his reggae-loving drug addicted little brother's latest protest. Babamunini Benjy was only five years older than me and had been like my older brother, always prepared to batter any boys who annoyed me in Masvingo. He would talk about Baba and how oppressive he was, imitating his facial expressions and prolonged cackles. I pretended to understand his concerns, as I had not fully developed a mind of my own.

Tete Mary had been processing college applications for Babamunini Benjy in the US. When she attended Mbuya's funeral, she had returned with his identification documents and academic certificates in order to register Babamunini Benjy at various universities in Nebraska. He had sounded more and more desperate to escape when we spoke to him only a few weeks before he died. I wished I had paid more attention to Babamunini Benjy's voice when I had last spoken to him. I may have detected his worsening depression and said something positive to save his life.

I could sense the shock in my brother's voice as he broke the news to me. I had hoped he was pulling a prank on me, but he was not. I was utterly heartbroken by the news and knew I would not attend Babamunini Benjy's funeral. The university semester had just begun, and I now knew my attendance at his funeral would not bring him back. My uncle's death caused tangible tension in our family. The strain in family relations was obvious when I visited Zimbabwe a few months later. Mhamha had been blamed for my uncle's death and that ravaged her heart and soul.

"What happened exactly?" I asked Tizai one evening as we sipped local red wine in his bedroom at our childhood home in Masvingo. "Mbuya's will stated that Baba was to take Babamunini Benjy under his wing and teach him how to run a business. Immediately after the reading of the will, Baba instructed Babamunini Benjy to pack his bags and return to Masvingo with us that evening to run the butchery Mhamha had been running," Tizai explained. Mhamha had resigned from her nursing career to run our family businesses on a full-time basis for no pay. She was generally held accountable for any mishaps within the businesses, while Baba got the recognition for their success. Mhamha was very hands-on with the businesses, going to wholesalers and breweries in person to ensure adequate stocking of the shops, then stock taking every month-end to ensure the takings were accurately accounted for.

Tizai went on to explain that Babamunini Benjy was still grieving for Mbuya and was reluctant to relocate to Masvingo immediately, but he was given no choice. Upon arrival, Mhamha handed over a fully stocked cold room to

Babamunini Benjy, but she expected to be paid back for the meat she had bought, as soon as Babamunini Benjy was able to do so. Being inexperienced in running a business, my uncle had been selling but spending all takings as they came in, to the point that he had no money left to restock his butchery. Mhamha began to ask Babamunini Benjy when he would pay her back for the butchery stock. He felt he needed the initial stock to start him off and did not need to reimburse Mhamha for it. Mhamha asked Baba to settle the issue, but Baba did not resolve it. Eventually, the tension between Mhamha and Babamunini Benjy led him to pay Baba a visit at our childhood home. Babamunini Tafara, Tizai and Mhamha were also present when Babamunini Benjy demanded that Baba deal with the butchery stock issue as a matter of urgency. Baba laughed off the request.

"You are the head of this family! If you do not resolve this issue Mukoma Davis, I will kill myself!" Babamunini Benjy demanded with teary eyes.

Baba chuckled and said to Babamunini Benjy, *"Shuwa ungatenda kunetswa nemunhukadzi? Mukadzi wauchagara nhaka ndafa?* Honestly, why would you agree to be troubled by a woman? The very woman you're going to inherit when I die?" then burst into a prolonged roar of contagious laughter. Babamunini Benjy was too depressed to laugh with Baba and remained silent the rest of that evening. Babamunini Tafara later drove Babamunini Benjy to the one room he rented in the *rokeshen* near Baba's grocery stores. It was not very far from the room where Peter had raped me.

The following day during his work lunch break, Babamunini Tafara decided to go and check on Babamunini Benjy at his butchery. When he got there, he was told by Mhamha's staff that Babamunini Benjy had not turned up that day. Babamunini Tafara went on to ask at a nearby *bhodho*, a communal eating restaurant, where Babamunini Benjy usually ate his lunch, whether they had seen him that day, but they had not. Babamunini Tafara intuitively knew, before he embarked on the journey on foot to Babamunini Benjy's home, that he would find him dead. His neighbours had seen him taking a shower in the communal bathroom that morning, before he disappeared into his room and never came out. When Babamunini Tafara peeped through a small window, he saw his brother hanging from the ceiling, then broke down the door. There was no suicide note.

"Babamunini Benjy was very depressed Ruva. He said he saw visions of people following him...he thought someone was trying to kill him. He would ask his friends to walk ahead of or behind him, due to paranoia of being killed," Tizai explained.

"But you guys were always high on the chronic though. Don't you think he may have been over-using it? Sounds like he was hallucinating man!" I replied.

Reports of Babamunini Benjy's hallucinations had led to the *kuchekeresa* accusations on Mhamha, that she had sold his soul to the spiritual realm for successful businesses. Following the public humiliation, Babamunini Benjy's friends from the *rokeshen* would intimidate and verbally abuse Mhamha on a daily basis, threatening to hit or kill her, shaking her car when she parked at the shops for her daily routines. Mhamha saw no way out of her quandary and began avoiding going to work when the harassment got out of hand.

The many years of emotional abuse she had suffered had taken their toll on Mhamha, and the witchery accusations had been the final straw. She began toying with the idea of returning to the UK to reinstate her nursing licence so that she could work and pay my university tuition fees. I encouraged this idea, which I sensed would heal Mhamha by removing her from the toxicity of our family. I had felt lonely, so the prospect of Mhamha coming to live in the UK was delightful, albeit selfish to Baba and my siblings. I also desperately wanted to rekindle the intimacy that I knew should have existed between Mhamha and me.

Within a few months of Babamunini Benjy's death, Mhamha arrived in the UK and went to live with Mainini Portia and Mainini Joy in Aldershot. I visited her during weekends when she was not working and would spend my university holidays with her when I could. Excited to rekindle our intimacy, I sometimes invited Mhamha to come out with me and have some fun.

"Let's go and watch a movie Mhamha. We can go and eat or drink after that; my treat!"

"Ah! And what would people back home think if they hear that I now go to watch films. I'm a married woman, remember? I can't be seen doing things like that. Nooo."

I found her responses amusing and always challenged her.

"But Mhamha, how does going to the cinema make you a bad wife? Who cares what people think anyway? Ok, what would you rather do for fun?"

"Perhaps we could go to London and buy some hair extensions, then you can braid my hair."

"Is it true Ruva, that you told Tete Gwinyai you believe I killed your uncle?" Mhamha asked me one evening when I was braiding her hair.

"Don't be ridiculous Mhamha, I'm your daughter. I would never say that about you. People commit suicide because they are tired of living and have made a choice to die. If I believed you were responsible for it, I would have said something to you, not to other people."

An expression of relief took over my mother's face then she said, "I did wonder what I ever did to you to deserve such judgement. Tete Gwinyai was going around telling people that even my daughter felt like disowning me for what I had done."

"Well I'm glad you asked Mhamha. I know you had nothing to do with Babamunini Benjy's death." With a heightened awareness that smear campaigns defined how our family operated to undermine their target's credibility, I felt deep empathy for Mhamha.

I had had two brief meaningless relationships with Zimbabwean men after Baby. The first was with a gangster cum fraudster who made me believe he was an import and export trader, Brian. I had been introduced to him by Janet and Jean in London and had always sensed something a bit off about him. The relationship ended when he slept with my older cousin, Moira, the daughter of Mhamha's older sister, Maiguru Chiedza. Moira had been living in the UK illegally and had asked me to introduce her to Brian who was apparently known among Zimbabwean circles for "sorting out papers". I was aloof to the issue of "sorting out papers", and I had been too busy studying and working to bother finding out what Brian really did for a living.

One morning, my younger cousin Chenai called me. She too had relocated to the UK, had overstayed her visitor visa and was living illegally.

"I think something really bad happened last night Ruva," she said.

After coercing her to divulge the difficult news, she said, "I think Moira slept with Brian." When I probed Chenai further, she divulged that she and Moira had arranged to see Brian so that he could produce some fake identification documents for them. In return for his service, he charged a discounted fee plus sex from Moira. I thanked Chenai for the information and immediately called Brian.

"I know what happened. Explain yourself!" I screamed.

"Your cousin is a whore, she made me do it! The sad thing is she doesn't even have hips as wide as yours or boobs as perky as yours, it was such a waste of time," he explained.

"Handina kana kutombonakairwa zvekuti ngatingozvikanganwai sweetie. I didn't even enjoy the sex; we may as well forget it ever happened sweetie." Shocked by his nonchalance I dumped him straightaway.

"Fuck you dude!" I said calmly then hung up the phone. I was hurt.

I met the second guy, William, while I was out clubbing with Janet and Jean, and they spoke highly of him. He was an IT expert who was more polished and sophisticated than Brian. However, he had a secret that he forgot to share when we got together. I had a friend who I had inherited from Tete Mary, Bridget. She lived in Paisley, Scotland, and had gone to the same mission boarding school as Tete Mary in Zimbabwe. I had met Bridget during my visit to Nebraska, where she had been visiting her fiancé. One weekend, I went to visit Bridget in Scotland and told her about my new boyfriend, William. It turned out Bridget's fiancé in the US was actually William's cousin. Bridget knew

William's secret, but said nothing about it during my visit. A few days later, when I had returned to university, Bridget who's recent attitude to me had been off, called me and said, "I didn't realise you were a homewrecker, just like your aunt Mary!"

When I asked her to explain herself, she told me William was married, and when I appeared shocked by the news, she thought I was feigning my response. "How can you not know that a man is married? His wife travels a lot, but when you go to his house, do you not see signs that another woman lives there?" she enquired. I had never been to William's home. I had met him whilst partying in London, and the few times I saw him thereafter, he insisted on visiting me at the university campus in Kent to save me travelling to his home in north-west London. Realising how stupid and naive I had been, I dumped William immediately and was put off dating for a while.

My sole intention for dating was to get married, so I never dated for fun. Disappointed by Janet and Jean for putting me through such unnecessary kerfuffle, I ceased contact with them and erased them from my memory. I decided to stay single for a while and heal.

Chapter 9

At some point during my second year of university, a man from Masvingo, Tawanda, who had pursued me unsuccessfully during my high school years, because I had been dating Morris, got in touch with me. He was based in Stamford, Connecticut and had caught wind of my regular visits to Omaha. He wanted to find out if he could meet me in Omaha the next time I visited. Tawanda was a few years older than me and had a celebrity status in Masvingo, because his father had been a prominent politician there. I was reluctant to date him for this reason.

I deliberately avoided being in relationships with men who resembled Baba and his family in any form. For that reason, I avoided dating the Masvingo elite. I loathed privilege and anything associated with it; I believed it was synonymous with dysfunction. Growing up, my experience was that many people seemed to despise and scrutinise the lives of privileged people and they always had something negative to say about them. I did not have many close friends of my age for that reason. Growing up, I usually was closer to older or younger girls, and barely anyone of my age. I learnt that privilege implied I had had an easy life and did not have to work for anything; yet the sad reality for me was I did in fact have to work hard for a lot of things, including parental love, which was supposed to be free and unconditional. I had to endure a painful three-year course at university to maintain the family image that Baba wanted me to sustain. I hoped that attaining a degree in Law would increase Baba's love for me. Mhamha had shown me love, which I failed to see because I was in pursuit of Baba's love.

After several weeks of courtship, I rationalised that things would be different with Tawanda because the relationship would be over a long distance. Plus, he was no longer living back home where he had been a luminary. I felt lonely and had not been in a meaningful relationship since the relationship with Morris had gone cold, so a new romance blossomed with Tawanda. I stopped visiting Tete Mary in Nebraska and spent the next two years travelling to Stamford every couple of months to visit my new love. He was living in the United States illegally and could not leave the country. He worked as a health care assistant, funded my trips to visit him, and this suited me well. Tawanda's financial and immigration status made him as ordinary as a man could get; this represented the opposite of my upbringing, and I loved it. Together we could start from the bottom and work our way up if we needed to. At this point, I hated my course and found it suffocating, so the trips to Stamford were a welcome relief.

Tawanda could not help but idolise me, which I found delightfully surprising. The relationship with him was my first proper adult relationship, which I learnt a lot from. I enjoyed the long-distance relationship, because through talking and emailing each other daily, we got to know each other very well. I fell in love with Tawanda and trusted him. When I visited him and went about doing normal things young adult couples did together, like dining out, going to the cinema, shopping for clothes and trinkets, and shooting hoops together, it slowly became apparent that Tawanda was in fact overprotective and jealous. At first, I misunderstood these behaviours and thought they meant I was loved and needed. It felt good to be loved and needed by a member of the Masvingo elite because they were not usually prepared to display their vulnerability or affection. However, Tawanda's character slowly began to reveal he may have had unfulfilled needs resulting from his upbringing. Endless bouts of sex which at times felt like punishment were one of his coping mechanisms, which I mistook for me being irresistible to him.

Tawanda was openly condescending to women, but he delivered his views in such a shockingly nonchalant manner that made me doubt the reality. He quite often said to me, *"Mwari pavakati mukadzi vaida kumuti mutadzi. When God named 'woman', He meant to name her a sinner,"* a Shona adage he had learnt from his elderly father. I often contemplated the unfortunate truth in the statement, which I felt was a painful reality for a lot of women I knew. Women were reduced to functional objects by society and were often punished if they did not live up to societal expectations, just like sinners.

Tawanda often laughed about his upbringing, joking about how his father's illegitimate children had randomly walked up to introduce themselves to him in supermarkets and other random places back in Masvingo. I found it intriguing that he normalised his experiences and wondered if he actually hurt inside but chose to mask his pain. In fact, Tawanda seemed too happy for no good reason, and laughed a lot about things I did not particularly find funny, in a way that subtly reminded me of Baba.

Tawanda did not like my clothes, which he felt shaped my body and made other men want me. He decided to buy me a new wardrobe comprising maxi skirts and other loose-fitting clothes he felt were appropriate for a woman in a serious relationship. Tawanda's views often felt more stifling than Baba's great expectations during my teenage years. I had worked so hard to liberate myself from my strict upbringing, but as my relationship with Tawanda progressed, I felt like I was taking several strides back to where I had begun. Tawanda could only tolerate very subtle make-up because his mother and sisters did not wear any. I did not find this expectation onerous.

Tawanda did not like the fact that I consumed alcohol because he did not drink, but I failed to give alcohol up for him. He also banned the few male friends I had at the time, which I found strange but complied with anyway. I was forced to abandon my relationship with Nigel; a sacrifice I found painful. Nigel had made several attempts to contact me, leaving voice messages, text messages and emails when I went cold turkey and shut him out of my life with no explanation. I was too embarrassed to rationalise to Nigel that Tawanda did not want us to be friends.

During one visit to Stamford, an anonymous person sent me an email, declaring that they wanted me; they watched me with Tawanda and they would be a better man to me than him. Tawanda had been reading the email on my screen from the sofa, where he was pretending to watch a basketball match. He raged towards me and bellowed in my face that I was cheating on him, despite the fact the email was actually sent anonymously. He broke a couple of chairs in his apartment and stormed out in utter indignation to harass his friends who lived in the same apartment complex. I remained in his apartment and only imagined who might have received facial fists for remotely seeming like they may have sent the email to me. The promise of a violent future presented by this incident agitated me.

On a separate occasion, I had gone to visit Tawanda, and whilst tidying up his bedroom, I had found used condoms under his bed and in his wardrobe. When I demanded enlightenment on such a clumsy discrepancy, he explained that a married friend of his had asked to sleep with his side chick in his apartment a few days before I arrived from the UK, and the friend must have forgotten to tidy up his mess. He went on to rationalise that if he had cheated on me, he would have done a better job of eliminating the evidence before my arrival. The condom incident marked the end of my trust for Tawanda. I was not too surprised by the revelation, because I had often wondered how he coped with his insatiable appetite for sex in my absence.

When I returned to the UK, I rekindled my relationship with Nigel, who was then going through a breakup with Karen. I told him about the condom sighting, and he affirmed what I already knew. I was not hurt by the discovery of Tawanda's infidelity, but I was disappointed that even a man who idolised me could not be satisfied by the one woman he seemed to have eyes for. I was, however, prepared to marry Tawanda, not for love or trust, but to tick the box my family expected me to tick. As my relationship with Tawanda progressed in the wake of an obscure future, I could not help but compare him with Morris, who I had once decided would be my ideal life partner.

A cousin of mine, Tete Gwinyai's eldest son John, lived in the UK and made a living out of his kleptomania. His behaviours which could have been tamed in his childhood were widely accepted as normal and sometimes applauded by our family. As a child, John had grown up in a well-off family and attended private school. His recurrent urge to steal had nothing to do with need, and he stole because he could, from his parents, family, friends, or anyone who had anything to steal. Interestingly, John never stole from me. Quite often, I found John occupying my room on campus after my trips to Stamford.

"Who let you in, John? I'm pretty sure I locked my room before I left!" I would ask my cousin incredulously. He would go on to explain how he had found the university housekeeper's office and stolen master keys to rooms he needed access to on campus. He then invited me to enjoy the copious amounts of groceries he brought with him, which made it difficult for me to ask him to leave. How could I ask John to leave? My cousin who had come to Masvingo on countless occasions and proceeded to Chivi with the rest of us during school holidays. All the adventures we had experienced together herding cattle, getting lost in mountains, then eating communally from the same plate each evening under Mbuya's protective wings. Despite the risks associated with sheltering John in my room on campus, he was my blood, so no alarms would be raised. That was how we had been raised.

John had indeed turned up during dark times when I had no money, or no time to work due to exam pressure or otherwise. Using money he had acquired fraudulently from banks and vulnerable rich women, he ensured I was fed and watered during desperate times. I felt guilty for *kudziya moto wembavha* – those who associate themselves with a thief also become thieves – a Shona proverb; but I was grateful for his help.

John dated several PhD students on my campus, whose money he would steal using methods I could never quite understand. John was handsome and charming, and women found him irresistible. He sometimes got caught and served time in prison, especially when he robbed established institutions with advanced surveillance systems. John wrote to me while he was in prison, and I wrote back to him, updating him on family news and encouraging him to do better so that he would not go back to jail. He seemed comfortable with going to prison and insisted that when he was incarcerated, he got time to introspect, network with more sophisticated criminals and better his criminal skills. John did better his skills each time he was released from prison, going to the extent of dressing up as a woman to trick surveillance cameras, or to withdraw funds from women's bank accounts. When the movie "Catch Me If You Can" was released, Frank Abagnale completely reminded me of John.

During my final year at university, I lived off campus in a shared privately rented house on the outskirts of Canterbury. I was too busy to nurture relationships with my housemates, between attending lectures, working, studying and visiting Mhamha in Aldershot during weekends, when I was not in Stamford visiting Tawanda. Out of the blue I received an email from an old friend from high school, Raviro. She wrote that she was in London and would love to pay me a visit, for old times' sake. She said she had missed me. I was sceptical about the visit, because I had not heard from Raviro after she left high school following our GCSEs, to attend a prestigious college in Namibia. Raviro had had a huge following of friends who I had become affiliated with through my friendship with her, but I sensed they did not like me. I did not have many friends in high school. Most people thought I was privileged, and I did not trust forging friendships with people who thought I was better than them. I preferred friendships that were not influenced by personal backgrounds we had no control of. Raviro and her friends had caused me a lot of grief in high school, and I had not forgotten it. I hoped she had finally matured into a kinder, empathetic and compassionate human being.

When I was in form one, a butch athletic student called Melody claimed she could beat anyone up, including all the boys in our boarding hostel. Her claim to have single-handedly trounced a set of twins in her hometown awarded her fear and respect. Melody had also been seen by a few of her friends grabbing boys by the collar and was deemed a gutsy 13-year-old. I had a good relationship with Melody and had no reason to fear or dislike her. One evening after a tedious two-hour prep session, I made my way to my dormitory and found all the girls congregated in a prefects' cubicle. I wondered why I had been excluded from the meeting, but I soon found that the assembly had been about me.

"Ruva we've been waiting for you. Come over and tell us your story," Precious invited me into her cubicle.

As I confidently walked into the meeting, 32 girls shuffled to create a ring at the centre of the cubicle. A few girls stood on their feet, others sat on top of the cubicle divider and stared down at me, and a few sat on Precious's desk swinging their legs forward and backward in anticipation. I stood still under the spotlight, my mind racing about what I may have done wrong. Perhaps my secret romance with Oliver who also boarded in my hostel had been discovered and I was about to be shamed for it. Perhaps I would be awarded a surprise recognition for something I had done well, but that was unlikely, because I barely did anything over and above expectations at that age. I wilfully circumvented difficult situations, and simply wanted to get by.

Avoiding eye contact with the audience, I smiled nervously and awaited further direction. At that point,

Melody stepped forward with her chest stuck out and said, "*Wakati unondirovaka iwe?* I heard you've been claiming you can beat me up!"

Utterly confused, and quickly trying to think whether I might have said something to someone that may have been taken out of context, I noticed Raviro and Chipiwa sniggering mischievously, in a manner I had witnessed when they got other girls into trouble by lying or gossiping. Other than my childhood scuffles with Tizai, I had never been in a proper fight. Neither did I have the appetite for bellicose jingoism. In that moment, I felt like I had been thrown into a wrestling ring unprepared. My performance in it would determine how everyone perceived me for the rest of my life in that school, and potentially thereafter. I had already witnessed sixth formers who had earned shameful nicknames in form one and had dismally failed to shake them off.

Contagious giggles spread rapidly in the cubicle until Precious banged her travel mug on the metal bedside cabinet on which she was perched. "Order! Ruva, what say you?" Adrenaline burst into my bloodstream, and without thinking, a shocker escaped my mouth. "*Yaa, ndokumamisa!* I'll make you shit!" I said to Melody as I confidently poked her inflated chest. The onlooking girls roared in utter shock, some of them jeering wide eyed, and others covering their open mouths. The interjections and murmurs that took over my dormitory could have been equated to "Oof!"

When I noticed Melody's chest deflating slowly, I realised I had won. Our boarding house had a strict anti-fight policy which if breached would result in immediate expulsion; and a fight incited by a prefect would have had devastating consequences. I felt my nerves calming down gradually as I remembered the school rules around fights and bullies. *"Wati chii?* What did you say?" Melody asked in a shocked voice. Although I was still trembling with fear inside, I had to respond in a louder confident manner, with sanguine authority. With my feet planted firmly on the ground, I stood a little taller, my hands cinching my waist, and leaning forward I declared, *"Ndaa-ti ndokumamisa!* I said I'll make you shit!"

"Ok, ok, order girls!" Precious said. "We don't condone fights here. Ruva and Melody, can you resolve your issues in a more mature manner please. Everyone else! Go back to your cubicles except for Ruva and Melody." When we stayed behind, I explained to Melody that I had no intention of beating her up and that the claims she had heard were false rumours. However, if the need ever arose, I would indeed beat her up. Knowing the line would never be crossed, we laughed it off and remained amicable thereafter.

On a separate occasion a few years later, following a playdate at Chipiwa's house during a school holiday, Raviro must have felt jealous of her exclusion, then lied to Chipiwa that I thought Chipiwa's home looked like a stable. Chipiwa actually lived in my neighbourhood and her parents' home was not too different from ours. When the confrontation from Chipiwa came, I was shocked by the accusation, which I denied. I apologised to Chipiwa anyway for the sake of peace. Similar incidents had erupted during my boarding school years, and they had confirmed what Mhamha had always counselled me about friends.

Raviro arrived in Canterbury on a Friday morning, with no travel bag or change of clothes, so I assumed she would return to London on the same day. Raviro had apparently left Namibia without completing her course because her stepmother had coerced her father to cease financing her studies, so she was now seeking a better life in the UK. Raviro was an illegitimate daughter of a wealthy doctor, but she had been raised modestly, much to her frustration, by her mother who was a schoolteacher.

Raviro said she had been staying with relatives in London, but she did not return to London that day, or the next. She borrowed my sleepwear, used my towels and everything she needed to get by. Within a few days of sharing my single bed in a single room with Raviro, I began to find the prolonged visit suffocating. When I asked Raviro what her plans were and when she would return to London, she casually responded that she had no plans to leave my room. With my tiny student budget, I bought her cheap new clothes to stop her from wearing my special clothes Tawanda had bought me in Stamford. I also bought all the food and toiletries she consumed. Raviro would watch television all night, despite knowing I had lectures to attend the following morning. I began to avoid my own home, spending longer hours on campus to get more studying done in preparation for my final exams.

Desperate to get Raviro out of my space, I offered her my papers so that she could work and earn enough money to stand on her own. I contacted the recruitment agencies I had not worked with for a while, notifying them I was available for work. When those agencies offered me work, I accepted the jobs and Raviro went to work on my behalf. In no time, Raviro was earning. When her money hit my bank account, she demanded it all on the same day, to which I obliged. With that money, Raviro bought herself luxuries, like chocolate and wine. She also bought phone cards to make international calls to her boyfriends in Namibia. I continued to buy all the food, toiletries and paid the bills. I had a landline in my room, which Raviro misused within the first two weeks of her arrival. When I learnt of the inflated phone bill, I contacted my service provider and asked them to block outgoing phone calls. One of the people she liked to call was Chipiwa, who now lived in London. I knew that when I was not present, the two gossiped about me because Chipiwa's attitude towards me when I picked up the phone was telling.

After a few months of living with Raviro, and not receiving any financial contributions to her upkeep, I asked her when she thought she would leave to find her own place. Raviro arrogantly responded, "And why would I want to leave this easy life? I'm not going anywhere!" she affirmed then ejaculated a prolonged laugh that induced a never-ending headache on my front left temple. Raviro had been in the habit of rearranging my room and misusing everything I owned. I miraculously managed to write my final exams whilst enduring the disturbance and discomfort of living with Raviro.

When I had had enough, I did not know how else to deal with the situation. As the summer holidays approached, I decided to hand in my notice earlier than contractually agreed with my landlord, and I was fortunate enough that he agreed to an early termination of our lease agreement. I arranged to disappear to Stamford for a while, then returned to live with Mhamha in Aldershot later that summer. When all was arranged, I announced to Raviro that I was leaving, and she could stay in the room and pay for it on her own if she wanted to.

By the time I had finished packing my belongings, Raviro had made alternative arrangements she did not care to disclose. Following Raviro's departure, Chipiwa called my landline expecting to speak to Raviro, but she had gone without updating Chipiwa of her whereabouts. An unsurprising allegation followed.

"Since you're around, I thought I should just ask. Raviro says you told her that I have no papers and am dating a guy who I hope will marry me for papers. She also said you told her that I'm doing a useless course, so that I can tell people back home that I'm doing something useful. Why would you say such hurtful things about me Ruva?" Chipiwa queried.

"Not again! Some things will never change Chipiwa. This sounds like high school all over again. I never said those things and I have nothing else to say to you." That was what I managed to say, then hung up, disconnected my phone and packed my headset away. Exhausted by meaningless friendships, I vowed to protect myself harder from toxic relationships.

I finally graduated with a 2:2 and my parents were extremely proud of me. Although I had not enjoyed the course, I was perpetually grateful for the effort they made to get me where I had got to in life, and the sacrifice they had made to separate, in order for Mhamha to finish funding my course. Prior to Mhamha immigrating to the UK, my parents had sold many of their prized possessions, including Mhamha's BMW, to get me through my first year of university. I on the other hand had worked tirelessly to earn a living, slaving away through 12 to 14-hour shifts on farms, bakeries and hotels to make ends meet. The goal was accomplished! My parents decided their first project had been delivered successfully, so they would relocate my siblings to the UK and get them into school younger to avoid a repeat of the extortionate international tuition fees they had had to pay for my education.

Baba travelled to the UK for my graduation with Tongai, who was under the age of 18 and considered dependent on Mhamha. Tizai was denied a visa to the UK because he was over 18 and no longer considered dependent on Mhamha. Runako was granted a visa but would travel during the Zimbabwean August school holiday so that she would begin school when the UK academic year commenced in September.

I travelled to Canterbury with my parents from Aldershot on graduation day. Beneath my graduation gown, I wore a panelled plum Chantilly silk and lace dress with a bead-encrusted sweetheart neckline. I accessorised my outfit with black leather pointed-toe kitten heels with an elaborate floral applique on the outer sides, and freshwater pearl studs. Mhamha had invested in a beautiful crepe antique-rose formal dress and jacket suit which was out of her usual price range. She accessorised it with a matching beige and chocolate structured sinamay hat and dark-brown leather mid-heels. We had made a special trip to Liverpool street in London and ventured into the more expensive stores near Petticoat Lane Market. While we were there, Mhamha identified beautiful African embroidered lace fabrics which she unashamedly announced would make superb outfits for my wedding.

"You look gorgeous Mhamha!" I proudly told her before we left for Canterbury.

"And you look beautiful *mwanangu*! Our own amazing lawyer. I am so proud of the woman you have become Ruva."

Baba wore a penguin suit beneath his graduation gown and cap from Oxford University.

Mhamha did not like driving on the motorway, so Baba drove to Canterbury and made it known that he also did not enjoy the challenge of driving on British roads. We kept the radio in Mhamha's car off to ensure Baba's two-hour drive was not made any more difficult by unnecessary distractions. We travelled quietly most of the way, and only spoke when commenting on other vehicles that offended Baba on the road.

"These haulage trucks! The UK ones are no better than the ones back home, bullying smaller cars out of their lanes without warning," Mhamha interjected.

"*Iiiiiiiiii* the number of accidents on the Beit-bridge road these days? *Aaaah* it's bad! The potholes!" Baba responded, then briefly summarised the latest car accident that had been headlining the news immediately before he left Zimbabwe.

When we arrived in Canterbury, Baba was upset by the fact that we did not know where exactly we were meant to park the car. He had also grumbled over the fact that we had to find the correct designated entrance into the Canterbury Cathedral, rather than use the main entrance which was easier to access. Perhaps he was agitated because he was not a morning person.

The Kentish weather was warm and fresh, and the atmosphere was exultant. The serenity of the graduation ceremony in the Romanesque pilgrimage cathedral was complimented by the pleasant weather. However, my whole being was flooded with a cocktail of conflicting emotions, because of the subtle tension Baba had managed to create that day, which kept me on the brink of tears. Uncalled-for grouchiness that made smiling on the official graduation photographs difficult had prevailed from the time he had woken up. At first, I thought I was overwhelmed by happiness and needed to shed tears of joy. But happy tears usually flowed out freely together with laughter. Something in my chest stopped my tears of joy from materialising. There was a ball of pain in my heart I did not want to acknowledge. It was a tightening that made me want to rip my sternum apart to set myself free.

I excused myself from my parents a few times to visit the toilet, where I had hoped to sob and let some of the pain out. But each time Mhamha came with me and uncharacteristically helped to freshen my make-up.

My graduation day had been a long-awaited opportunity to prove to Baba that I was sufficient, but I felt like I had not done enough to make him happy. I was also consciously and proudly aware of my resilience, having overcome three years of intellectual torture, just to make

Baba proud. However, the only time Baba had seemed happy was when passers-by recognised his Oxford graduation gown and stopped to comment on how impressed they were by him. Only then did he release a prolonged chuckle of genuine pride.

A big celebratory function organised by Mhamha followed, where many well-wishers joined my family and I at a party in Aldershot. Mainini Portia, who had managed a nursing home congratulated me and expressed how shocked she was that "a person who could not handle something as simple as shit, could complete something as complicated as a degree. *Munhu anotadza kubata duzvi chairo dhigirii wakarikwanisa sei?*" We were all tipsy and burst into roars of laughter.

Baba said a proper celebration needed to take place at our rural homestead whenever I returned to Zimbabwe, because it was my ancestors who had made it possible for me to graduate. So, we had to appease them by acknowledging their input in my success.

As was the norm, everyone wanted to know what was next after my graduation. Baba's expectation was a good job, or marriage, had to follow. However, neither my parents nor I could afford to pay for the Legal Practice Course, and my chances of getting a training contract with a 2:2 were next to nothing, so a "good job" was wishful thinking on their part. I decided to take a year out to work and raise money for a master's degree at the University of Surrey. That plan would buy me time to decide whether to get a good job or get married next.

Runako eventually travelled to the UK and I went to pick her up from Gatwick airport by train. I barely knew my sister, who I had avidly written to but had only received two responses from during the few years I had been in the UK. Runako was the youngest in our family and was seven years younger than me. When I left home for boarding school at the age of 13, she was six years old. During the six years that we lived under the same roof, she had been the typical lastborn who could do no wrong and barely tasted the peak of my parents' proactive parenting years. She had been known to throw vicious tantrums, delivering the loudest screeches, jumping into her blankets on scorching hot afternoons to demonstrate her discontent, sometimes delivering a puddle of urine on freshly polished floor, and never getting reprimanded. Our family always joked about Runako's childhood antics, as we did about everything else.

When I relocated to the UK at the age of 18, Runako was 11 years old and still in primary school. When she turned 13, Runako was sent to the same boarding school that I had attended. In a school where I had left a solid track record of leading by example, excelling in numerous ways – academically and in the extracurricular realm, Runako unfortunately endured most lastborns' nightmare. The constant comparison of herself to me was relentlessly inflicted on her by my parents, schoolteachers and the wider community.

In the letters Runako had written to me, she explained that she found letter writing challenging, but she missed and loved me, which I thought was adorable. She explained that she was fed up with fighting with Tongai and Tizai, a familiar predicament which I too had endured as a child when Tizai and I partook in what felt like epic karate fights. She had also stated that all her friends and her school prefects were my "fans", and repeatedly declared that she wanted to be just like me. Runako decorated her letters with slogan artwork sprinkled on all pages.

"Like Big Sis', like Lil' Sis"

"You set a good example."

I found Runako's innocent declarations sweet but unsettling. Whilst I found it flattering to be adored by my little sister, I pondered why anybody might want to be like me when I barely knew who I was. I had never deliberately wanted to be like anybody else but had lived Baba's dreams all my life. I knew I was not perfect and was trying to find myself. I decided to spend some time with Runako to get her settled in the UK and to get to know her better. I hoped to discover unique attributes about her so that I would encourage her to embrace those aspects about herself. Within the first few weeks of her arrival, I took Runako to the Kent coast to introduce her to the sea, and to London for a tour and showed her all my favourite shops. She seemed very excited about her new life in the UK.

Tawanda had been proud of my accomplishment at university and threw me a party when I went to visit him after my graduation. However, when I mentioned furthering my education through a postgraduate course, he seemed intimidated by my progress. I communicated my expectation to get married in the near future and wanted to know if his values and objectives were aligned with mine. Tawanda who had a rare type of closeness with his friends said he was not ready to get married. Some of his friends were in their 40s and remained happily single. I by then was not so keen on marriage myself, because it was obvious most people my age were not rushing into marriage, but I certainly wanted to have a child. Cervical screening tests had revealed that I had abnormal cancerous cells, so having a child before potentially losing my womb had become my priority. Tawanda was not ready to have children either, especially out of wedlock and that immediately turned me off.

Baba thought my abnormal cervical smear test result was a sign that *Kurova guva* or *Magadziro*, the beating of Mbuya's grave, was overdue. *Magadziro* was a ritual performed by Shona people a year to two years after burial of the deceased for their spirit to be brought home, so that it did not wander causing problems. If the ritual was not done on time, the spirit of the deceased would become restless and either become a ghost or torment the family by other means. Mhamha did not entertain such cultural biases as they were deemed satanic and incompatible with her Christian faith, and as such rubbished Baba's view. Early Christian missionaries in Zimbabwe had preached against *kurova guva,* which they equated to worshipping ancestors and therefore a sin against God.

I knew that by going for a postgraduate course, I was merely delaying the inevitable. My parents expected me to get married and have children very soon. Other than Tawanda's lack of interest in getting married in the foreseeable future, there was a slight cultural complication I knew my family would over-inflate if they could get away with it. Tawanda was of the *shumba mutupo,* lion totem, which was the same as Mbuya's, so according to the Shona culture, he was deemed a very close relative.

Marrying Tawanda was therefore forbidden, unless he was prepared to pay the price to sever the relationship. *Chekaukama* was a special ritual to break the relationship before a totem inter-marriage. The man intending to marry a relative was expected to find a completely white cow and present it to the wife-to-be's family, as a symbol of cleansing the abomination. I had no appetite for the inconveniences commensurate with totem beliefs, which was very likely to affect me if I married anyone from Masvingo, where almost everyone was related by totem.

I ended the relationship with Tawanda, most unusually. I paid him a final visit, where I packed all my belongings including those I usually left in his closet and drawers to mark my territory. When he took me to the airport, Tawanda's intuition was spot on.

"Ruva, look me in the eye and promise me you will be back."

I could not do it. Discussing difficult topics had never been my strength. I left him whimpering, as I walked through the security gates and headed for the departure lounge. I did not look back and wave at Tawanda as I had done many times before. When I arrived in the UK, Tawanda called my mobile phone to check I had arrived home safely, and I gathered the strength to tell him that our three-year relationship was over.

My family, who had no idea of Tawanda's immigration status and career prospects, had been excited that I might marry someone with a recognisable name, so the news of the breakup was a huge disappointment for them.

Chapter 10

I decided to get in touch with Morris, who I had never broken up with officially. We had not been in touch for around three years, but he had visited me in several vivid dreams, some of which were lucid; an occurrence I took as a sign that his soul was calling for mine. We quickly rekindled our love, and the relationship was a whirlwind from there on. We had both dated other people and the relationships had not been like ours. We had yearned for each other during our separation and could not stay away from each other following our hasty reconciliation. Morris was in his final year at university and I was going to begin my post-graduation course – a master's degree in European Politics, Business and Law. When I told Morris about my cervical cancer scare, he confirmed he would be there for me no matter what happened. We both wanted to have children as soon as we completed our courses, and to get married at some point in the near future, so our intentions seemed fully aligned. I stopped taking contraceptives and began working overtime to fund my trips to Zimbabwe to visit Baby.

I travelled to Zimbabwe in April and in June 2004. A second graduation party was thrown for me in April by Baba, for the purpose of showing me off to his people and to appease our ancestors. It was an extravagant affair that involved Baba hiring a bus to transport several of my former primary and high school teachers and other well-wishers to Chivi, where we found a huge turnout of his constituents awaiting my arrival. During that visit, our family was shocked to learn that Tete Mary had had a baby girl in the States. She had kept the pregnancy a secret, the father of the child was not known, and she had been too ashamed to disclose the pregnancy. Tsvakai had moved in with Tete Mary, knew of the pregnancy, and had been sworn to secrecy. I could not believe I had been left out on such a beautiful journey. I immediately started budgeting for a trip to visit Tete Mary. I had not been to visit her for nearly four years, or at least since I began dating Tawanda. In the meantime, Tete Gertrude was commissioned by Baba to go to the United States immediately to assess Tete Mary's situation, with a view to return to Zimbabwe with the baby if need be.

In Bulawayo, Morris and I spent our time rambling across town, visiting art galleries and museums, wining and dining, shopping for trinkets and curios. He swiftly began to feel like Baby again. One of my married aunts, Tete Primrose, lived in Bulawayo at the time, so I would stay at her house where we would discuss in great detail my relationship with Baby and where it was going. My aunt, who was very rigorous with particulars expected me to divulge details about everything, including Baby's penis size and shape, and why we did not feel ashamed of holding hands in public. "Is it a Russian or Vienna sausage?" she would ask with a mischievous leer, to which I would respond with a detonation of uncontrollable giggles.

I was very close with Tete Primrose, who had herself been brought up by Baba's hand. Her notorious delinquencies had awarded her beatings that had been traumatic for me to watch as a child, yet here she was, happily married and raising good children. I always wondered whether she had managed to forgive Baba's fierce parenting methods; we never touched on the sensitive subject. Because I respected Tete Primrose's home, and deliberately avoided awkward confrontations by her husband, Babamukuru Francis, I could not have sex with Baby there. I often fabricated a story about leaving town, for Babamukuru Francis's benefit, then booked into a local lodge where I stayed for extended weekends. Baby, who also respected his parents' home, did the same. I had not yet been introduced to his parents or been to their home. Tete

Primrose would drop me off at the lodge and pick me up when I was ready to return to her house.

I loved spending time at the lodge with Baby, where we hibernated and drenched each other with unending love and attention. The lodge was close to town and we only left when we ran out of provisions. It was a self-contained sanctuary with a large bedroom, bathroom, lounge and kitchen. Adorned with aristocratic colonial décor, solid antique mahogany furniture, old original paintings of wild animals and white war generals unknown to us, the lodge was a true escape from reality. The bedding was one of my favourite touches. Ironed cotton sheets with a higher than usual thread count by Zimbabwean standards, paisley print quilt covers, all made me feel at home, like one might feel when visiting a warm-hearted classy grandmother. Being at the lodge gave us an opportunity to be ourselves without judgement.

Baby and I went on extended food shopping sprees at specialist grocery stores, bought numerous ingredients to experiment with, then cooked together. When we bathed together, Baby would ask me what I thought about, and I sincerely expressed all my fears and ambitions. I would ask him what he thought about, and Baby expressed his hopes and desires. We talked for hours on end, planning our perfect future. We would stay in the bath enjoying glasses of wine, until the water became colder than the atmosphere. Very rarely, when we felt exhausted from coital fun and games, we would go out clubbing or to enjoy a night of Jazz at a quiet bar in town. Quite often, Baby borrowed his mother's little red car which he fondly nicknamed "The Batmobile".

Baby taught me to drive in The Batmobile. We spent hours starting and stopping, him touching my thighs when giving direction. We kissed and fondled when the driving became exhausting. The Batmobile was in fact the venue of our first proper consummation, an uncalculated event driven by prolonged galactic yearning, which took place on my second night after arriving in Bulawayo from the UK.

On the first evening, my cousin Imogen, Tete Gwinyai's daughter, and I had travelled together from Harare to Bulawayo in a *muchovha*, commuter minibus. We arrived early evening and found Baby waiting for us with an enormous grin. Baby and I had not seen each other in over three years and were unsure of how to act. He looked at me with a piercing gaze full of love, forgiveness and desire. I blushed and could barely look him in the eye. Following drinks at a coffee shop in town, Baby drove us to Tete Primrose's house in The Batmobile. Baby stayed for dinner and then had to return to his parents' home.

I escorted him outside, where we talked quietly, then shared the most delectable promising kiss. We stood in the dark, in a very tight embrace, our bodies heating up, throbbing and needing more, but we could not justify taking things further on the first day of our reconciliation, so we let go until the next day. Babamukuru Francis was out of town, so Baby and I had returned to Tete Primrose's house in the evening after a day of romance in town. We had dinner, as we did the previous day, then I saw Baby out. This time, we went and sat in the back seat of The Batmobile for a few minutes, where verbal conversation rapidly advanced to physical communication suffused by ravenous desire. We ripped each other's clothes off, then devoured each other in quick breathless feats of aching want. We could not take our time because the encounter was risky. Tete Primrose might have come outside to check on us, and that thought niggled me. The deed was quick and dirty, and it left us wanting more. We knew the future was perky!

In the days that followed, Baby finally introduced me to his mother, Mhaiyo, who seemed to like me very much. I had brought her gifts from the UK and braided her hair, which she was grateful for.

I arranged a week-long trip to the Victoria Falls, where Baby was obliged to accompany me. We stayed at The Kingdom hotel where we had an amazing time and gelled as if there had not been a separation. I was amused by Baby's enchantment by aeroplanes; that domestic flight to our first holiday together was the first time he had boarded a plane. We had an amazing time together, walking around, sightseeing, booze cruising on the Zambezi, wining, dining and having plenty of sex. It was during that trip that we spontaneously stopped using condoms, an irresponsible move that intensified our heated romance. We did not stop to think or care about where our whirlwind was going.

We returned to Bulawayo exhausted, but not of each other. During these early days of rekindling romance with Baby, Tawanda could not come to terms with the fact that I had got tired of his taking me for granted and had moved on. He managed to investigate my Zimbabwean telephone number and often made interrupting calls while I was with Baby. Tawanda would declare his undying love for me and Baby listened in to ensure I repelled Tawanda effectively. On one call, Tawanda cried into the phone, begging me to visit his aged mother who was unwell and dying in Masvingo. I empathised with him, but I could not engage in any behaviour that might have given him false hope. While I was in Zimbabwe, Tawanda worked on Mhamha in the UK, by calling her daily and begging her to help to patch the relationship up. He bought Mhamha an outfit, which made her feel uncomfortable, then began threatening to commit suicide if I did not reconcile with him. I empathised with Tawanda but remained steadfast.

On one occasion, when the international trade fair was running in Bulawayo, our usual lodge was fully booked, and so were all decent hotels and bed and breakfasts in the town. We had endured a prolonged period of abstinence due to the ongoing event, and we desperately needed to lay. We resorted to buying a newspaper to find accommodation contacts in the most uncouth areas of town. We were in luck and found a room in a dingy hostel on the outskirts of the metropolis. The rooms were rentable by the hour, so we booked one for a couple of hours. We had felt the need to manufacture a story behind why we required the room.

Accommodation owners in Zimbabwe took the liberty of making intrusive enquiries and felt obliged to deny access where they felt reasons for use of their property were not above-board, or moral. Baby and I decided to say we were a married couple who had been on a long journey from South Africa and were taking a break before proceeding to another town, because I was pregnant and exhausted. The story was plausible because I was overweight. We turned up at the hostel and the lady owner at the check-in desk immediately recognised me as a member of my family. I denied any knowledge of my family and said I was probably a look-alike. The conversation made me feel uneasy, as such dialogue would. When I met random people in different towns, who stopped me to ask if I was related to my aunts or uncles who had been involved in historic scandalous infamy, I despised my association with them.

My close affiliation with disgrace made me impatiently await marriage, so I could shed off my maiden name. The plight of being recognised plagued different family members for varying reasons.

Once, Babamunini Benjy had contracted a sexually transmitted disease while Mhamha was still working as a nurse in Masvingo. He had gone through the pains of saving up money and travelling to Chiredzi by bus to seek treatment where he thought he would not be recognised. He had arrived at a small clinic where a nurse who had worked with Mhamha in the past immediately recognised him. The nurse had played the fool by treating him silently, then immediately telephoned Mhamha to inform her of Babamunini Benjy's visit. Upon my uncle's arrival back home, he had found Mhamha waiting for him with some cash talk.

"So, you thought you were clever by travelling all the way to Chiredzi for treatment of *siki*? You're going to die of AIDS if you're not careful!"

Back at our family home in Masvingo, only Baba was living there. Tizai had been enrolled on a Fine Art course at a South African art institution in Johannesburg, as he was the only one of my siblings who had been denied a visa to the UK. During the times Tizai was home visiting Baba, he had consistently contacted me to report his frustrations around Baba's clandestine and hypocritical behaviours. Amongst other things, the man was openly having extramarital affairs with local and foreign women, and for some reason kept a stash of weed in his bedroom drawers, which Tizai and his friends helped themselves to.

"There is waaaay too much of it for one person Ruva, and quite a lot for Baba to notice any shortage." Tizai had insisted whilst justifying his pilfering.

Before his death, Babamunini Benjy who had the ability to identify users, had also asserted that Baba was a ganja addict. I therefore was not completely surprised by Tizai's discoveries, or that he had been in my parent's bedroom rummaging through their privacy. This was a practice we developed together many years back as very young children.

We were bored kids living on a secluded property with no structure to our days, or enough activity to keep us positively occupied, an issue that was later resolved by sending us to boarding school. Other than video gaming Pacman, Tetris and Super Mario, riding our bicycles and browsing a small encyclopaedia collection, we did not have much else by way of entertainment, and we were quite often restless. The encouragement to read for leisure at home was inadequate. Other than our school reading books, which we usually did not read, and forged our parents' signatures on reading record cards, there were very few storybooks made available to us during our childhood. Over time, we grew accustomed to entertaining each other.

At some point, Tizai and I had both identified that soon after we were sent to sleep, on the rare nights Baba was home early, he would collect some videos from his bedroom, which were played at very low volume but incited strong rackets of merriment by my parents. We decided to investigate this mystery, and through that inquisition discovered pornography. We watched the shocking biology lessons religiously each time an opportunity presented itself; when our parents were at work, when our housegirl was busy laundering at our detached utility room, and when our younger siblings were out of sight.

During my visit to Zimbabwe in July, Tizai was returning to South Africa to begin his second year of art school. Before Tete Gertrude drove Tizai to the Harare International Airport, he gave me his favourite blue sweater, which I found unusual. Tizai appeared depressed and had lost a huge amount of weight.

"So, what were you up to in Masvingo then?" I asked him as we drove to the airport.

"Just hanging out with a few friends, but mostly keeping to myself. I've been painting a mirage. I left it on my dressing table to dry. If you go to Masvingo before returning to the UK, put it somewhere safe for me please."

A few weeks later, when I had returned to the UK in August 2004, Tizai sent Baba an email, informing him that he had dropped out of college to become a paid artist, and would change his name and contact details. He would be out of touch for a while and would return home in December 2004. Immediately after receipt of his email, we tried frantically to find Tizai, hoping to change his mind. We called and sent text messages to his mobile phone, we sent him emails, we telephoned his college, we asked relatives and friends based in South Africa to try and find him, but none of that effort brought Tizai back. After a while, Baba's attitude and advice to us as a family was there was no point in trying to find someone who did not want to be found. Tizai had said he would return, so we were to relax and await his return. Baba's counsel was always received as dictum, so we complied with his directive.

Those days, when I was not visiting Baby in Zimbabwe, I worked part-time for a charity organisation in Aldershot and supplemented my income by braiding hair and working one-off catering shifts as a waitress or kitchen porter at restaurants and nursing homes. When I was not working, Tongai who was into producing his own music would show off his latest beats made on an MPC player, which he had proudly purchased after tirelessly working in fast food restaurants and nursing homes. He also liked to disc-jockey and would make us sample the latest Jamaican dancehall, Hip Hop and Afrobeats.

Runako was a mid-teen and was busy acclimatising herself to the UK culture. Her transition from Zimbabwean culture seemed seamless compared to mine, with no strict expectations imposed on her by my parents. She had not been conditioned to comply the way I had been. She did not seem to get the lectures I had received from my parents or any adult relative who may have felt compelled to participate in my communal upbringing; Runako made friends with whoever she wanted, and she could even answer back to my parents. I could not decide whether my parents had got tired of parenting, or whether they simply expected my siblings to follow the footsteps of the one child they had invested the maximum disciplinary effort in.

I on the other hand was undergoing a major identity crisis. It had become apparent that Baba, the man I had been conditioned to emulate had been acting all along and his mask had finally fallen. I had completed a degree to appease Baba, but my qualification did not seem to satisfy his insatiable appetite for achievement and perfection. To make matters worse, the qualification did not represent my true self. I simply did not feel like I had been born to become a lawyer. As if that was not bad enough, I was about to embark on a master's degree I was not interested in, simply to justify my "spinster" existence. In addition to that, my strict upbringing, expectations of my parents and the Shona culture did not seem to match the environment I now resided in.

None of my age mates were chasing marriage. Even Tawanda who was Shona and a few years older than me, was not ready to get married simply to appease societal expectations. My new priority was to have a child and I was no longer sure about marriage, for obvious reasons. The need to escape my upbringing through marriage no longer seemed like my only option, but there was something about getting back with Baby that cemented my original objective to tie the knot. I felt under pressure as I embarked on what seemed to be a lonely and burdensome dilemma, and I could have stopped to breathe, but I did not know how, so I continued to play the game.

Chenai, Moira, Mainini Joy and Mainini Portia also lived in Aldershot, so our sense of family and community was strong. Chenai, Moira and I often went shopping for clothes for retail therapy. We attended local parties and nightclubs together and were living our best lives. Moira eventually moved to Sheffield where she began a new life. Chenai stayed in Aldershot where she dated a young man who consistently broke her heart.

Chapter

11

My master's degree commenced in September 2004 then I began making arrangements for Baby to visit me at Christmas. I would introduce him to my family then. Everything went according to plan. His parents paid for his flight and it felt great for Baby to reciprocate a visit. This would be a good opportunity for him to experience the UK and decide whether he would want to immigrate permanently.

I decided to squeeze in a one-week trip to the United States towards the end of November, to visit Tete Mary, her new surprise baby, Sophia and my cousin Tsvakai who still lived with her. Our reunion was epic! We had last seen each other in Nebraska, and now my aunt and cousin had relocated to Atlanta, Georgia and there was a new addition to the family. Sophia was already nine months old when I met her for the first time, and I was completely captivated by her. She was a beautiful, easy baby, who seemed to love me back. It felt good to be loved by a baby. Tete Mary, who we knew by then was allergic to marriage seemed so happy and fulfilled. There was no man in sight and her "baby daddy", as they call unmarried fathers of children in the United States, had once shared an apartment with her but moved to another State as soon as he learnt my aunt was pregnant.

Tete Mary now owned this adorable little person who loved her unconditionally, and she did not even need to put herself through the misery of marriage to attain this. I secretly envied her situation. I knew then that I too would soon have a baby of my own. After a few days of shopping and sightseeing with Tsvakai, who had volunteered to stay out of work to babysit Sophia while Tete Mary was at work, I returned to the UK, heartbroken that I had had to leave so soon.

Baby's first visit to the UK coincided with Baba visiting for Christmas. The two actually met at Harare airport at the check-in desks. Tete Gertrude had driven Baba to the airport and as she knew Baby, she took the honour to introduce him to Baba as *"shamwari yaRuva"*, Ruva's friend. Baba was receptive and thankfully did not cause any awkwardness. When they boarded the flight, Baby who had been avoiding Baba in the departure lounge, found to his horror that he had coincidentally been allocated a seat next to Baba. A few minutes of uncomfortable silence had felt like hours, as the two tried to get acclimatised to each other's presence. Baby wondered how he would survive the trip and considered feigning deep sleep all the way to the UK, then to his relief, Baba was upgraded to a first-class seat. The two did not have any other encounters until they reached the arrival hall at Gatwick airport.

Mhamha and I had been waiting for our men, wondering who would come out first; and if they appeared from the baggage reclaim together, who I would run to first, Baba or Baby? Luckily, Baby appeared first, and I introduced him to Mhamha while we waited for Baba to emerge. Mhamha adored Baby, and Baby thought Mhamha was the sweetest lady he had ever met. "I can see where you got that beauty from," Baby would tease me in Mhamha's presence from time to time thereafter. When Baba finally turned up, Mhamha whisked him to her home in Aldershot by car, and I travelled to my university with Baby by train.

I lived on campus at the University of Surrey in Guildford and occupied a single en-suite room, which was my little holistic sanctuary in a block designated for postgraduate students. My room was immaculate, with crisp white jacquard bedding, white towels, scented candles, and a couple of small plants. I had never been with a man in such a confined space, so I had to learn to relax when Baby decided to eat his saucy spaghetti bolognaise on my bed whilst watching tv. I noticed with internal indignation every sprinkle or crumb of food that he carelessly dropped on my bedding. Sometimes he enjoyed a glass of cranberry juice whilst relaxing on my bed, which he used as a coaster. I would wipe after his mess and pick after him, and hint that he ought to be more responsible. Baby seemed surprised by my shogunate attitude. He had only ever been with me in Zimbabwe where I unconsciously switched to holiday-mode. But something about the UK made me inadvertently uptight.

I took Baby on tours to London, Canterbury, Isle of Wight and other places I thought he might enjoy. We spent Christmas at Mhamha's house in Aldershot, where he was well received. We had never continuously spent that amount of time together, so we began to feel negative energy building up between us. One day, we had gone shopping for presents Baby would take back home at the end of his visit. Back at my room, I started removing price tags off clothes we had bought, because I thought I was being helpful. This annoyed Baby and he called me "stupid!" for doing so. Nobody had ever called me stupid. Well, except the few times Mhamha had beaten me up as a child, screaming "schupet! schupet!" Perhaps that was what triggered me! In a fit of rage and shock, I stormed out of my room, left Morris on his own and went to Mhamha's house in Aldershot. After a couple of days on his own, he must have got tired of waiting for my return, then he arranged for a cousin of his, Maynard, who lived in

Luton to pick him up from Guildford. Morris left my room with all his belongings and did not communicate.

After several days of no communication, Baba advised me to call Baby and make a peace offering. "Honestly Ruva you are being very childish. You recently dumped a good man who could have married you, and now you want to dump another, after everything you've been through together? Come on! Most things are fixed by the little word 'sorry', even if you don't mean it!" he stated matter-of-factly then served a prolonged chuckle, in a manner that made me feel like I was placing too much weight on a very menial issue. My gut did not agree with Baba's perspective, but after much coercion and reluctance, I did get in touch with Baby and said I was sorry.

I began to realise that Baby was not the boy I had fallen in love with in high school. A dark cloud of misery seemed to encapsulate him, and I could not understand why he was so bitter. I was unsure whether the bitterness was a result of something I had done or said, or whether it was completely unrelated to me. After Christmas, Baby returned to Zimbabwe.

Perhaps due to time lost when we fell out during his first trip, we immediately began making plans for Baby to return to the UK the following Easter. I resolved that upon his return, I would be a little more acquiescent, and allow Baby to direct our daily activities as he saw fit. I would deliberately make him feel like he wore the pants in our relationship. Baby did return, and we had a much better experience than we had before. I found myself seeking Baby's approval for menial decisions that did not require his input, to make him believe I respected him. I would ask him what he thought of every outfit I wore, and whether he liked my makeup, to make him think he could control me. Before we left my university room for any outings, I handed him cash, so that he would pay all our bills from his own wallet, to make him feel like a real man. I had bought darker bedding, so that his clumsiness on it would not bother me, and he had begun cleaning up after himself. It seemed we had both become more mindful of being more courteous to each other, to avoid unnecessary fallouts.

When we survived that three week holiday with no glitches, we felt ready to spend the rest of our lives together. I loved Baby in a way I could never love another man, and our successful cohabiting bout encouraged me to commit to being his ride or die. I would be his cherub and whore who did whatever it took to make him happy, from feeding him soul food for mains, to serving him lap dances for dessert. Baby was receptive to my service, in a way that made me know I would always be his one and only.

In July 2005, I travelled to Zimbabwe to visit Baby. He had decided he would emigrate to live with me, so we agreed to secretly get married in court, in Bulawayo. That would be the easiest way for him to live with me legally in the UK. The marriage was for practical reasons, so there was no romantic proposal. I had bought two cheap gold wedding rings for the event. On the day of the civil wedding, we arrived at the magistrate court around 10am. It was a sunny but cool morning, and we stood outside the court nervously, hoping no one would recognise us and ask what we were doing there. We were called in by a court officer when it was time to tie the knot, which we did with no glitches. Two of Baby's friends, Tanaka and Kundai, witnessed the secret civil ceremony, and Baby became my husband. After the proceeding, Baby drove us into town in The Batmobile, where we enjoyed a hearty brunch at a swanky restaurant.

In the days that followed, Baby suddenly seemed bothered by my food consumption and subtly hinted that I needed to lose weight.

"You need to manage your relationship with food Ruva. I don't think it's healthy."

I had never considered my love for food as "a relationship" that needed to be managed, so I took no notice of Baby's unrelatable remark. When I had not shown any signs of submission, Baby mentioned that Mhaiyo had commented I was fat, and queried whether I had a *mubvandiripo*, a bastard child. He went on to explain that my pooch, which Mhaiyo had noticed in one of the photographs from our Victoria Falls holiday made her question my maternal status. No one had ever negatively commented on my weight or body shape before, and I was unsure how to react to what Baby was saying, so I ignored it as well.

When Baby and I were in Harare, he stayed at his older sister Valerie's home and I at Tete Gertrude's, but we tended to do sleepovers at either of the hosts as our relationship developed. Valerie and I had known each other for years, from the time Baby and I had dated in high school. During my school holidays spent at Tete Gwinyai's, I had always gone to visit Valerie at her office in Harare city centre, or sometimes at her flat near town, before she was married. Valerie was easy going and welcoming, and Calvin was a private school educated frisky who loved his drink and to entertain his guests. I found it hilariously bold that he always had his latest HIV negative test certificate framed and hung up on the wall directly in front of the main door into their home for all to see. Valerie and Calvin had a huge circle of fun-loving friends who we went on holiday with once.

Around 10 couples all travelled to Nyanga to stay in a large, self-catered lodge over an extended weekend. We had all contributed money to buy food and alcohol and paid a local chef to churn out five-star meals for us twice a day. The beautifully built chalet was a haven of tranquillity, and of course we disturbed the peace there, when we got drunk and played card and board games into the early morning hours. Other than one couple fighting publicly over a *small house* who had text at the wrong time, the trip to Nyanga was awesome.

Baby and I would lie-in and only emerge from our en-suite room when we had completely depleted our energy from relentless morning sex. We found Nyanga absolutely serene and stunning, as we drove up and down its winding roads on the mountains, and as we walked around the neighbourhood where our chalet was located. Along the way to and from Nyanga, Baby and I stopped to buy curios and crafts we would use to decorate our home in the UK. The anticipation of spending the rest of our lives together grew by the day, and we could not wait for Baby to graduate and move to the UK.

During that visit, Baba who seemed nervous about my whirlwind romance with Baby instructed me to introduce Baby to a great aunt of mine who lived in our childhood neighbourhood. Vatete Guvudzai was Sekuru's first cousin who held our family patriarchy together. She was considered an evangelical extremist who lived and acted straight and narrow. She had herself married a virgin at the age of 40 and was well respected for it. Her husband, Babamukuru Pukunyani apparently paid an extra cow to thank our family patriarchy for the honour. Vatete Guvudzai had no television in her house and owned a very old stereo on which she rarely played gospel music. She was consulted for all serious matters in the family, such as marriages and divorces, because she was the only person who cared to maintain moral traditions alive. Baba had huge respect for Vatete Guvudzai and knew that if I or Baby declined the introduction, it was a sign that our relationship was not serious. When I told Baby about the invitation, he reluctantly agreed to go, not because he was not serious about our relationship, but because he was aware of the tedious bureaucratic activities my family loved to impose on others. Baby's family did not have strong relationships with distant and wider family, so it always surprised him when a seemingly distant relative exercised clout over our family.

We arrived in Masvingo by bus and took a taxi to Vatete Guvudzai's house. We were shown to our separate bedrooms where we would spend the night, and we left our luggage there. Three of her older children had by then flown the nest, but her youngest daughter was home, helping to make us feel comfortable. When we had sung hymns, said numerous prayers, read several bible passages and enjoyed a well-prepared traditional meal, Baby was grilled about his intentions by Vatete Guvudzai and Babamukuru Pukunyani, who was a leader at their church. They asked him about his family background, his studies and how he felt about me. With a stern gaze that pierced into Baby's soul, Vatete Guvudzai announced that now that she knew who Morris was, she did not expect him to let her down. A few days later, Baby and I cried in each other's arms at Harare International Airport.

I returned to the UK with an aching heart and could not stand the separation anxiety that resulted from leaving Baby in Zimbabwe. When I was alone in my university room, missing Baby, his remarks about my weight began to play on my mind. So, I decided it was best to lose the weight to end the judgement. For the first time in my life, I went on a diet for a man and his mother, and I lost ten kilograms. Coming off the contraceptive pill certainly helped to accelerate the weight-loss.

While I celebrated a healthier, lighter body, the sacrifice I had made felt huge and burdensome, because I had not done it for myself. Interestingly, it did not occur to me to question why Mhaiyo who was overweight herself would have made such comments about my weight. Her own daughter, Valerie was twice my size, and in any case quite obese. Her husband Calvin had intimately nicknamed her "Gonyeti" to reflect her haulage truck size. In fact, most of Baby's female relatives were proudly massive, but I never stopped to question why my weight was such a big problem for Baby and his mother. I had from a young age worked out and kept fit, and that had remained my priority, rather than being skinny.

I returned to Zimbabwe for Baby's graduation in October 2005. I went straight to Bulawayo, where I stayed at our usual lodge and was heavily involved in preparations for his graduation and farewell party. Mhaiyo and Baby's father, Bambo, were ever so kind to me and treated me like their own, which made me wonder whether Baby's feedback on my weight by his mother was true. Perhaps it was their lack of entitlement, but something about Baby's family made me feel at ease.

I attended Baby's graduation ceremony with Mhaiyo, Bambo and Bambo's sister, Tete Miriam, the mother to Baby's cousin Maynard who lived in the UK. It was a glorious sunny day with blue skies and a gentle breeze. The mood was light, and we were all filled with pride as Baby walked up to be capped by Robert Mugabe. After the graduation ceremony, we enjoyed a party that lasted into the very early hours of the morning. A few old faces from high school turned up, including Tanaka, as well as Baby's relatives who had travelled from all over the country for the event. A few days after his graduation, we began preparing for our return to the UK to begin our new life together.

I was not on speaking terms with Baba, so I did not visit Masvingo during the October visit. Following his text message incident in the UK the previous year in the summer, the tension in our family had only got worse thereafter. Baba, who had been in the habit of shopping for other women while he was visiting the UK was not remorseful about the incident and his offensive behaviour thereafter. Mhamha, out of deep frustration, had decided to unleash details of previous incidents of Baba's philandering, which she had grown completely sick off. I had advised her to leave the abusive relationship before it made her unwell. Mhamha did not understand the concept of emotional abuse, as culturally the only abuse Zimbabwean women acknowledged was physical abuse. Any other hurtful behaviour presented by men was supposed to be endured silently. She too cried for help from her elders, who issued her the Shona retort, *Kurohwa warohwa? Kudya wadya? Kukwirwa wakwirwa?*

Mhamha was chronically heartbroken but felt she could not possibly leave her husband at her age. It would have been completely shameful to do so, plus she feared being alone, and starting again. "Can you imagine me undressing for a new man Ruva? Your father is the only man I have ever known, so your suggestions to move on are unthinkable." Mhamha felt obliged to stay and try to sort out the mess. I was informed by my aunts that I had broken Baba's heart by meddling in the affairs of his marriage and indeed trying to end it by encouraging Mhamha to leave him.

I felt Mhamha's pain and could not stand Baba or anything to do with him. One of his brothers Babamunini Tafara, lost his life to AIDS at the age of 43 about a month before Baby's graduation. He was survived by his wife, Mainini Gemma, with two sons Matthew and Kudzai, and one illegitimate daughter, Nyarai. Nyarai was born to a woman who had been working for Mbuya during a time when the boys in Baba's family were growing up and experimenting with sex. When the woman became pregnant, she was unsure who the father was between Babamunini Farai and Babamunini Tafara. It was only after Nyarai was born that it became obvious who her father was.

It was never clear whether Nyarai's mother had in fact been gang raped, because the Shona term used to describe what had happened to her was ambiguous. *Akapindigwa*, meaning "they entered her room", was how the act of trespassing servants' quarters and molestation of female workers was sugar-coated in the rural areas. The female workers would never dare to report the privileged boys, because their reports would be of no consequence, and may have resulted in termination of their employment.

I was too angry to pass my condolences to Baba and his whole family, who I had told off for mistreating Mhamha. I had no business speaking to them. I also did not travel to Chivi to pass my last respects at my uncle's grave by placing a small pebble on his headstone, as was expected traditionally when relatives missed funerals of close family.

I loved Babamunini Tafara dearly. He was one of the calmest, content and ever so ordinary people I had ever known. He taught at a local secondary school in Masvingo and lived a very humble, slow, frugal life. Babamunini Tafara was notorious for being irresponsible with the little money he earned as a teacher, often disappearing for days on end after payday every month. He often left his house on a Friday afternoon, promising his kids he would return shortly, as if he was going to the local corner store, only to return home on Monday evening after work. His younger son, Kudzai, once famously said to him, *"Daddy musadzoka manje manje!*

Daddy please don't return soon!" because the poor child naively thought "soon" meant "late".

Babamunini Tafara was stubborn and spoke his mind ever so gently and did not care when his well to do siblings made fun of his simple lifestyle. He always complained that Baba pressurised him to marry Mainini Gemma when they were both too young. Babamunini Tafara had been a groomsman and Mainini Gemma his partner, at a wedding of one of Baba's friends, VaJongwe. Babamunini Tafara was in his early twenties when immediately after that wedding, my Mainini Gemma, who was a late teen sister of Mai Jongwe, got pregnant and my uncle was forced to marry her to avoid souring the relationship between Baba and VaJongwe.

I had many fond memories of Babamunini Tafara, my favourite being when we travelled together from Harare to Masvingo for over six hours; a journey that would have taken less than three hours under normal circumstances. We travelled in his banger which he fondly nicknamed "Candle in the wind", stopping for at least half an hour at most bars along the way. The stops allowed him to buy himself a beer, whilst giving the car engine a chance to cool down. Tizai, who was now missing in South Africa had been in the car with us, and we often asked my uncle how long was left till we got home. He bought us soft drinks and crisps, which cheered us up momentarily. We were very young and impatient at the time and would have been travelling back home to our parents' home after a long school holiday visiting family. Babamunini Tafara who was a chain smoker responded, "There is no hurry in Africa!" with a cigarette stuck in his mouth. He explained matter-of-factly, that if we went any faster without giving his car a break, his candle in the wind would blow out permanently.

When our whining got out of hand, he took longer than usual to return to the car at the next stop, but when he turned up, he had a sizzling hot whole freshly grilled baby chicken placed on a newspaper. Tizai and I looked at each other in hesitation before using our unwashed hands to tuck in. We found that it was the best chicken we had ever tasted, which Babamunini Tafara had flame grilled himself.

My uncle was very handsome and had a weakness for women, which led to his untimely death. On the day he died, Babamunini Tafara was said to have requested a hot drink, and his wife made him hot chocolate. He subsequently spewed the drink and began to lose consciousness. Mainini Gemma called a taxi to take Babamunini Tafara to hospital, but he died on his way there. Mainini Gemma was suspected to have poisoned my uncle's drink, to speed up his death. Her bitterness for an unhappy marriage and contracting HIV from my uncle were cited as her motives for finishing him off.

As was traditional, Mainini Gemma, the younger rebellious *muroora*, was not expected to remarry a stranger, so was offered *kugarwa nhaka*, wife inheritance. This Shona practice involved the deceased wife selecting a new husband from her deceased husband's older and younger brothers and cousins, in order to keep her in the family. If the woman had sons, then they too would join the queue, and if they were selected by their mother, it meant the deceased's wife was not interested in remarrying. On the day of *kugarwa nhaka*, the nominated men sat in a straight line, and Mainini Gemma was expected to take a bowl of water to the male of her choice, so that he would wash his hands to seal the union. Mainini Gemma offered the bowl to her older son Matthew, which caused much disappointment to my uncle's rural cousins who had been hopeful and oblivious to what had killed Babamunini Tafara.

In Bulawayo, Tete Primrose phoned to try and talk sense into me. She asked why I was treating my mother like a friend – did I not know that Baba's behaviour was normal? What was he expected to do when Mhamha decided to migrate to another country and leave him behind? I had no right to meddle in my parents' marriage and was now considered a *mhunzamusha,* homewrecker, by the whole family; to which I responded:

"I did not hold a gun to my mother's head to make her speak. In fact, I do not recall ever asking her to divulge the state of her relationship with my father; but she did. I am not going to stand by and watch Mhamha being abused by a man who doesn't love her and by his relatives who have been completely cruel to her for as long as I can remember. I am not interested in talking to you or Baba until you stop hurting Mhamha," then hung up.

Chapter

12

B aby and I arrived in the UK on a cool October Friday morning. I was confident about our happy future and was ready to live my life to the full with the love of my life. Our secret marriage was taboo, so it remained concealed and we guarded it vigilantly.

Prior to attending Baby's graduation, I had moved out of Mhamha's house and found a room to rent in a shared house in Aldershot. Mhamha subsequently moved out of Mr. Khan's terraced house in Aldershot, to a detached three-bedroom house in a quaint little village in Worplesdon, not very far from Aldershot, where she lived with Tongai and Runako. Her new neighbourhood was extremely quiet and picturesque. The house move into an unfurnished house motivated Mhamha to purchase chocolate leather sofas and white goods, which she intended to take back home when she returned to Zimbabwe.

Mhamha knew my "boyfriend" was coming to live with me following his graduation, and had queried our planned living arrangements, and I honestly informed her of our intention to cohabit. Inevitably, Mhamha expressed her discomfort with the arrangement. What would her church elders and other family members back home think, if they caught wind of the cohabiting arrangement? *"Kuchaya mapoto? Mmmm hazviite izvozvo. Vanhu vese vanotiziva vagotii nazvo?* Cohabiting? Mmm nope. What would people who know us think?" My parents would have preferred it if Baby initiated the traditional marriage, *roora* proceedings by paying a token deposit towards my bride price, to show that he was serious about our relationship. In Shona culture, *roora* involved the gifting of wealth, *pfuma*, to the bride's family to thank them for bringing up a marriage-worthy girl child. Historically, the bride price had been paid to compensate the bride's family for loss of labour when the bride moved away from her family.

I told Mhamha I was not prepared to marry a man I had not lived with for a while. I had to be certain of our compatibility first, before committing to the life-long sentence of marriage. Reluctantly, Mhamha gave us her blessing, on condition a timeline for traditional marriage proceedings was provided to Baba very soon. By then, she had begged me to forgive Baba, as he was soon coming to visit her in the UK for Christmas. I said I would think about it. A few days later, for the sake of maintaining peace, Baby and I gave Mhamha a provisional date of the following April, for the *roora* proceedings. The pressure to officialise our union traditionally was intense for Baby and I who were very content with our secret civil marriage.

On the morning we arrived from Zimbabwe, we dumped our luggage in our room in the shared house, then proceeded into town to register Baby with several employment agencies. By the end of that day, he had been offered a temporary job, which he started on the following Monday. I also got a temporary contract working near Baby's job. We signed up for evening waiting and kitchen porter shifts. Christmas was fast approaching, so we were flooded with work, due to numerous Christmas parties in the county. Shifts we worked on together seemed quick and painless. I sometimes caught Baby looking at me in wonderment while I polished silverware towards the end of the shift, and we would smile at each other, yearning to cuddle up in our modest space at the end of the night. Mhamha, who had bought a better car for herself, sold us her old banger for £50. We were able to therefore, travel to and from work easily.

One evening, Baby and I were travelling in our banger to do a silver service shift in a nearby town, when he ignorantly took an illegal right turn onto a one-way road. Flashing blue lights grabbed our attention, and we knew we were in trouble. Baby was stopped by the police who had been driving behind us. A colossal white armed police officer dressed in black asked Baby to step out of the car and present his driving licence. He wanted to know where we were going. Baby had never been stopped by the police, other than in Zimbabwe where the police were always dismissed with a bribe. In the American movies he liked to watch, Baby knew that police interactions never ended well for young black males. Clearly intimidated, he quickly stepped out of our banger. Baby wore a slim fitting waiting penguin suit that accentuated his lean form which I found attractive. He adjusted his bowtie and stated we were going for a catering shift, in a slight stammer that revealed his feigned confidence.

"How much are you going to make this evening?" the police officer asked.

"£30 before tax," Baby boldly replied.

"You made an illegal turn, and the fine for your offence is £30. If I fine you, you're going to lose all the money from your shift tonight."

The traffic officer muted for a while, pondering enforcement action, as we watched him, worried we were running late. Some hotel managers had a tendency to deduct half an hour off timesheets as penalty for a few minutes of lateness.

"As it's Christmas, I'll let you off this time. I can see you're from Zimbabwe. Do be more careful next time, yeah?" the police officer said in authoritative English accent. We were both relieved, but Baby remained shaken the rest of that evening.

Sometimes we left our daytime jobs and went straight on to evening waiting shifts, starving and unsure when we would eat next. On such days, we strategically swiped piping hot bread rolls and potatoes from serving dishes en route from the kitchen to the tables we served. These practices often resulted in the burning of our upper palates, something we laughed about when we were not working. We often wondered why the aristocratic restaurants and hotels we worked for did not feed staff before service. There was always plenty of leftover food thrown away at the end of our shifts. Frustrated by this stinginess, Baby and I began the practice of loading bottles of wine and champagne into black refuse bags during our shifts. We took the bags out as if we were going to throw out rubbish, then carefully placed them in the boot of our banger. Oblivious to the value of the stock we pilfered, we felt the free drinks compensated the hard work we were undoubtedly underpaid for.

When Baby and I were not working, we went sightseeing or visited friends and family. We attended one live concert in London as a treat. I had found solace in Baby and was grateful for his presence in my life. Life was good.

Despite ceasing contraceptives for over a year, my period had unfailingly appeared month after month, until about a month after I started living with Baby. I had not been actively trying to get pregnant, but the religious appearance of my period each month had started to worry me, that I might not be able to have children. One morning, I became aware that my period was late. I was working in a mundane call centre job which allowed my mind to wander endlessly. I decided to buy a pregnancy test during my lunch break, just to check, although I did not actually think I would be pregnant. Baby had on several occasions joked that I might be pregnant, but I was not aware of any biological changes within my body, so I rationalised that the chances of my being pregnant were very slim. I took the test, and it confirmed I was in fact pregnant. A wave of exhilaration took over my being in a way I had not expected. Sitting in the toilet cubicle at work, I fumbled for my phone and held it for a moment, wondering if Baby would be as excited as I was with the news. I took a big breath and dialled his number. With feigned neutrality, I delivered the news, and to my relief Baby was ecstatic. We were going to be parents! The feeling of love and veneration that prevailed between us in the coming weeks was immeasurable. We spent most of our free time in our room, smothering each other with fuss and attention.

I avoided visiting Mhamha, who would have undoubtedly picked up on the pregnancy. Mhamha was highly intuitive, and had had a dream at the time, where two pumpkins were growing out of the ground. One of them was healthy and normal, but the other pumpkin was stunted and showing signs of death. She predicted that two people in the family were pregnant. One pregnancy would be carried to full term and the other would miscarry. A few days after Mhamha's dream, my older cousin Moira, announced she was pregnant with her second child.

I was very close to Moira. Growing up, we shared similar interests and challenges, and she was like an older sister to me. Moira had had a challenging upbringing with an emotionally abusive and unavailable father who covered up all his weaknesses with money. Moira had suffered punishments including being sent out on the streets at night for very minor misdemeanours. Growing up, it was not uncommon to visit their home and find Maiguru Chiedza locked up in her sewing room to escape her husband. My aunt was known to lock herself up for days on end to protect herself from her husband, Babamukuru Gilbert, when he was going through his episodes. We never found out what it was Babamukuru Gilbert would do if Maiguru Chiedza had set herself free during his mysterious episodes. Moira, like me had yearned for the love of her father, that resulted in her being impregnated by a covert abuser at the age of 16. The event hindered her studies, but she did well at GCSE and proceeded to A level despite having a baby.

Moira's pregnancy had resulted in the tightening of my sanctions in my life, and I had had to work overtime to prove my goodness to my parents who were extremely worried that I too might get pregnant prematurely. Moira was forced by her father to get married to Alan, who had impregnated her. Moira had habitually dated men who were "beneath her" and Alan was no exception. The man, who had been sweet and loving to her during their courtship transformed into an abusive monster as soon as they began living together. He seemed to punish Moira daily for having been brought up privileged. I was eventually allowed to rekindle my friendship with Moira after she got married, because the shame of getting pregnant out of wedlock had been absolved. Marriage also seemed to automatically grant women respect in the Shona culture.

One school holiday, when I was around 15, I went to visit my cousin Moira at her one-bedroom apartment where she lived with her husband Alan in Harare. It was the same school holiday I had encountered Geoff. Moira who had been trendy and well kempt now looked like an exhausted poor woman. She looked like she was hurting, but she did not speak about her pain, so I could not understand what was sapping her energy. One night, when we had said our goodnights and gone to bed, I was shocked to be awakened by Alan's penis thudding on my face. I was sleeping on the floor in their lounge when the violation happened. I asked him to leave me alone or I would scream. Alan said I would hurt Moira's feelings if I alert her to what was going on, and he would tell her that I had been the one begging him for sex. When I threatened to go and wake Moira up straightaway, he left me alone.

The following morning, I wondered how Moira could not have felt her husband missing in bed. I wanted to tell her what had happened, but in my naivety, I believed Alan's threat. I could not face being in her house, knowing what I knew, unable to raise the alarm, so I left prematurely and went back to stay with Tete Gwinyai, who was living with Tete Mary. I told Tete Mary what had happened and sought advice on what to do. I was surprised by her response. She said if I told Moira the truth, she would simply direct her anger at me and hate me for it, not her husband. She advised me that if I was not interested in Alan, my best course of action was to avoid him and situations that presented the opportunity for him to chase me. Following my encounters with Peter, Geoff, Thomas and then Alan within the same time frame, I had felt like prey kicking the can down the road. I never went back to Moira's house, and I would only see her when she was visiting her parents' home.

A few years later, Babamukuru Gilbert who was a wealthy businessman, sponsored Moira and Alan to relocate to the UK. Moira seemed a lot better than she had been in Zimbabwe, although she was still with an abusive husband, who by then beat her up whenever he felt justified to do so. The freedom that came with living in a first world country must have boosted Moira's confidence and somewhat ameliorated her restricted life. She could at least now leave their home to work and interact with other people, a condition that would always bring some fresh air to any woman in an abusive relationship. Alan's philandering escapades had multiplied, and he seemed to be having an affair with Moira's paternal cousin. Alan was bad news.

During my first year at university, Moira invited me for a night out to celebrate her birthday. Alan would take me and Moira night clubbing, with a few other friends. I had travelled from Canterbury to Luton where they lived, and I was very excited to visit Moira, who I had not seen since arriving in the UK but spoke to often. We arrived at a dingy nightclub where we enjoyed some cocktails. After a while, I was shocked to see muscular naked men bouncing onto a t-shaped stage with large phalli hanging freely for all to see. I had never been to a strip club before, so I did not know how to react. There was a minimal male audience in the nightclub, but many women unashamedly screamed in excitement as the men on stage vigorously swung semi-flaccid penises off oiled sculptured bodies. I did not realise it was okay for women to be openly comfortable with mental fornication.

If Alan had not been there, I may have joined in the screaming; but I was embarrassed and did not know what to do. I heartily sucked my cocktail through a straw, avoiding eye contact with anyone, and accepted the event as an induction to liberties enjoyed in the first world. I wondered if women were allowed to dance naked too, whether they would be called whores for doing so, and whether they cared. I wondered why no one had warned me that we were going to a strip club. I would have thought a bit more about how I really felt about it, and I may have rehearsed a more appropriate reaction. As the night progressed, the naked male dancers had become a common sight and I had eventually relaxed.

At the end of the night, Moira's friends dispersed, and we carried on to her home where we stayed up to chat then eventually said our goodnights. I slept on a sofa in the lounge, and as I was drifting into sleep, I felt a body trying to squeeze onto the sofa, breathing heavily behind me. I was shocked to find Alan at it again. I jumped and sat up, to ensure he would not overpower me whilst lying down, then he began brandishing his phallus through his pyjama bottoms' open fly, as if he expected me to pounce on it. He was begging me for sex, again!

"Please Ruva please! *Ndongoisa musoro chete*, I'll insert just the head only!"

"*Hezvo!* Fuck off Alan, you disgust me!"

"You think I spent all that money for nothing? Taking you out to a strip club, buying you drinks all night? You think I did all that to get nothing from it? Mate, do you know how expensive that was?" His honeyed tone had become more guttural.

"Did I ask you for any of it? Did you not take us out to celebrate your wife's birthday? Get away from me before I scream for help Alan!"

"Don't do this to me *sha*! I know you're horny Ruva. After seeing those naked men all night, I know you need a man. *Haikona kunyara zvako!* Don't be shy, I can give it to you right now!" Alan pleaded like a child begging a friend for a toy swap, desperately squeezing the head of his penis harder, as if he urgently needed to hold back his urine; so as to signal that my refusal to concede caused him immense pain.

"No thank you! I am sure Moira needs you more than I might need any man, so leave me alone please, you dirty dog! *Uri mbwa yemunhu iwe!*"

This time I was older and feistier, so I used my harshest facial expression and voice to curse him, pushing him away from me as hard as I could, then promised to tell Moira everything. Alan nearly fell onto the coffee table, then he quickly got up and knelt beside me. He threatened to turn it on me if I told Moira.

"*Usada kuziva nhema wazvinzwa*! Don't try to be clever for nothing Ruva!" he hissed obnoxiously. "If you say anything to Moira, I'll tell her it was you who was begging me for sex." He shot a piercing look into my eyes, as if to check whether my pupils would dilate in response to his familiar unsubstantiated warning. I looked away and rubbished his threat.

"*Nxaa*! Don't be ridiculous Alan! You're the one coming onto me. You're the one who has left your wife sleeping and now you want to tell Moira that I was begging you for sex? Are you okay upstairs?" I let out a gasp of frustration and clicked my tongue again.

"Try me!" Alan whispered, as he got up slowly to return his member into his pyjama pants.

The next day, I called a taxi and left Moira's home a lot earlier than planned. All the way to Canterbury from Luton, I wondered how I would break the news to my cousin. When I arrived on campus, I called Moira and blurted out what Alan had done. I felt bad for hurting her feelings, but something had to be done about Alan. Following the call, I did not hear from Moira for a very long time. She stopped responding to my calls or text messages. Over a year later, Moira got in touch with me, acting as if nothing had happened, and we picked up from where we had left. At this point in her life, Moira was having an affair and her marriage to Alan was practically over.

A few years after the incident with Alan in Luton, we were at Mhamha's house in Aldershot and Gogo had come to visit. Mhamha's sisters, my maternal cousins and I were enjoying a long night of wine, cheese, crackers and plenty of girly talk. Mhamha was out working on a night shift, as she usually did. When Gogo got drunk, she told us some of her youthful stories and tips on what and what not to do in marriage. She would tell us to refuse doggy style in bed because only loose women agreed to be treated like a dog in bed. "How is a man meant to reach those inaccessible folds and angles Gogo?" I teased her. "A real man can reach them without treating you like a dog!" She insisted. We would burst into fits of uncontrollable laughter, wiping off tears and suppressing the urge to drain our bladders, lest we missed juicy parts of the conversation. Gogo humorously narrated how she had put up with her late husband, Khulu's philandering, in a way most modern women could never relate to. She would run Khulu a bath in which she doused permanganate, then cooked him the most delectable meal, when she knew he was returning home from his mistresses.

We would then shower Gogo with probing questions around her unique ways of keeping a man, and where on earth she got that high level of tolerance from. Our girly yabber carried go on for hours and hours, until we passed out in the lounge or crawled to bed. On this particular night, when we had got quite drunk, I must have inadvertently touched a nerve when Moira screamed at me, "…but you fucked my husband!" Unsure I had heard her correctly, I asked her to repeat what she had said, then explain herself. Moira explained that Alan had told her after I reported him to her, that he had in fact been having a long-term affair with me. Alan claimed he had been sleeping with me from before they relocated to the UK from Zimbabwe.

When I asked Moira why on earth she thought I had told her about the incidents with Alan if I had been having an affair with him, she offered the most shocking explanation. Alan had apparently told Moira that I wanted to take things further and had asked him to leave Moira and make me his one and only. But, because he loved his wife, he refused to take things further with me, and out of bitterness, I lied to my cousin that her husband had been bugging me for sex. It dawned on me then, that this was why Moira had slept with Brian a few years back. Although the incident had broken my heart, I eventually appreciated the fact that Moira helped to unveil Brian's true colours before I had fallen too deep for him.

Without taking a moment to think, an uncharacteristic response shot out of my red wine stained mouth.

"Well I do not fuck uneducated douchebags with no potential! I am not attracted to them and never will be. Go and tell that husband of yours that maybe if he retakes and passes his GCSE's I might just think about fucking him," and that marked the end of an otherwise amazing evening.

I was furious and perplexed by how men managed to get away with their shenanigans. I was particularly put off by their ability to make women absolutely cruel to each other, as we had become in that moment. It seemed Tete Mary had been right after all. Moira did hate me for revealing her husband's true colours, and that broke my heart.

Moira eventually left her abusive husband and lived her life to the full. She moved to Aldershot during the time I completed my undergraduate degree and lived there while I waited to begin my postgraduate course at Surrey University. Moira, Chenai and I enjoyed many delightful escapades together before Moira decided to move to Sheffield, where she met a new love of her life, Tendai. They seemed to love each other very much, despite the fact that her lover was ordinary, and Babamukuru Gilbert could not get his head around that discrepancy. Moira was happy, and I was happy that she was happy and now expecting a baby with Tendai.

Baba had by then arrived for Christmas in December. He seemed mellow about Baby and I's cohabiting situation and surprisingly did not drag us into uncomfortable conversations about it. He clearly was conscious of how fragile my tolerance for him was. Any wrong move, however small, would have tipped me over to write him off. We had a merry, albeit exhausting Christmas. I wondered if anyone had picked up on the fact that I had avoided alcohol. By this time, Baby and I had already picked a name for our baby. I kept a pregnancy diary where I devotedly made note of the minutest details of my pregnancy, including how I felt, how Baby felt, what I ate, what we did, what we hoped, what we thought, what we planned. It was truly an amazing time for us.

One evening before the New Year, I began spotting. Baby rushed me to the Accident and Emergency at Surrey Hospital, where we were horrified to learn that our baby's heart had stopped beating and I was miscarrying. The hospital staff had comforted us by stating that only a scan could confirm the status of the pregnancy, but as it was between Christmas and New Year, the scanning department was shut, so we would have to wait until the first working day in the New Year. The indifference with which the situation was dealt with was shocking to us. We returned to our room, feeling distraught, but hopeful that the baby was still alive. We politely declined New Year's Eve party invitations and stayed cuddled up in our room, hoping, praying, wishing, for positive news in the new year. On the day of our appointment, we went back to the hospital for our scan. By then, we had convinced ourselves that our baby would live. I had for some reason stopped bleeding, which raised our hope.

After many hours of waiting, our turn came to have the truth revealed. We saw our baby's little body on the screen, but a heartbeat was nowhere to be found. Baby and I broke down into a distraught snivel. The soreness of our broken hearts seemed to worsen as we embraced continuously outside the scan room. I knew we would not cope with this predicament on our own, so I innately telephoned Mhamha's house. It was only after Mhamha picked up and asked what was wrong, that I realised she was unaware of my pregnancy, so I should have rehearsed how to break the news of the miscarriage to my family. I wailed into the phone for a prolonged period, feeling helpless and unsure of what to say. When I managed to catch my breath I blurted, *"Ndanga ndine nhumbu…*I was pregnant…" then continued mourning. Mhamha responded in a calm knowing voice,

"Come home…" and so we left the hospital and went to her house, which was only a five-minute drive from the hospital.

Baby and I found my parents were waiting for us with warm cuddles and words of comfort. They told us they had lived through a similar experience themselves before I was born. A few days later, I had to undergo a procedure to remove the remains of the foetus from my womb. Mhamha kindly volunteered to take me to hospital while Baby worked. Due to his temporary working arrangements, if he missed work, he would not get paid. As we were only starting off a life with no savings to our name, every penny counted for us. In the hospital ward, a pessary that would induce labour was inserted into my vagina and I almost immediately felt contractions. Mhamha held my hand and comforted me, sometimes keeping the mood light by cracking jokes. I was not comfortable with that sort of attention. I somewhat felt like I did not deserve it. After several hours of excruciating lower abdominal pain, I was wheeled into a theatre, received anaesthetic and underwent the procedure. I woke up hours later, with Mhamha at my side, but no baby. I had given birth to a dead baby I would never see. My whole world felt shattered and a dark cloud of sadness engulfed me. I returned to Mhamha's house where Baby picked me up after work later that day.

I received phone calls from well-wishing relatives who assured me that miscarriages were very common, and Baby and I should not waste energy mourning over it. Some advised that the best remedy for a miscarriage was to get pregnant again. Some audaciously mentioned they had deliberately terminated several pregnancies in their lifetime and were shocked by how easily they got pregnant again each time. Baby and I returned to our room where for the next several weeks, we cried ourselves to sleep.

Baba was uncharacteristically kind about our situation. He was too kind in fact, in a way that made me suspect I had significantly increased my *roora* worth by proving I could bear children. My suspicions became stronger when Baba repeatedly told Baby that he did not need to rush to marry me simply because I had accidentally got pregnant. Each time we went to visit my family in Worplesdon, Baba would gently say to Baby, "There is no need for you to marry my daughter simply because you made her pregnant, especially now that the pregnancy has been lost. You only marry for love, son. Not because you made my daughter pregnant. You will be blessed with another child." Baba's reverse psychology made Baby feel pressured to firm up his promise to pay *roora* in April. Baby knew that until he fulfilled his promise, Baba's overstated words of consolation would keep coming. He knew he had officially "damaged" me and there were financial consequences for it. Those ramifications would multiply if he took longer than necessary to rectify them.

Without pre-warning me, or considering how he would fulfil the promise, Baby blurted back to Baba before he returned to Zimbabwe, "I love Ruva, so I will pay the *roora* in April as promised." I should have been excited by Baby's announcement, but I was not. Although I was smitten by Baby, I would have preferred to wait and test the resilience of our relationship first. Men had consistently hurt and disappointed me, and although I knew Baby would never hurt a fly, him calling me "stupid!" during his first visit to the UK had thrown me off. I could not fully trust him until I had uncovered the reasons behind his bitterness. His commitment to Baba therefore completely derailed my plan to maintain our public dating status while remaining secretly married. That plan had been my mitigation against the risk of Baby ever disappointing me. It would have allowed me to walk away from him quietly without family or societal judgement, had the need arose.

A few weeks after I miscarried, I heard a rumour that Mainini Portia was shocked I had been pregnant and had miscarried. She had apparently been relieved that I had lost my baby and could not understand the stupidity behind "a UK law graduate importing a boy with nothing, all the way from Zimbabwe to give her a bastard child". Her words hurt me deeply, but I was too fragile to confront her directly, so I wrote her a letter instead, telling her exactly what I thought. I did not bother to find out the reasons behind Mainini Portia's hurtful opinion, so my letter was long and unkind, highlighting all the bad decisions she had made in her life that I had heard her own sisters gossiping about.

When Mhamha heard about the letter, she advised me to never write such letters again, because words could never be erased from the recipient's subconscious. *"Siyana nema cup final mwanangu.* Stop writing these cup finals my child!"* Mhamha pleaded, then she urged me to apologise to Mainini Portia, reiterating that she had been through a lot in her life. I did eventually apologise, after a few months of procrastination. Mainini Portia had had a difficult first marriage to an abusive doctor in Zimbabwe. After many years of emotional and physical torment by him, she relocated to the UK where she had worked as a nurse and progressed to manage a nursing home where I had dismally failed a job trial a few days after arriving in the UK. Mainini Portia had now left the nursing profession and ran her own beauty parlour business. Now remarried to a rather eccentric middle-aged English man called George, she seemed happier and empowered. Mainini Portia often sounded stern, and perhaps slightly harsher than she intended to. Becoming more mindful of the journey she had been through helped me to refrain from judging Mainini Portia unfairly when she spoke her mind.

Chapter 13

In search of new brighter beginnings, Baby and I spontaneously moved to another town. We had been struggling with living in a shared house anyway and had endured our food going missing in the fridge, sharing a dirty bathroom, and noisy altercations between the Zimbabwean landlady and her Nigerian boyfriend.

After Mainini Portia's comments about my importation of a "boy with nothing" from Zimbabwe, I suddenly felt secretly ashamed of a situation I had otherwise been proud of. As far as I was concerned, I had found a man with the potential to fulfil all the societal goals that were being imposed on me and love me truly as a bonus. But it seemed my progress had not been good enough. Manini Portia's views somewhat groomed a fear in me, that my own family and the wider Zimbabwean community would have negative views of my relationship and attempt to sabotage it somehow. I had seen so many good relationships ending prematurely due to unnecessary drama, false rumours, or otherwise. So, it felt necessary to flee the plague of enmeshment.

Baby and I agreed that moving away from Surrey would enable us to live more autonomously. I remembered that I had often seen a factory off the motorway when I travelled to and from Kent during my undergraduate studies in Canterbury. We decided to look for a flat to rent near the factory, with the hope that Baby would get a job there in future. We found an ideal two bedroom flat in Chatham and moved there at the beginning of February. We only had enough money to pay for a deposit and first month's rent, so we both had to find jobs very quickly. We managed to buy furniture on credit, and we settled into our cosy home in no time.

I, for over a year, had been buying bedding, kitchenware and other such goods to prepare for our ideal home. The hopes and dreams we had had for what seemed like a lifetime were finally materialising. Happiness began to return into our lives and my menstrual cycle resumed. By the end of February, I was pregnant again. Within a few weeks of moving to Kent, Baby had been offered a job at the city council's call centre. I subsequently got an administrative job in a bank call centre, where I processed pension transfers. I could not afford the luxury to have any feelings towards the job. It paid the bills, so I neither loved it nor hated it. We, however, could not afford to pay the rent for the first month, so we took out a high interest loan from a loan shark who came to collect weekly instalments from our door for the next few months. Having recently moved to the UK, Baby did not have a credit history and my credit rating was poor, due to all the debt I had accumulated whilst studying at university. This did not bother us too much. We were grateful to have each other and to be expecting a baby again. Baby drove in our banger to his work in Maidstone, and I walked a round trip of five miles daily to my job. It did not take us long to become frustrated by our jobs, which we were overqualified for. We were reporting into experienced individuals with no qualifications who felt threatened by persons of our calibre. Baby and I began to proactively look for ways to improve our situation.

Within a couple of months of settling into our new life, a newspaper advertisement from the factory appeared. They were running a graduate scheme and were looking for chemical engineers! We had aligned our career intentions with our action to move to Kent, so we believed the synchronicity of the job opportunity was not an accident. Baby was accepted onto the scheme and would begin his new job as a graduate engineer in May that year. We were ecstatic that our intention had manifested. I continued to search for a professional job, but I was turned down for being inexperienced but overqualified. The career advice available to law graduates was for them to attend graduate law school in order to attain legal practice qualifications. A training contract would also be required, and these were usually available to law graduates who had attained upper second-class degrees or better. I had no access to funding for the Legal Practice Course and was unlikely to get a training contract as I did not have the required grades. In addition to this, I did not enjoy Law, so my desire to pursue a legal career was minimal. The dissertation for my master's programme needed completing, but as my pregnancy progressed, my energy levels depleted, as did my motivation to complete the course. I had after all signed up for it to buy time. Now that Baby had come to live with me and we were expecting a baby, there was no real need for me to complete the course, so I parked it, hoping my motivation would return in the near future.

In April, my *roora* ceremony took place as promised. Baby and I were in the UK, while the event took place at my childhood home in our absence. A running commentary was provided to us by my cousins and aunts who were present, through phone messaging, calls and social media. Baby's father, Bambo, and his brothers, together with Baby's older brother, Daniel, and cousins made up the entourage that went to pay my *roora* on behalf of Baby. We were getting married traditionally simply to please my parents, and this made me very upset. It was a Saturday and we had travelled to Surrey to visit Mhamha. The realisation that I was still very angry towards Baba for disrespecting Mhamha became amplified by the *roora* event, because I felt Baba did not deserve to be paid for my upbringing. The derailment caused by discovering Baba was not the man I thought he was had triggered an identity crisis which pushed me to detach myself from him and his culture. I particularly began to loathe the patriarchal elements of that culture.

When I heard Baba had ordered Bambo to sit in a corner on the floor, like a naughty child, and state the purpose of his visit when he arrived, as was customary, I wanted to phone and curse Baba. Mhamha pleaded with me continuously to calm down and not take these events to heart. After all he had done to her, to us, why was she fighting his corner? Baba apparently wanted to recover the university fees my parents had paid and wanted to be compensated for the derailment caused by my mother's relocation to the UK when she came to work for my university fees. But had Mhamha not stayed on after my graduation to escape him and his abusive culture? Baba had been rubbing his hands too for the damage caused by Baby when he got me pregnant.

The *munyai,* spokesperson and messenger for the groom, was VaJongwe, a common family friend who Baba and Bambo had known for a very long time. A long list of groceries had been presented to the *munyai* by Baba to pass on to Baby's family to bring the provisions on the day of *roora*. Complying with the list was a sign of respect. I felt sorry for Baby who had arrived in the UK with nothing to his name only six months ago. He had no savings, was living from hand to mouth and expecting a child before year end. Baby had sent a token £200 to his parents as an earnest contribution towards part of the bill they footed on the day. I felt sickened by the itemised *roora* charges, which were negotiated and partly settled as follows:

- *Vhura muromo*: Icebreaker, or loosening of mouths. The father of the bride would not name the bride price until the *vhura muromo* was paid – £300 (paid)
- *Ndiro*: At the beginning of the proceedings, the *munyai* asked for a plate, the *ndiro* where the monies would be placed when requested. When handed over, a float was immediately placed on the plate by the groom's family - £150 (paid)
- *Zvibinge*: Damages for any transgressions by the groom. One such misdemeanour was the sitting of Baby next to Baba on the flight to London, regardless of the fact that the crime had been beyond Baby's control. Another was the issue of my travelling to Zimbabwe for Baby's graduation and not proceeding to visit Baba in Masvingo afterwards. Baby should have ensured that I set foot on the soil of my ancestors - £1,000 (outstanding)

- *Mavuchiro*: The groom was expected to clap his hands in a specific way called *kurova gusvi*, to grab the attention of his in-laws. This fee afforded the groom a right to perform the clap as and when required during the ceremony - £150 (paid)
- *Matekenyandebvu*: Damages for any disrespect the bride might have shown her father growing up - £250 (paid)
- *Kunonga kwanyakuwanikwa*: A sum the bride was required to pick from the plate as a gift, which she could use to buy household goods for her new home - £500 (outstanding)
- *Vana tete nevanun'una*: A sum picked from the plate by aunts and sisters of the bride, in order to buy the bride kitchen utensils and other household essentials as gifts for the wedding - £500 (paid)
- *Rugaba*: This was the most crucial part of the *roora*, also known as *kubvisa pfuma*, which translates to "parting with wealth" - £5000 (£1,000 paid; £4,000 outstanding)
- *Kupinda mumba:* After the *rugaba* stage was completed, the groom's entourage was officially made part of the household, following payment of the requested fee - £150 (paid)
- *Danga raBaba*: Live beasts for the bride's father – 8 head of cattle (4 paid; 4 outstanding)
- *Mombe youmai*: The mother of the bride's cow was

the most important cow, which had to be alive, as it was expected to produce offspring to prove that the union was blessed – 1 heifer (paid)

- *Mafukidza dumbu*: A gift of covering of the belly given to the mother of the bride to thank her for carrying the bride in her womb and to appease her maternal spirits - £500 (paid)
- *Pwanya ruzhowa*: Literally translates to "breaking the security fence"; these were damages Baby had to pay for impregnating me out of wedlock – 3 head of cattle (paid)
- *Mabhachi*: Also known as "majasi" were gifts of clothing for the bride's parents, comprising full outfits from head to toe – Baby was to buy outfits for Mhamha and Tongai, to wear to our white wedding (outstanding).

How were these charges justified and why was there no input from me in deciding these fees? The proceedings reduced me to a commodity, and within a few hours, I was sold! I also wondered why most of Baby's "wealth" was being paid to Baba and not Mhamha who had played a significantly larger role of birthing and raising me. The event lasted a full day, and Baby and I were relieved when it was over and done with.

Under normal circumstances, traditions and culture provided safety and security within families. I had been brought up to respect and fully comply with the Shona culture. However, within our family, that culture was restrictive, static and unchallenged. It was used to further various personal agendas at the detriment of others, usually women. Having experienced the ordeal and death of Tete Vimbai, the suffering of Mhamha, Maiguru Chiedza, Moira, Tete Gertrude, Mainini Gemma and many other women, I could now see that our culture was tailored to boost male egos and put women down. It was a culture designed to erode my sense of self and my self-esteem in addition to promoting inequality.

What a farce this was! Men paying money to other men in exchange for well-trained obedient women they could abuse freely going forward, with no repercussions. If the *roora* process was truly about gratefulness, why did women not pay dowry for husbands who kindly donated their sperm as and when the women desired to reproduce – as was my case? If this event was genuinely about thankfulness, I should have been paying dowry to Baby's family to compensate them for the loss of a son to a girl living in the diaspora. If the two families were equally grateful for each other, then no one should have been making any payments at all.

In order to supplement our income, which was very low, we drove to Surrey every Friday after work, and I would braid the hair of at least five clients over the course of the weekend.

My clientele in Surrey was very reliable and I had struggled to establish new clients in Chatham. The trips to Surrey would earn me up to £300 per weekend and this made it worthwhile for us. I would therefore work all weekends braiding hair, and then Monday to Friday at the call centre, where I walked to daily; while Baby settled into his new professional job. We had both got involved in maintaining our flat, cleaning, doing the laundry, shopping for groceries, cooking and ironing. However, as Baby took on more responsibility at work, I found myself running our flat on my own. Life began taking its toll on me.

Around July, when I was around six months pregnant, I started bleeding, and a dark cloud of sorrow hung over us again. Although we had been ecstatic to be pregnant again, the fear of losing the pregnancy again had prevailed. I phoned Mhamha and told her about the bleeding. She tried to calm me down and explained that bleeding was normal during pregnancy. She encouraged us to go to A&E immediately and keep her updated. She would be praying for us. When we arrived at the A&E, I was scanned, and my abdomen was examined. Our baby's heart was beating, but I had contracted a urinary tract infection that had induced the bleeding. After taking some bed rest and completing the antibiotics course, the bleeding stopped, and things got back to normal. A few months on, my temporary job at the bank call centre came to an end. I was too far gone to find another job, so I stayed at home for about two months before the baby was due. I spent that time nesting, and hand knitting a multicoloured blanket for my child.

My body had changed tremendously, and although I felt like I had lost control over my own body, I loved how I looked. A linea nigra stretched vertically down my belly from the sternum to my pubic bone. I enjoyed standing in front of a full-length mirror to inspect such changes and wondered why they might be happening. My belly was large and round, and my belly button, which I had never seen before popped out. I experienced chronic back ache due to the baby's weight. I also suffered with carpal tunnel syndrome in my wrists, so it became quite difficult to complete basic household chores. A stuffy nose made me snore loudly and wake myself up, resulting in broken sleep. I felt exhausted and impatient to have my baby. My breasts had become enormous as oestrogen and progesterone hormones caused the milk ducts and milk-making tissue to grow. During the final trimester of my pregnancy, I started producing colostrum, a clear sweet fluid that Baby enjoyed sucking on during our mating sessions. The baby kicked vigorously when she heard Baby's voice and when he touched my belly.

My family and friends arranged a baby shower where they generously presented everything I needed for the baby. My friends from Canterbury attended the baby shower, and I was delighted that Belinda made it too. Runako coordinated the event with Baby. A rather strong friendship had developed between the two by then.

Mhamha bought most of the baby's furniture and knitted several little outfits for her. A scan had confirmed by this time that our baby would be a girl. Prior to the scan, I knew instinctively that I was carrying a girl, and Baby and I decided she would be called Mayananiswa. Mhamha had forecast a girl too due to my slim linea nigra. My midwife also predicted a girl due to her heartbeat rate. Colleagues at work had foreseen a girl as well, due to my raised bump. Many people prophesied a girl due to my clear fair skin during the pregnancy. In October, Mhamha, who I had emailed my latest pregnancy photos replied to my email, telling me that I looked "truly majestic" and that she loved me.

Mhaiyo, Valerie and Daniel's wife Memory text me regularly to check on me. It felt uplifting to receive emotional support from Baby's family from Zimbabwe. Mhaiyo and Bambo began making plans to visit us after the baby was born.

Baby continued to take on more responsibility at work, working overtime and always very busy. He worked night shifts, extended day shifts, and was never home. I realised towards the end of the pregnancy that

Baby and I had not had an opportunity to spend time alone as a couple before the baby's arrival. Feeling desperately lonely, I wondered whether the prospect of parenthood made Baby anxious, thereby needing to escape to work. I worried he would not be fit enough to support me during labour. Staying sober throughout the pregnancy was taking its toll on me, and I wished I could drink to ease my worries. I began experiencing nightmares, including one where Baby was best man at a friend's wedding and the maid of honour who was his partner was seducing him, despite knowing he was married. I rationalised the dreams were reflective of my insecurity, that I might never be the same woman after childbirth and that Baby might lose interest in me.

At this stage during my pregnancy, I should have customarily gone through *masungiro,* the return of the wife to her parents during her first pregnancy, as Tete Vimbai did, when she had James. Due to an absence of Baby's relatives, the fact that no one would have been available to look after me at Mhamha's house, exacerbated by erosion of the Shona culture commensurate with relocating to the UK, and mere ambivalence on everyone's part, *masungiro* did not happen. Two days before my due date, I had a final hospital check-up which confirmed the baby was in good labour position. Her head was down three fifths, facing my back, lying on my right side of my womb. All was going as planned. I was ready for childbirth and I was not afraid.

Chapter 14

In November, I had a show at 2.45am and my labour commenced around 5am on the predicted due date. I was ecstatic when the pains began, because not only was I sleep deprived and exhausted by the pregnancy, but I felt desperately impatient to meet Maya. I had become colossal, like a beached whale, and suffered with sleep apnoea. It was a Monday morning when the contractions began, and little did I know they were to last four days. I had already had a taste of contractual pains when I miscarried earlier that year, so it was not the pain of contractions that distressed me, but the prolonged infliction of agony drove me to delirium. Baby drove me to the local hospital that day, and we were turned back because my cervix had not begun to dilate. My contractions were also seven to ten minutes apart, so I was not yet in active labour.

Mhamha had had four caesarean sections, so she projected that I would end up delivering my child by surgery as well, something she affirmed throughout my pregnancy. As a child, I had had a phobia of dentists. I had not got into the habit of brushing my teeth twice daily until I went to boarding school at the age of 13. Mhamha had therefore taken me to the dentist countless times before then, and she helplessly watched me lapsing into panic attacks and terror fits which required my little body to be restrained during the uprooting of molars, premolars and canines. Mhamha had as a result reached the conclusion that if I had a phobia for dentists, there was no way I could give birth naturally. How she had made the connection between my fear of dentists and natural childbirth remained unclear to me. I decided this would not be the case, even if it killed me. Whilst acknowledging there was no right or wrong way of giving birth, I planned the delivery of my child in great detail and was determined to push it out regardless of the consequences. I was going to deliver naturally to prove Mhamha wrong.

I was not prepared to bear any scars as a result of the birth. I had exercised religiously during the pregnancy and fully relied on the elasticity of my birth canal to not let me down. I had not expected to develop any stretch marks either, and I had done well until the 38th week of my pregnancy. Doctors and midwives had commented during antenatal appointments that my stomach muscles were very strong and elastic, and I took this as confirmation that my abdomen would not disappoint me. Burgundy-like marks had appeared from nowhere on my smooth supple stomach one morning. I stood naked in front of a full-length mirror, examining the foreign meandering superfluities on my body. Had an invisible entity poured trickling syrup over my belly and disappeared? I was dismayed by them.

Mhamha arrived on Tuesday morning, to wait for her first grandchild's arrival. Tongai had driven her to Kent and returned to Surrey immediately as he was in college studying for his A levels.

Mhamha took me for a long walk in the morning to try and speed up the process, then for a run later that afternoon, but the baby was not ready to come out. I was exhausted by the intermittent contractions in my lower abdomen. They came in waves that felt like the bites of several soldier termites pinching away on the same spot repeatedly. The relentless nips stopped and started for hours on end, and the burden of labour weighed me down.

On Wednesday morning, Mhamha and I repeated the tedious exercise rituals to encourage progression of the labour. By Wednesday night, my contractions had progressed to shorter, sharper sting sensations that made me think my core had been invaded by yellow jacket wasps. However, my cervix was still not dilating, and my membranes had not ruptured, so my waters remained intact. I was fatigued by the pain and needed relief.

We returned to the hospital where a decision was made to sweep my membranes. A midwife stood at the bottom end of my bed with her right hand gloved. She scooped a generous amount of lubricant from a tub on her trolley, then stiffened her fore and middle fingers in readiness to rupture my amniotic sac. "Ready?" she asked in a Scottish accent, then I nodded hesitantly to consent. Her cold hand penetrated my vagina and firmly swayed left, right, centre and down, in a manner reminiscent of Shaka's cow horn formation. Following that intervention, we were sent back home where I quietly paced up and down, huffed and puffed, clapped my hips and wiggled my toes in incomprehensible pain.

Since Monday, Mhamha had been trying to phone Baba to alert him I was in labour, but his mobile phone was not reachable. He eventually picked up the phone and said he was busy at a conference in South Africa. The look on Mhamha's face left me in no doubt that Baba did not want to be bothered by her.

On Thursday morning around 2 am, active labour commenced with contractions less than two minutes apart, and we were all certain I was ready to give birth. Baby drove us to the hospital where I was placed on a wheelchair on arrival, as I could not walk anymore due to excruciating labour pains. We were finally directed to the labour ward, where the screams and cursing of other women giving birth provided brief comic relief.

"Damn! What was I thinking! I am never ever doing this again!" one woman yelled.

"Noooooo! I'm gonna die, I'm gonna die, I'm gonna die!!!" another woman screamed.

The histrionics reminded me of our childhood years, when perpetrators had dramatised the corporal punishment process and got tortured further for it. I had found that screaming and dancing around in pain encouraged the beater to prolong the ordeal, so I learnt to not react to pain. I was certain my delivery would be quiet and dignified. A few hours later, I was moved into a sterile delivery suite. The room was extremely clean and white and was adorned with intimidating gadgets that would be employed if anything went wrong. I had opted to use Pethidine, plus gas and air as my painkillers, and refused an Epidural. I had found the notion of inserting a needle into my spine terribly unnerving.

My contractions were monitored closely, as my cervix distended steadily. The first inspection confirmed I had only dilated to three centimetres. This announcement was met by shocked, impatient grumbles by the stakeholders in my birthing suite. It was difficult to comprehend that all the pain I had suffered until then had only resulted in such minute progress. Time could not have moved any slower for me. Seconds had felt like minutes, minutes like hours, hours like days and days like months! I rolled to the left, then to the right, lied on my back, sat up, knelt, clenched my teeth, pinched my waist, tapped my feet on the floor, and all sorts of doings in response to labour pains. I was also exasperated by the number of times I had opened wide, during the pregnancy, and now more frequently towards the end of it. Female and male nurses and doctors, all turned up when they saw fit to spread my legs and insert their limbs inside me. It felt degrading, and I had no choice but to comply. I empathised with Baby who judiciously monitored these intrusions. His exclusive rights to my pudenda were temporarily suspended, and he loathed the apparent lack of science to back up this infringement. I also felt self-conscious about my *matinji*, stretched labia minora, that our housegirl, Sisi Fungai, had dutifully pulled when I was ten years old – what did they all think of this oddity?

Sisi Fungai had assumed the role of agony aunt to me and my young cousins when they visited our home. She would tease us about our growing busts and buttocks and tell us we would soon be married. She had dubbed the labia stretching sessions our "secret ritual", where she would come into the bathroom daily before my bath and pull the vertical folds of skin in the middle of my vulva. When I went to visit her during her days off and we ran out of things to talk about, she invited me to lie on her bed where she inspected my progress down below. She said *matinji* would enhance sexual pleasure when I grew up, and if a man ever "tasted" me, he would never leave me. I had no idea what that meant at that age, but understood the lengthening had to happen before I began menstruating, otherwise the opportunity would be missed forever. When my labia had proven stubborn, our housegirl resorted to tying knitting wool to two golf-ball-size stones and tying the opposite end of the wool to my tiny labia in a knot. I then had to stand for lengthy periods of time to enable the weight of the stones to do the job for her. This secret ceremony caused me immense anguish, but I never thought to inform Mhamha about it. How could I, when we had never spoken about our genitalia, save for when we were reprimanded for poking each other's "wee wees" as kids, during what we thought was sex?

At the end of it all, I failed to achieve a length that Sisi Fungai was proud of. She had humongous ones that shocked Tongai as a young boy when he had walked in on her during a shower. He had kept the finding to himself until one day during a family gathering, he screamed "Sisi Fungai! Sisi Fungai!" The room went dead silent to allow the child to speak, then Tongai went on to shout, *"Futi chinhu chenyu chaakutoenzana necha Tizai!* Your thing is now nearly as long as Tizai's!" and a barrage of suppressed laughter followed. I was not particularly impressed by the aesthetics of *matinji* and endured a lifetime of hiding and tucking them away as a result. On this day, they were out and plain to see, but I had to let go of the ego concomitant with fretting about such miniscule tribulations. I took comfort in knowing that Baby loved my *matinji*, as he loved me and my imperfections.

A second inspection confirmed dilation to four centimetres. All this while, I writhed and squirmed in tremendous pain. An affliction worse than the worst menstrual cramp combined with the worst case of constipation. There were a few more inspections before one affirmed dilation to six centimetres. A subsequent inspection unearthed eight centimetres. All this while, the anguish was increasing, to what now felt like an army of bullet ants attacking my core already wounded by termites and wasps. An injured core where menstrual cramps and troubling constipation convened to create a meticulous concoction of brilliant pain. To top it all off, the sensation of a sledgehammer propelling into my lower spine was gradually developing. For a moment I marvelled at the resilience of the human body. How it could endure such torture and return to normal function thereafter was phenomenal. How any woman would want to experience such pain more than once was even more remarkable. It was at this point I remembered the Shona word for childbirth, *kupona*, which literally translates to "survival". I fully understood then, that when a woman went into labour, they were faced with the prospect of death; their own death, their child's or both. When they successfully gave birth and remained alive, they circumvented death and survived.

When I became fully dilated to 10 centimetres, I was overcome by a need to defecate, so I requested to use the bathroom before giving birth. My midwife allowed me to get off the bed, knowing fully I would not be able to walk a single step. The toilet sensation I felt was actually the baby on its way out. I quickly returned onto the bed, unable to close my legs, and remained on my knees, then felt the need to push. At the top of the bed, I grabbed the gas and air pump with my left hand and sucked unreservedly for much needed pain relief. I felt myself getting high.

On my right, Baby braced my torso and whispered into my ear everything he could to keep me enthused. "You can do this baby", "you're stronger than you think", "our baby is nearly here, you can do it Ruva", "I'm so proud of you", "you're doing really well my lovely", "I love you Ruva", "hang in there sweetness", his free verse bestowed strength in me. At the bottom of the bed, Mhamha and the midwife dealt with more gruesome undertakings. They took turns to check the baby was moving correctly down the vaginal canal while one of them plugged my anus with a thick towelling cloth, to prevent faecal matter from shooting out when I pushed. The midwife's instructions were clear, to push, and pant, and push, and pant, as I summoned the strength of muscles throughout my body to eject the baby, until its head crowned.

I could not deal with the pain any longer. I was sure I was going to die, so I meditated a quick prayer for forgiveness. I felt indebted to Mhamha and Baby for their presence. I would die surrounded by the most important people in my life. I suffered severe pressure around my perineum as the baby's head journeyed through my cervix. It felt like the worst carpet burn a hundredfold. I was overstretched in a relentlessly obstinate way that promised a detonation of delicate muscles, and I had absolutely no control over it. The feeling resembled watching a child over-inflating a balloon, to the point that it would certainly pop and slap them in the face, yet they continued to blow and flout your warnings to stop. I suffered the ring of fire as my tissues stretched around the baby's head. Surrendering my whole being to the universe, I allowed nature to take its course. My child's head travelled slowly through me, undisturbed. To ensure it was delivered unmutilated, I breathed softly, as one would to allow free passage of the largest stool of their life. I suppressed the urge to control the inevitable descent, hoping I would not tear. The constipation sensation had graduated to a feeling of imminent diarrhoea, ready to explode. The baby was coming!

I was undeniably lapsing into insanity when the midwife announced the baby's head had protruded, but the umbilical cord was wrapped around its neck. My cervical muscles savoured minor temporary relief as the head was out, but the shoulders were yet to pass through. I had to push slowly as instructed, while the midwife attempted to unwind the cord from the baby's neck. In that instant, I was consumed with fear and anxiety, that at that very last moment I might mess it all up and kill the baby. It was this angst that gave me the final urge to see the process through. Not once did I scream during this ordeal. Like a child hoping their chastisement would end soon, I suffered in silence and channelled my energy to where it was required. When the moment came, I groaned deeply, teeth clenched, his arm clamped, pushing as hard as I could one last time. My head was spinning, my mind had departed, my whole being was shattered, and my vagina in tatters. Then, I heard Mhamha screaming.

"Oooooh, my grandbaby is here!" At 3.15pm, Maya shot out, and I instantaneously collapsed face down onto the thrifty hospital pillows in eternal gratefulness. I felt insanely powerful.

Baby proudly severed the conduit that had attached our daughter to my womb during the preceding nine months using an enormous steel clinical pair of scissors. Moments later, an injection that would reduce the size of my womb and help the placenta to come away, was administered into my right thigh. I became mindful then, that I had not heard Maya crying. "Is she okay?" I asked with concern. Mhamha and Baby stood next to the midwife as she wiped the baby and wrapped her in blankets. Maya was fine but was sedated by the gas and air I had taken during labour. She was also exhausted by her protracted traumatic journey into the world. Baby held her briefly, then Mhamha took her from him and brought her to my arms. As I held my child for the first time, kissing and talking to her, I was overwhelmed with unconditional love and said, "Hey beautiful…what took you so long?" Mhamha stood next to me, then without notice positioned the baby for breastfeeding from my left breast.

Although I had intended to breastfeed, the feeling of a dependent little child sucking my breast for lifeforce threw me off. At that point, the midwife returned to the bottom of the bed and instructed me to push the placenta out.

For a few hours after the delivery, Mhamha frantically tried to call Baba to tell him he was now a grandfather. His sisters had been informed of the news and he may have received a text message from one of them, when he decided to return Mhamha's calls and offer his congratulations. Mhamha, who was by then perpetually heartbroken by Baba's philandering and had got into the habit of sharing her frustrations, decided to divulge a bitter memory to me. She revealed how surprised she was by history repeating itself. She recounted how Baba had left her on her own during labour, when she gave birth to me. He had gone to start celebrating early with a lady friend and left Mhamha to face labour and the subsequent caesarean section alone. She reminded me how lucky I was to have a husband who stayed to witness his daughter's birth.

Chapter 15

I was discharged from hospital the next day, on a Friday. It was Baby's birthday, and we joked about how he might have shared a birthday with our daughter had my membranes not been swept. I had spent the morning learning to wash a real baby and helping her to latch onto my breasts for colostrum. Baby turned up with Maya's car seat and we left the hospital to face our new life as parents.

Mhamha, Tongai and Runako were waiting for us at home, but they had to return to Surrey later that day because Mhamha needed to return to work. Baby and I felt an overwhelming responsibility when Mhamha left, as we became conscious of being alone with an infant for the first time. Later that evening, Baby's cousin, Maynard, his wife June and their two children arrived to see us and the new baby. The following day, Baby's colleague and friend also came to visit, with his wife and new-born baby who was a month older than our daughter. Our days were filled with taking phone calls and listening to voice messages of congratulations, receiving flowers, changing nappies, washing the infant, and our nights were plagued by intermittent sleep and breastfeeding an eternally hungry baby.

Passing water was excruciatingly painful for me, due to a vaginal graze resulting from natural childbirth. Every time I went to urinate, I took a jug of cool water to pour over my vulva to cool down the burning urine as it trickled through my healing vagina. Each time I squirmed and wondered if I would ever be able to have sex again. I religiously began pelvic floor exercise rituals to tighten my pelvic muscles. I did mine in ten sets of ten, tightening my vaginal walls as if there was an object inside for ten seconds, then releasing and tightening again, ten times.

The process of milk production never ceased to amaze me. The mere sound of Maya crying would trigger a warm tingling sensation as my breasts swelled and filled up with nutritious liquid that would eventually erupt from tiny cracks I never knew existed in my nipples. I had thoroughly researched the back-office production of milk in my breasts and found it fascinating.

Exactly a week after Maya was born, we were lying in bed feeling exhausted after a restless night. Maya, who had started suffering from colic, was sleeping between Baby and

I with my breast in her mouth, when Mhamha rang on my mobile phone. It was around nine in the morning and I guessed she had been on a night shift, possibly checking on me quickly before making her way home to sleep. I considered not answering the phone, as I felt too tired to speak, but I intuitively picked up. After exchanging brief pleasantries, Mhamha solemnly announced, "I have just received very sad news. I've been diagnosed with cervical cancer." I was not aware of any symptoms she had suffered, so I struggled to digest the news and impulsively reassured her, "You'll be fine Mhamha." She told me she was dying, to which I said, "You can't die now Mhamha, you have so much to live for, so you will not die." When the call ended, the news sunk in slowly.

A dark cloud of depression tattooed my life that day. The joy I had felt for the arrival of Maya progressively disappeared as arrangements for Mhamha's healthcare plans developed in the weeks that followed. Mhamha had unfailingly attended cervical smear screening tests when they were due, and the results had always been normal, but she had started bleeding abnormally a few months after her previous screening and was tested for cancer. She had advanced cervical cancer, so she was scheduled for a total abdominal hysterectomy in February of the New Year. The thought of Mhamha ever becoming seriously ill or dying had never crossed my mind – she had been the only consistent source of love and stability in the family that everyone took for granted. It was unthinkable that her existence and strength might ever become threatened and compromised. The thought of Mhamha suffering from cancer was even further removed, because after Mhamha abandoned her career as a nurse to run our family businesses in Zimbabwe, she had volunteered at a local hospice where she provided end of life care for cancer patients in Masvingo. Although there was no real logic to my thought process, it made no sense that a person who had voluntarily cared for cancer patients might be inflicted with such bad karma and suffer from cancer themselves.

Mhaiyo, arrived at Gatwick airport during the first week of December. Baby and I took Maya with us to the airport. Mhaiyo was ecstatic to see her granddaughter, and asked to hold Maya, but I was worried she might drop her. As a paranoid new mother who was slowly lapsing into depression, I did not contemplate the awkwardness of my response, and I refused to hand the baby over to Mhaiyo. Baby took our daughter from my arms and passed her to his mother. Mhamha had requested that we passed through her home in Worplesdon to introduce Mhaiyo, who she had not met yet, so we drove to Worplesdon from Gatwick. Mhamha was very excited to meet Mhaiyo and had made us a lavish cooked breakfast to welcome her, and we took many photographs.

We left for Kent later that afternoon and spent the next few days playing the role of tour guide to Mhaiyo, showing her the seaside along the Kent coastal towns. Bambo was due to arrive in the UK shortly after Christmas, as he needed to work on Christmas day. He had worked on Christmas day and bank holidays for as long as Baby could remember. As a result, Baby's family did not celebrate special occasions including Christmas and birthdays. My family on the other hand, marked celebrations extravagantly, with offerings, copious food intake and plenteous drink. Special occasions were always a good excuse to overindulge, cross boundaries and conveniently forget any offences that might occur.

We spent Christmas in Surrey with my family. Baba had by then arrived from Zimbabwe and would see his first grandchild for the first time. He seemed very happy to see Maya and joked that he and my aunts in Zimbabwe had grown very anxious about my prolonged labour. They had been tempted to encourage me *kudura*, a confession made by pregnant women who would have cheated on their husbands. It was a Shona cultural belief that a baby would not come out before its cheating mother confessed. I did not find the joke funny. To me, this cultural reference was simply a projection of Baba's own behaviour. He also managed to notice that I had grown "very fat".

I found myself trying to find opportune times to slip away to breastfeed my daughter privately. I felt ashamed of unleashing my enormous breasts publicly and feeding my baby confidently like other women. I often thought of the breastfeeding women I had seen on buses and markets growing up in Zimbabwe. I particularly envied the ones who left their breasts hanging out even when they had finished feeding their babies, talking endlessly as if they had forgotten the simple task of returning their mammary glands into their blouses. Why could I not be like them?

I experienced occasional breast engorgement due to irregular feeds. Christmas day progressed quickly as I was too tired and sober to participate in any drama. I had quietly observed that Baba's Christmas gift to Mhamha was a dildo. His offering to Mhamha had nothing to do with me, but it made me furious! Mhamha had by then got into the habit of loading me with details of Baba's marital delinquencies. The gift, as far as I was concerned, was inferred confirmation that he had completely lost interest in Mhamha. Plus, what a thoughtless gift for a woman who had been diagnosed with cervical cancer!

On boxing day, I woke up with a fever and lumpy red-hot inflamed breasts. Baby drove me to a local walk-in clinic where I was diagnosed with lactation mastitis and prescribed antibiotics. The build-up of milk in my breasts due to irregular feeds had resulted in the blockage of some milk ducts, which led to the infection. My areola had also cracked, and my nipples had become raw due to the baby's failure to latch on to my breasts properly. My breasts felt unusually warm to touch and I felt fatigued and nauseous. What followed were days of excruciating soreness, due to feeding from fractured udders.

Feeding times had developed into a warzone, where I unleashed and reluctantly dangled my breast in anticipation of Maya's remorseless devour. She would scream helplessly, as she tried to angle her mouth for the breast. I lowered it to her ever so slowly, only to swipe it away as I squirmed in pain when she enveloped only my nipple, which felt and looked like it was detaching from the rest of my breast. Maya would scream desperately louder, and I felt very guilty for failing at this very basic task of feeding a hungry baby. I would eventually squeeze the lower half of my breast to create an oblong shape that allowed my whole areola to fit into her mouth. Out of frustration, Maya would dive onto the breast and lock her mouth around it with exceptionally firm vigour that abruptly brought the short war to an end. Panting fleetingly, she stared into my eyes and sucked the life out of me, then calmed down gradually as the warm liquid flowed into her little body, to fill her up with vitality and reassurance. Our tedious feeding ritual carried on for several days, which felt like several weeks.

I occasionally resorted to using a breast pump to relieve myself and feed the baby from bottles, as the pump's suction was a lot kinder than Maya's voracious orifice. This option was not appreciated by Maya, who preferred to latch onto me for comfort. The antibiotics healed me eventually, but my first impression of breastfeeding was very much unpleasant. I produced so much milk thereafter, I felt like a cow! I would breastfeed the baby until she filled up and belched, then pumped excess milk into bottles until I filled up all available containers. I would on many occasions subsequently stand in a warm shower for prolonged periods to allow some of my milk to drain out. Baby had walked in on me during one of my showers and exclaimed "Eeeew!" when he saw milk gushing out of my swollen breasts like torrential rain. He also continuously hinted that he missed having "them" to himself. I decided then that I hated breastfeeding and needed to find an excuse to stop.

Mhamha regularly phoned me to check on my breastfeeding progress and would not be easily convinced of seizing this vital maternal task. Once during a visit in Worplesdon, I had gathered the guts to tell her straight up that the rightful owner of my breasts wanted them back. She gave me a brief gaze of surprise, then stated matter-of-factly that there was no reason why Baby could not share my breasts with Maya. She went on to giggle as she provided graphic details of her own experience I did not need to know.

"Baba used to love suckling. You know he loves milk! Sometimes he had my right breast simultaneously as you suckled my left one!" I had to stop her right then,

"Gosh Mhamha! That's too much information!" then we burst into mischievous titters.

When Bambo finally arrived, I barely spent intimate time with Maya. Amid Baby's parents and Baby taking turns to hold her, I was left yearning to hold my own child, so feeding time was my only excuse to take Maya away and enjoy bonding time alone with her. As a result, I quickly fell back in love with breastfeeding. I would take as long as possible to breastfeed, usually until one of the trio queried if I was still at it. Feeding time never felt ample. Mhaiyo had instructed Bambo to bring with him some Cerelac, a sugar-filled cereal porridge, which she preferred to feed the baby to keep her fuller for longer, as my breastmilk was deemed insufficient. My two-month-old Maya did not respond very well to the watery porridge which was being administered to her in a bottle. Mhaiyo wished she had brought some *Ntolwane*. I had never heard of the medicine and Mhamha, who was a nurse had never been in the habit of resorting to traditional medicines when we were growing up – she understandably preferred clinical pharmaceutical healing solutions. The only traditional herbal treatment I had received was *Zumbani* green tea, which Mbuya had relied on heavily for treatment of colds and flu. I hated the treatment, which involved enduring enclosure by a thick blanket whilst facing a steaming pot of boiling water with *Zumbani* immersed in it, a suffocating and uncomfortable experience for any claustrophobic children. I was relieved there were no traditional medicines to experiment with on Maya, as I was sceptical of their suitability on a new-born baby.

When I was not breastfeeding, I cooked, cleaned or organised a tour of some sort. We took my parents in law to Canterbury, Bluewater and nearby towns in Kent. I would always mess my clothing with overflowing milk from my full breasts – a happening that felt embarrassing to begin with, but later became normal to me. We also took them to London on a joint trip with Baba and my siblings. I felt completely run down during this time.

In mid-January, a few days before my parents in law were due to return to Zimbabwe, Baba requested a family gathering at our flat in Kent. We all assembled as instructed. In predictable fashion, I had ensured there were sufficient provisions to feed and water all invitees present. When the eating was done and the drinking was underway, Baba announced that he expected Baby and I to have a white wedding in April. A few months earlier, Baby and I had toyed with the idea of getting married the past December but had resolved it was impossible. We had a new-born baby, I had not been working, Baby was on a miniscule graduate trainee salary, and that situation had not changed. So, our automatic response was negative. We were in no position to fund a wedding.

Baba said the wedding had to happen while he still held a prestigious position in politics – he may not win the next election, so it was important for the wedding to take place before then. My parents in law may have hinted that Baba's expectations were rather ambitious, but Baba said he would expect them to provide drinks only, and he would fund everything else. Claiming to have organised and funded many weddings in the family in the past, Baba said his own daughter's wedding would be a breeze. This statement was followed by a contagious roar of laughter, which seemed to give all stakeholders some confidence that Baba's expectation could be and would be fulfilled. Incredibly, it was agreed the wedding would take place in April and sounds of merriment echoed into early morning hours.

After my parents in law returned to Zimbabwe, Baby, Maya and I went to spend the weekend at Mhamha's house in Surrey. On the Saturday morning, Mhamha was unusually late arriving home from her night shift. When she finally arrived home, she looked like she had seen a ghost and presented palpitations. Although Mhamha had cancer, she had not displayed any symptoms, so I was surprised by her demeanour. When I asked if she was okay, Mhamha handed me an envelope full of newly developed photographs. I sniffed in a whiff of photo ink as I opened the package, unsure I wanted to see what she had seen. I was still half asleep, having had a late night as was the case when Baba was around. I started perusing the photographs and felt my stomach churning. I immediately ran to the toilet to vomit, then I turned around and dispensed explosive diarrhoea. I had seen numerous images of Baba, having sex with various women in hotel rooms, on different occasions. They were performing oral sex on him; he was taking pictures of them at work. Most of them were morbidly obese, which I found surprising given that Baba had been calling me "fat", yet I was not half the size of the women in the pictures, and I had just given birth. None of them were stunning, or half as beautiful as Mhamha. They all appeared foul and clammy. Some of them simply reminded me of Bubbles and Desiree from Little Britain. I felt traumatised that I had seen my own father's erect penis and felt too weak to leave the bathroom, but I had to.

I wobbled back to Mhamha, trying to think of what to say to her, how to console her. I tightened my core, looked her in the eye and told her sternly that she needed to leave Baba. I had delivered this speech many times before, but this incident was undoubtedly the ultimate deal breaker.

"You can't continue to suffer like this Mhamha! You have to leave this man, for your own sake. For your own sanity! And dignity!" I pleaded with my mother.

"Not until he tells me he doesn't love me anymore," was her predictable response.

"Does he tell you that he loves you?"

"He does!"

"Unprompted?"

"That's none of your business!"

"It is now!"

"Listen, we have invested so much time and so much more into this relationship. I will not allow some cheap whores to displace me and take over everything I worked for.

Practically all my life! He's been my one and only since I was fourteen! I love my husband and he loves me!"

"Well, that may be true Mhamha, but love alone is not enough. He certainly doesn't respect you. And he doesn't adore you, or make you happy. You're not his favourite sweetheart anymore."

"He will stop when I return home!"

"When?"

"I am fifty-one Ruva! I will not leave my husband at this age. We've come a long way, and I have been coping…" Mhamha paused to wipe away tears she had been fighting hard to suppress. "My only wish is to have him by my side as we get older and begin to enjoy the fruits of our labour…our grandchildren, more graduations and weddings, celebrating our children's successes. But your father seems to be going the other way, getting younger as I'm getting older. Throughout this marriage, he has shocked me with his behaviour, time after time, I never get used to it. Each heartbreak hurts exactly like the first. I can't believe I am still talking about heartbreak at my age Ruva. And I am ashamed to admit that after all these years, I will never know who that man really is."

I felt the pain in each and every one of Mhamha's words. However, I had never invested as much effort as she had into a relationship that caused so much pain, so I struggled to understand why she would not give up on it. I wanted to cry, then I wanted to punch Baba in the face, and I wanted to unknow him. I could not comprehend how a learned, well-respected man like him could turn out to be such a familial washout. "Now that you have cancer, you need to exist in a stress-free atmosphere that will not worsen your illness," was all I could say to Mhamha to end our conversation.

As we were speaking, Mhamha had been mentally preparing for a fight with Baba. When she had shown the pictures to Runako who was also utterly disgusted by them, Mhamha made her way to her bedroom to start a world war. She woke Baba up and invited him to comment on the photographs. We heard Baba shrieking on top of his voice that Mhamha was sick in the head, and only sick people would do what she had done.

What had in fact happened was, upon Baba's arrival in the UK, he dismantled his phone, and hid the different components of it in different locations. He had placed the phone battery in a coat pocket, the sim-card in a side pocket of a bag, the memory card in his wallet, and other parts elsewhere. Mhamha had observed for many days that Baba, who was addicted to his mobile phone, was not using it often, and when he did, he did so privately. Mhamha hunted down Baba's phone then when she discovered it was dismantled, commenced the project of putting together the jigsaw. When she finally put the phone together, it was password protected, so she took its memory card to a photography store and asked them to print any images saved on the media. We were all disgusted by Baba and could not look him in the eye. He did not know that we had seen his photographs.

By February, Baba had returned to Zimbabwe, and we were left to face Mhamha's hysterectomy on our own. Although the operation was successful, Mhamha requested radiotherapy to ensure that her cancer was completely eliminated. Due to her experience working for a cancer hospice in Zimbabwe, she knew that operations deemed successful did not warrant total elimination of cancer. When Mhamha was denied this treatment option by the specialists looking after her, she decided to go to Zimbabwe to heal in the sun, and to start preparing for my wedding. Mhamha had stayed in hospital for nearly two weeks and seemed to be in a lot of pain. I had not until this point realised the seriousness of her predicament. I did not think anyone in the family had. As Baby was working and we shared one car, we only visited Mhamha in Surrey during weekends, where I would sit next to her hospital bed and look at her helplessly, toing and froing between grocery stores to buy her some essentials. I felt heartbroken each time we returned to Kent, knowing Mhamha needed looking after. I was by then quite depressed and needed looking after as well. Tongai and Runako who still lived with Mhamha visited her daily in hospital. I spent the week looking after Maya, preparing for the wedding and calling Mhamha daily.

As I coordinated bridesmaids' outfits and matching groomsmen's suits, we had to decide who would be in the bridal party and figure out their dress, suit and shoe sizes. Often enough, I received coercive messages to ensure at least one of each of Baba's siblings' children took part in my wedding. My aunts vigorously campaigned that a daughter of Babamunini Farai, Beauty, who I had never met, be added to the bridal party. I invited Runako, Imogen and Tsvakai's younger sister Tarisai to be my bridesmaids. I also had to ensure Mhamha's family was fairly represented in the bridal party, and all my maternal cousins who took part were flower girls. A good friend of mine from high school, Rudo agreed to be my maid of honour and I was very flattered by her commitment to fly to Zimbabwe from the UK for my wedding. Daniel would be best man. Baby's friend Kumbirai, who had been loitering with him when I visited him in Karoi, would be a groomsman. A few of Baby's cousins would be groomsmen, including Maynard's younger brother, Noel, who would travel from the UK for the wedding. In total, the bridal party comprised 15 people: 10 adults and five children, all of whom required robing and adorning.

We had very little money to spend on the wedding, so everything was planned on a very tight budget. I had initially found a wedding dress on eBay, but when it turned up it looked dreadful on me, so I returned it. Before Mhamha travelled to Zimbabwe, she surprised me by travelling to Kent, taking me to a local wedding dress shop, and buying me a designer wedding dress which had been on sale. I was eternally grateful for this gesture of love and support. Mhamha travelled to Zimbabwe in early March. By then, we had bought some blank wedding cards, which needed to be decorated, completed then distributed for the wedding in April. Mhamha took this task with her and would give me regular updates on how she was progressing with the wedding preparation on the other side. I felt extremely worried about Mhamha's wellbeing. She had not healed but had to prepare for my wedding on her own.

In mid-March, only a few weeks before our wedding, Baba demanded a *roora* instalment, to be delivered before the wedding. It had been a whole year since he had received the initial token bride price payment from Baby and that was not good enough, he said. As if he had not bulldozed us to wed in Zimbabwe on three months' notice, on the basis he would sponsor the function, Baba brazenly offered a brusque justification for his absurd request.

"*Imimi,* I have a wedding to pay for and the money has to come from somewhere!"

We were aware of the worsening economic situation in Zimbabwe, so as far as we were concerned, we did not need to wed there, and certainly not at such short notice. I felt like Baba did not deserve compliance to his unreasonable commands because he had done nothing lately to deserve that right.

It had been over a year since we had acquired the high interest loan to pay our first rent instalment. The unwavering weekly visits from our loan shark collection agent still haunted us like a virus. We had had to employ all sorts of tactics to explain Mike who had relentlessly rang our doorbell every Friday at 6.30pm to Baby's parents during their visit.

"It's that guy from the Jehovah's Witness," we explained one time.

"Oh, it's just someone trying to sell us windows," we lied another time.

I explained to Mhamha that Baby and I did not want to wed in Zimbabwe, and we did not need to. All our friends and most people with whom we had meaningful relationships no longer lived in Zimbabwe. Mhamha could not help me much on the matter, as Baba was adamant the wedding had to take place "back home". At this point, we had not paid for our flights and were struggling to cope with daily living expenses. Baby and I were both only 25 years old, trying to get to grips with parenthood, still trying to learn to live with each other, and still in the process of growing up. We were doing our very best to establish ourselves as first-generation immigrants in the UK, and also trying to conform with societal norms from a place we had once called "home". But we were wrapped in manipulative fog and could not see where we had come from and where we were going.

We had no option but to apply for another loan, which we would repay over a seven-year term. We were lucky enough to get a £7,000 loan. Baba received the *roora* instalment, we paid for flights and other wedding expenses. The wedding would take place.

Chapter 16

I travelled to Zimbabwe during the first week of April 2007, with Runako and Maya, then went straight to Masvingo to prepare for my wedding. I had always dreamt of a garden wedding, or in the worst case, a wedding in a marquee doused with fresh blossoms, draped in silk and satin fabrics. This could have been at my childhood home, or at the Great Zimbabwe resort, but Baba said easy access for the crowds was key. A wedding was never for the bride and groom, he said. It was for the public to turn up and witness, so a wedding reception in the centre of town was ideal. He also stipulated that a second reception at the family rural homestead in Chivi, where I had had my second graduation party, was compulsory the day after the main wedding reception. He had guesstimated a turnout of around 1000 wedding guests for the town wedding, and an unlimited number for the rural wedding, where he expected his political constituents to turn up in large numbers.

For the town wedding reception, my parents booked a dining hall at the local polytechnic college; an architectural aberration that could have won the Carbuncle Cup. To try and sabotage my nightmare, I had taken with me balloons, vases, tealight candles, table confetti and other elegant decorations to Zimbabwe from the UK, hoping to create the wedding I had dreamed of. I had on my wish list other fantasies that were quickly thwarted by the economic crisis that prevailed in Zimbabwe at the time. There were no classic or vintage cars to hire for the couple and bridal party. Neither were there horses and carriages or a limousine available for hire or otherwise. Such frills were common at most weddings in the diaspora. I had bought foil helium balloons, but there was no helium to fill them up. It was not all doom and gloom, however. A family lady friend from our town, Mai Zorodzai offered to decorate the dining hall for me, and I was very grateful and hopeful for a miraculous transformation of the venue.

When we arrived home, Mhamha, who had not yet healed, had been struggling on her own with the craftwork required to complete and circulate the wedding invitations. She may have completed only a third of the target number of invitations and Baba, who had promised to deliver the completed invitations had not done so. He said he had been inviting guests by word of mouth, as was customary, but had recently spent most days in bed, apparently very moody, Mhamha explained. In the spirit of anticipation for the wedding, Runako and I joined Mhamha in making the invitations and distributing them to neighbours and friends.

About two weeks before the wedding, some political leaders arrived at our house to announce that my wedding venue would be used for a political rally, so we had to find somewhere else to wed. This was all too much for me to take in. Everything seemed to be going horribly wrong and I needed the nightmare to end. Baba, in a bid to appease his political cronies had submitted to the announcement without challenging the men. Mhamha who was utterly annoyed by the selfishness and audacity of the politicians stood up to the men and told them to "go to hell!" They left our house with tails between their legs, and I felt very proud of Mhamha for standing up to the bullies. As the wedding day beckoned, relatives from all over the country and those travelling from the UK began arriving.

My great aunt Vatete Guvudzai, who I had introduced to Baby after our secret civil marriage visited me at our childhood home one evening, for a customary ritual that should have been performed by Baba's sisters. She gave me advice on how to live happily with my husband during my marriage, based on the Shona culture and Christian morals. Although my great aunt was straight and narrow, she had an amazing sense of humour and I was very fond of her.

As I grew older and proved compliant, I was a good girl to her, and she treated me as an ally. Her visit turned out to be a fun evening of feminine talk and giggles, where she imparted advice based on how she conducted her old-fashioned but long and successful marriage.

Baby arrived in Masvingo one week before our wedding. We had missed each other desperately as this was the first time we had spent time apart since we began cohabiting. Three weeks apart had proven too long for us. He stayed with me at my parents' home, where we relished a delightful reunion. There was something deliciously errant about making love with Baby in my childhood bedroom. The lilac walls, the white burglar bars on the windows, blue and white lacy polyester curtains Mhamha had made during one of her many home improvement projects, cream wooden pelmets with remnants of cartoon and red heart stickers I had stuck on as a child, old floral cotton sheets I had cried in when I missed Baby during school holidays, bought when I had got older and stopped wetting my bed. A solid mahogany dressing table with trifold mirrors and a matching stool with a maroon velvet seat, the more mature incongruous furniture my parents had bought during my mid-teen years. Nothing had changed.

It was the very place I had received numerous beatings for various reasons growing up. It was indeed the place I had been beaten up by Mhamha for the defilement that deemed me unsuitable for marriage. And yet here I was, in that room, with the man who loved me with all my imperfections. Baby and I spent all our free time in my bedroom, when we were not running errands. Our countless bouts of sexual congress bestowed me swollen lips and furnished my neck with raised ruby love bites. Mhamha jokingly commented that the madness had to stop, because it would affect how I looked in the wedding photographs.

When all my bridesmaids had arrived, we decided to have the equivalent of a hen do, in the lounge at our childhood home, under Mhamha's watch. Rudo, Runako, Beauty, Imogen, Tarisai, the flower girls - Moira's daughter, two of Chenai's younger sisters, Tete Primrose's daughter and I, bonded over food and drinks, and danced the night away. Our home was ablaze with feminine screeches of excitement and cackles of merriment. I felt overwhelmed by the love that surrounded me. On the same evening, Baby and the groomsmen also congregated at a chalet near our home and enjoyed a stag do, by way of BBQ and drinks.

Our wedding ceremony would take place at the local Roman Catholic church because Baba and Baby were Catholic. Baby and I were supposed to receive marriage counselling before the wedding, in order to comply with Roman Catholic protocol, but due to our logistical challenges, and because of who I was, we were allowed to attend only one session, which felt like a perfunctory exercise solely fulfilled to serve a bureaucratic expediency. We had not been attending church in the UK, so had not received any marriage counselling or training either. Due to the short notice for the wedding, there was no qualified priest to officiate the marriage on the day of the white wedding. Baby and I therefore had to be married by a qualified priest the day before our white wedding, with Runako and Daniel as witnesses to the signing of our marriage certificate; our second and known marriage certificate. The disjointed nature of the wedding preparation was strenuous, but we carried on avidly and unconsciously.

The hyperinflation and economic crisis in Zimbabwe at the time deemed most of my expectations of a memorable wedding pretentious and superfluous. Most of my family thought as long as all guests were fed and watered, everything else was a bonus at the wedding. In fact, small details around presentation of the bridal party and appearance of the wedding venue, were rubbished as unnecessary tedious endeavours that my family claimed to have not seen before. Most weddings of Baba's relatives had indeed by default taken place at our rural homestead, decades before my time, where such details may not have mattered. I was therefore pioneering the seizure of this cycle, an arduous process for my family who did not seem to appreciate my "anglicised" taste. These views seemed like mere excuses to me, because my highly esteemed family would have been invited to several modern weddings which demonstrated that weddings in Zimbabwe had evolved. The fact was, everyone was secretly struggling financially but hid behind the excuse that modern weddings were alien to them. It was far more important to maintain the facade that our family was still rich, than be honest that the legacy had diminished simultaneously with my grandparents' death.

I frequently questioned if we had ever actually been rich. Other than the illusion of truth resulting from repeated mendacities, and the way society had treated us, I had never felt rich.

After the signing of our avowed marriage certificate, we had to carry on with last minute preparations for the wedding. The bridal party rehearsed the bridal dances, called *masteps* in Shona. In predictable fashion, the bridesmaids teased and flirted with the groomsmen in a manner that somewhat vexed me. A few of the groomsmen were married and I did not want their wives to blame my wedding if things got out of hand.

Runako and Beauty were kindred free spirits who seemed to gel very well and had attached at the hip. Together, they seemed to play mind games involving teasing men with the intention of frustrating them. They called it *kuzvimbisa bhibho*. I initially dismissed it as over-excitement, but I could not understand why anyone would flaunt themselves to a man if they had no intention of taking things further. As they consistently burst into victorious predatory giggles after *kuzvimbisa bhibho*, I sensed a whiff of sadism in their behaviour. Perhaps I empathised with the targeted men, maybe it was my perfectionism, or probably my fear of rape, but I was not convinced that *kuzvimbisa bhibho* was a justifiable pastime. Concluding that I may have been judging Runako and Beauty harshly, I decided *kuzvimbisa bhibho* was none of my business and carried on as if I did not notice it.

I hated to imagine what Baba would have called me for doing the same, but when I saw him laughing about the blatant chaos roused by Runako and Beauty, I was in awe of his duplicity. I could not help wondering which Baba was real – the one who had raised me or the one I now knew.

We barely knew Beauty who had been rejected by Babamunini Farai as a baby and had been raised by her mother in a *rokeshen*. Beauty and her mother now lived in the UK and happened to be in Zimbabwe on holiday. Mhamha was concerned that the blossoming attachment between Runako and Beauty was unhealthy and would not end well. Beauty's uncouth influence on Runako was obvious, and Mhamha was bothered by it. "*Aka kakazhangandirawo aka! Mmm kuchenjeresa kwacho.* She is too wayward!" she had murmured to me when we were cooking in the kitchen. I knew from personal experience what that statement meant. Mhamha intended to dismantle the friendship.

Contrastingly, Baba and his sisters cheered Beauty on. "You're Farai's daughter indeed! Behaviour and all! Ha ha ha! Oh, did you see her facial expression right there? Oh, my goodness! Doesn't she look just like her father?" they said, chuckling harmoniously. This was the sort of thing they did to bond with illegitimate children of late uncles who had finally been welcomed and accepted in the family. Such children always seemed to display over-compensatory behaviours which provided a new source of entertainment in the family. As Baba's own children began to question his character, he seemed to invest in relationships with relatives who desperately needed a father figure. They managed to provide him with adoration and submissive compliance without questioning his character too much, and he gave them precious intermittent attention when it suited him.

While *masteps* progressed, I ensured all ingredients had been delivered to the technical college kitchen in readiness for preparation the next day. I also had to ensure that decorating the church and the technical college dining hall was underway. Mai Zorodzai who offered to decorate the wedding reception venue was very empathetic to my expectations. She was a well-travelled well to do lady whose wedding to a local doctor I had attended as a little girl. It had been a glamorous poolside garden wedding at the Great Zimbabwe hotel, which had made a lasting positive impression on me, as I had not been to a wedding like that before. It was such an honour for her to volunteer her time and effort to get my wedding to as close as possible to my dream wedding. She magicked several yards of brand-new satin fabric to drape along the high table and the central aisle, then went to the local botanical garden to borrow most if not all their tropical potted plants.

The various titanic florae ranged from Travellers palms, banana trees, Elephant ears, Fishtail palms, Fan palms, King Sago, Chocolate dancers, Swiss cheese, Rubber plants, giant ferns, and many more. She managed to transform the wedding venue into a botanical wonderland, which absolutely dazzled me with joy and gratitude. The metallic balloons, table confetti, table and chair covers and sachets in the colour scheme of sage green, silver and white looked absolutely remarkable in the botanic nirvana the decorated venue had become. I had managed to source fresh white roses and arum lilies for table centrepieces, aisle flower arrangements, the bridal bouquet and bridesmaids' posies, through an Interflora agent in Harare.

Maiguru Chiedza, who was based in Harare, had pre-warned me about the ridiculous cost of wedding cakes in Zimbabwe and that even after paying through the nose, the cake ingredients would be improvised, and the end product compromised. The cake was a crucial element of the wedding; its taste and appearance had to be impeccable. After sampling several offerings in the UK, I had decided to buy six matured fruit cakes which I found sensibly priced online. I took these in my hand luggage to be decorated upon arrival in Zimbabwe, which a friend of Maiguru Chiedza did beautifully. Maiguru Chiedza arrived with the cake and fresh flowers from Harare the day before the wedding. She also kindly offered several of her luxurious cars, which she fuelled and drove to Masvingo with the help of her son, Richard and a few drivers. These were used to chauffer the bridal party and VIPs.

Although everything I had dreamt my wedding would be was not happening the way I had hoped, contributions towards the frills I valued, were the efforts that would make the day memorable for me. Relatives from out of town and a few from out of the country, began arriving the night before the wedding. When we were not ferrying relatives from where they had been dropped off by public transport to our house, we were at the venue checking progress of the decorating, or with the bridal party checking that *masteps* were on point. We retired to sleep around three in the morning, simply because we had no energy left to continue preparing for this one-off event.

At 5.30am, I woke up feeling exhausted and demotivated. When my alarm sounded, I realised for the first time that I had overlooked visiting a beauty parlour to get my nails prepared and my eyebrows shaped. I got out of bed to see if I could find instruments to salvage the situation. I found an old worn emery board and a nearly empty bottle of pale nail polish in my underequipped make-up pouch. I managed to shape my natural nails and apply the nail polish. I did not have any cuticle remover or nail polish remover to tidy up the edges of my nails or nail polish that had absconded the edges of my nails, so I used my teeth to bite off my overgrown cuticles and the nail polish overspill. I did not worry too much about my unshaved legs and toenails, because I wore stockings and closed toe Mary-jane heels beneath my wedding dress.

My blunt tweezer was useless, so I borrowed a razor blade from Mhamha to attempt shaping my scanty eyebrows. I took a quick bath in a bucket, a practice that had become normalised in Zimbabwe due to irregular water supply. At the time, water would be hoarded in large two hundred litre containers from friends and family living in areas where water was not being rationed. Small amounts of water were subsequently drawn in metal pails and heated up on fire, because availability of electricity to heat up the water on cookers was also intermittent. The hot water would eventually be transferred to communal plastic buckets which were placed in bathtubs or showers for a token cleanse. Some pedantic people like myself, would have a secret stash of disinfectants to sterilise shared buckets, bathroom and shower floors before use, to mitigate the risk of contracting athletes' foot or worse infections.

After my meagre bath, I put on my undergarments and dressing gown in order to sort my hair out. I had spent a full day micro-braiding my own hair earlier that week; attaching fibres of straight human hair to my un-straightened Afro hair. In an ideal world, I would have been more than happy to wed in my kinky Afro hair, but that would have caused so much controversy, because society generally shamed women who did not "fix" their hair. The week I arrived in Masvingo, I had bumped into a former school mate who unashamedly asked, "*Nemari yese yamunayo, uri kuchata nechoya icho mumusoro?* With all the money you have, are you really going to wed with those pubes on your head?"

Hair shaming was particularly ruthless in Zimbabwe, where it was used to poverty and body shame women. Those who did not sew on weaves, braid their hair or wear wigs were generally considered ugly and struggling financially. And because a wedding was a show for the people, it was better to conform to societal expectations by attaching fake hair to my head.

Dorothy, a hairdresser from Mhamha's hair salon had promised to style my braided hair, but she arrived tipsy and could not remember the hair style we had rehearsed earlier in the week. Dorothy did attempt to design a beehive-type style, but I had to dismiss her due to her incompetence. I managed to style my own hair in the end and placed a crystal encrusted tiara on top. I did not have a fancy cosmetic collection, so my make-up was very minimalist.

When I was satisfied with the frilly part of my presentation, I stepped into my A-line corset gown. Its off-shoulder sleeves and chapel train were encrusted with crystals and freshwater pearls that matched my tiara. All things considered, when I finished preparing myself, I felt like a fairy princess and was very pleased with how I looked.

Mhamha came into my room to usher me out. She had got a tailormade outfit designed, using beautiful turquoise and pearlescent beaded African lace fabric she had found near Petticoat Lane. She accessorised it with a matching wide veranda hat and looked royal. I was happy for her, that her wishes had come true. When Mhamha kissed me on my cheek and told me I looked beautiful, an emanation of euphoria gushed over me.

Maiguru Chiedza's Mercedes picked me up from my childhood home just before 7am. The church ceremony was due to begin at seven o'clock. Tete Gwinyai and Tete Gertrude were in the car, giving directions to the driver. We arrived in town and instead of heading for the church, we drove around town to kill time, apparently because the church was not ready. I felt impatient. I later discovered that Tete Gwinyai had deliberately made me late in order to make Morris nervous. She had managed to plant a few rumour mongers at the church, to suggest I was a runaway bride who was not going to show up. This drama had for a short while caused mild apprehension, but everyone found it hilarious in the end. While we drove around town, Baby was invited for a confession by the Catholic priest who would lead the wedding ceremony. Baby, who had not attended a single church service since relocating to the UK was taken aback by the expectation to confess before the ceremony. Without giving the discussion due thought, he confessed to *upombwe*, adultery. The concerned priest coerced him to elaborate, to which Baby explained we had had our daughter out of wedlock, thereby committing a sin. Baby, whose Shona was intermediate, meant to say he had had sex out of wedlock, a point lost in translation that we laughed about for days on end.

Due to Baby's confession, made up on the spot, the main theme of our wedding ceremony was centred around the fact that we had had a child out of wedlock and had done the right thing by getting married to purge the sin. Because Baby and I had got married secretly before we had Maya, we found the redemption unnecessary, and the sermon tediously irrelevant to us. There were some beautiful elements of the sermon I would cherish forever. My boarding school headmistress Mai Zawiza was one of the bible readers; this was a pleasant surprise for me. The sermon was dramatic, with the priest using his silk epitrachelion to tie Baby and I tightly together at the waist to demonstrate that we had been tied eternally in God's name and no one could undo the knot.

Most of our guests had gone to bed very late the previous night, so they struggled to stay awake during the ceremony. At the end of the sermon, VaJongwe who had been *munyai* during my *roora* was tasked with directing the wedding to ensure everyone was at the right place and time, doing what was expected of them. As we exited the church, avid ululation graced the air while guests sang and danced, and confetti were thrown into the air to rain on us like a gentle spring drizzle. Baby and I got into the same car, which headed towards a local hotel where we had arranged to have our official wedding photographs taken in its tropical garden.

At the photoshoot, VaJongwe micromanaged the process and it was done in under an hour. The most important people were directed to the photoshoot, but quite a few significant relatives were missing; and we were under too much pressure to notice. My parents, Tongai, Runako and the rest of our bridal party joined us. Most of Mhamha's side of the family were not present. Only the flower girls and Richard who had driven one of the cars in the bridal convoy were present. Mainini Rosey, Gogo and her sisters, together with other important close relatives had been shipped straight to the wedding reception venue. Baba's sisters and Baby's relatives were all present.

VaJongwe barked instructions relentlessly, and the snaps were shot, without due consideration to shadows, un-straightened jewellery, and other small details I felt made the distinction between good and bad photography. It was a beautiful hot day with blue skies, but by the end of the photoshoot, we were all fatigued and sticky. The hotel was only a five-minute drive from the technical college where our reception was held. We arrived at the venue to find that the DJ who had been hired to play music had not turned up and was unreachable by phone. The DJ had been seen extremely drunk the previous night and was likely still recovering. Tongai and a few other volunteers set off to find him, while the bridal party made their way to the designated banqueting area in the dining hall.

Mainini Gemma, was one of the key organisers who had not slept a wink to make the wedding a success. Despite appearing frail and unwell, she had led the other women who produced a majestic spread for the bridal party, and I was eternally grateful for her efforts. We were served a delicious meal comprising a variety of local delicacies; oxtail, goat curry, organic free-range boiling chicken, served with sadza, a variety of salads and a selection of soft drinks. The photographer took this opportunity to take caricature photographs of the bridal party eating, aiming for embarrassing shots when individuals had their mouths wide open, or picking meat from in between their teeth. I was not impressed by his sense of humour.

By the time we finished eating, the DJ had been found, watered, fed and sobered. The bridal party stood in order at the entrance of the hall, where they entered the hall, performing *masteps* through the aisle decorated by fresh blossoms. Feet exploded into dance in response to local *sungura* music and South African *kwaito*. Backs and waists writhed like snakes to central African *rhumba* music, necks flexed to Jamaican dancehall as dancing partners *dutty-*whined and showed off their boogying skills. Women ululated, girls screamed, men whistled. The morale was high and there was much enjoyment as the bridal party danced their way to the high table.

Throughout the day, despite the bursts of enjoyment and delight, I could not help but feel the painful absence of my loved ones who could have been there. The ones who had died prematurely and the ones who now lived in the diaspora and could not make it to my wedding. My uncles, Tafara, Farai and Benjy, my aunt Vimbai and her son James who would have been a teenager by then. Tete Mary, her daughter Sophia and my cousin Tsvakai in the US. My other cousins Moira, Chenai. Mainini Joy and others in the UK, Sekuru Tonderai and his family. John. Well, John had given up on the UK and returned to Zimbabwe a few months after my graduation. He had then proceeded to South Africa where he managed to pull-off multi-million-rand scams as part of a sophisticated gang. He had been caught and was serving time at Pollsmoor prison. I worried about him a lot, but instinctively knew he would be okay. Then there was Tizai. How could I ever fully enjoy my wedding without Tizai? Without knowing whether he was dead or alive?

The absence of my brother from my wedding hurt me more than the joy of getting married. I wanted him there, and I needed him back permanently. But it seemed the more I willed Tizai to return to us, the more his unlikely return was amplified. Ever since his disappearance, we had heard several rumours and accounts of Tizai's whereabouts from various people. Some people claimed they had seen Tizai in Johannesburg and he was fine, others said they had seen him in Cape Town struggling. Others said they saw him from across the road somewhere and when they called out his name, Tizai ran away and disappeared into the crowds. These accounts usually came from locals who expected money for a drink after the conversation, so when we eventually picked up that trend, we concluded the stories were simply heartless formulations created as bait for our petty cash.

In traditional fashion, the rest of the wedding was dominated by long speeches and guests announcing their gifts and pledged offerings. Unsurprisingly, there was no huge turnout of guests; there may have been up to 300 guests, as opposed to the predicted 1000. The reception was over by 6pm, which suited us well. Our wedding gifts were handed to us and we made our way to a local hotel, where we spent the night before proceeding to our rural home for the second reception the next day. Tete Gwinyai, whose businesses and lavish lifestyle had all vanished due to gambling, attempted to borrow the money that had been gifted at our wedding, to be paid back before we returned to the UK, and I politely declined the proposal.

The next day around 9am, a cavalcade of balloon-strapped cars made their way to our rural homestead in Chivi, for the second reception. The cars hooted as they exited the main motorway and cascaded on a bumpy dust road for at least two kilometres towards what was once my grandmother's castle. As we drove towards our homestead gate, I wished Mbuya had been alive to witness my wedding. The sun presented a bearable scorch, the turquoise sky was cloudless and energising, instilling a feeling of stability and loyalty commensurate with the occasion. Women ululated in excitement as cars arrived and slowly found appropriate positions to park. Some removed beautiful multi-coloured batik fabrics wrapped around their waists to reveal feminine floral and polka dot dresses that would later need protection from sitting on gravel during speeches and mealtimes. The batiks were dramatically waved in the air then strategically placed on the dusty well-swept yard to form a carpet for the bride to tread on. I stepped out of the car with my groom and we slowly made our way to the brick and mortar dining room that had been built by my grandmother.

Some men whistled euphorically and shook hands with arriving guests while others, who had probably never driven in their lives, appointed themselves to direct parking cars, vigilantly and dramatically providing exaggerated signage. Traditional wedding songs were sung, as guests were handed soft drinks in bottles. Some were given *7days* in beer gourds, mugs and recycled plastic containers – an indigenous traditionally brewed beer which took the local women seven days to brew. Others were handed sweaty bottles of cold lagers fished out of ice-filled metal buckets. The more expensive spirits were subtly distributed to VIPs who sat next to small ice buckets discretely tucked under their seats or pushed behind their handbags.

Although the bridal party wore the attire from the previous day, they did not make much effort in making up their faces or styling their hair. I wore no make-up at all and tied my braids into a ponytail. The atmosphere was relaxed and authentic. There was no one to impress and there were no expectations comparable with pretentious city wedding receptions.

At the edge of Mbuya's yard, a small tent had been pitched and decorated with some of the décor from the town wedding. When the bridal party had eaten in Mbuya's dining room, they danced their way to the small tent. A DJ was hired to play music, which caused much excitement to the local rural folk, who would have ordinarily had to walk significant mileage for such entertainment. There were a lot of familiar and unfamiliar faces, all full of love and authenticity.

As we made our way to the tent, I was shocked and disgusted to experience firm handshakes coupled with discreet scratches by men's forefingers inside my palm. The dirty practice was a tactful way that usually rural men communicated they wanted you. They would grab your hand firmly, scratch, wait for that confused look of aversion, then stare straight into your eyes with a look of hunger. Even on my wedding day, some sleaze balls had the audacity to present the violating scratch, with Baby standing right next to me. When the encroachment happened, I yanked my hand away, clicked my tongue and moved forward with no eye contact.

When we settled at the high table under the tent, several hearty speeches were made, many gifts were given – chickens, goats, reed mats, beautifully hand decorated clay pots, hand carved wooden cooking spoons and figurines, some of which we could not carry back to the UK due to luggage weight and customs restrictions. A group of elderly women sang a memorable acapella, "*Murume itsikidzi* – a man is a bedbug*,*" illuminating how abusive men sucked the lives out of their wives and left them dilapidated. We all found the song hilarious although I could not personally relate to its lyrics. Some traditional wedding practices that had taken place at the town wedding were repeated for spectacle to the rural folk; cutting the wedding cake, feeding each other and kissing thereafter. This also manifested a popular Shona proverb, *Ukama igasva, hunozadziswa nekudya* – a relationship on its own is a half measure, the full measure is attained by sharing of food. The party continued till around 10pm, then we returned to our hotel in Masvingo. The next day, our wedding guests dispersed and returned to their homes. Baby and I travelled to Bulawayo to spend time with his parents.

When we arrived at Baby's childhood home, I had to perform traditional duties that were usually conducted in a formal ceremony after a wedding. *Kuperekwa,* the handover of the bride by her family to the groom's family, was a procedure that marked acceptance and welcoming of a *muroora* into the groom's family. Under normal circumstances, my paternal aunts would have chaperoned me to my in-laws, with all the presents received at our wedding, to show my in-laws that I was ready to start my new home. We would have arrived at their gate and I would have sat down covered in a blanket called a *kwiriti* and would have not moved or uncovered my face until my in-laws gave me a token amount of money, *kushonongorwa*. I would have got up, moved a few steps, sat down again and not moved until I was paid another token. I would have repeated this process until I reached their kitchen, or lounge, thus symbolising formal acceptance of the bride into their home. Family, friends and neighbours would have sung songs to welcome me into my new family. The following day, my delegation and I would have had to wake very early in the morning to sweep the yard and boil water for the in-laws to bath with. Each person who took a bath would have had to make a token payment to me.

In my case, however, the ceremony was nominal, and none of my aunts were able to escort me for *kuperekwa*. Tete Gwinyai blatantly explained she did not believe in the institution of marriage and her participation in *kuperekwa* would have been inauthentic. Tete Primrose would have been best placed to usher me to Baby's family, but she had relocated to Harare. My other aunts did not have the financial means to do so. Upon arrival at Baby's home, there was no crowd to celebrate my arrival as *muroora* and to welcome me into my new family. Tension had also been roused by the fact that most members of our bridal party had disappeared and switched off their mobile phones. Memory was apprehensive and wanted me to confirm if Runako was with Daniel, but I was clueless about their whereabouts and felt helplessly awkward.

I ran a bubble bath for Bambo and Mhaiyo separately in their bathtub, then prepared for them a hearty meal of sadza, oxtail and pumpkin leaf vegetables. They made token payments of 20 US dollars each, making me officially part of their family. Baby and I could not afford a honeymoon. As a treat, we used some of the funds we had received as wedding gifts to book ourselves into a high-end lodge out of town, where we stayed for two nights. We spent one day resting and recovering from the wedding, and the other site seeing at Matopos. Mhaiyo volunteered to look after Maya, who I had stopped breastfeeding a few weeks before the wedding. This was the first time I was separated from our six-month-old baby, so our pseudo honeymoon was plagued by separation anxiety.

Chapter 17

When Baby and I returned to the UK to face the deflation that followed our wedding, I needed to look for a job in order to start servicing our newly acquired debt. My previous job applications since completing my undergraduate course had been met by the same predictable unconvincing response. I was "overqualified but not experienced enough". I therefore did not look forward to resuming my job search. Baby's parents had gifted us a property in Zimbabwe for our wedding, so we began trying to sell it, so that the funds could service our new loan, and contribute towards purchasing our first property in the UK.

I found it interesting that Bambo had worked, first as a teacher and then as an executive who climbed his way up to senior management in the private sector. His career path would not have excited my family. What I found more fascinating was that Mhaiyo had never worked. Yet the two had educated their three children in boarding schools and owned several properties in Zimbabwe, all acquired through sweat. Not once had I ever heard Bambo bragging about what he owned. The boy beneath me who had been looked down upon by my family had parents who could gift us a home, and my elite father gifted us a loan, for a wedding we did not need to have.

Mhamha had gifted us a cheque for £1000 for our wedding, but I was reluctant to bank it. I knew the gift was a huge sacrifice for Mhamha who had been on sick leave for a few months and saving up for Runako's university tuition fees. We would hold on to the cheque until we absolutely needed the money.

Upon our return, Baby immediately distanced himself from me and got back into excessive working patterns. He was completely emotionally unavailable in a way I had not experienced before, so I was unsure what to do. Since the rekindling of our relationship, we had experienced a heightened, unbearable need to melt into each other, as quickly as possible. The separate sense of self had become secondary to the relationship and we had begun to feel each other's feelings. I, on the other hand, had become addicted to consulting with Baby on every single thing I did. What had begun as a strategy to convince Baby that I could be a submissive good girl after he called me "stupid", had turned into a permanent reality, and my way of milking his scarce attention.

Without Baby's usual display of affection, I felt stumped, and he would not say what troubled him. One day, he had been using his laptop then forgot to log out of his account before leaving for work. A compulsion to check Baby's online activity washed out my self-control. The hope to find enlightenment regarding his sudden change in behaviour justified my invasion of his privacy.

Baby had several pages of pornography open on his internet browser. I was rather shocked by the discovery, mostly because I thought our relationship was open and honest, and that Baby would have mentioned his pastime to me. When we were dating over a long distance, he had occasionally emailed me pornography videos, which at the time made me think watching it on videos was far better than him acting it out with other women, so it gave me a sense of security. I could therefore not understand why the videos were still important to him now that he had a wife he had daily access to.

When I got tired of looking through his browser history and activity, I noticed that Baby had not logged out of his email account either, so I decided to have a look through his communications. At first, there was nothing worth worrying about; initially a few emails between him and his habitually philandering friends and cousins, them describing their latest escapades, him cheering on but never revealing his own adventures. What kept me reading was the need to find out how Baby truly felt about their conduct. His encouragement of their gross behaviour kept me interested. As I scrolled to older emails, I came across one from an old friend of his, expressing shock that Baby had finally settled to marry me, instead of the white girls he hung around with at university.

This was a surprising revelation, given that Baby, who hated to talk about the one relationship he claimed to have had during our breakup, had named only Thandi as his ex. I kept going, until I came across an email exchange with a woman who he missed and referred to as "sweetness". The dates of the emails revealed the exchange had happened while Baby was in my room at the University of Surrey. He was apparently giving this sweetheart Angie, an update on how he had travelled well and was staying in a town called Guildford. In the email, he conveniently omitted revealing why exactly he had visited the UK and who he was staying with. I was furious!

Without giving it much thought, I forwarded the email exchanges to myself, then waited for Baby to return home from work. My struggle to discuss difficult topics delayed the imminent confrontation. But the sight of Baby when he returned home from work sent waves of raging energy into my throat and my lips parted to ask a question I never imagined to ask only two weeks after our wedding.

"Who is Angie?"

Instead of giving me a straightforward response, Baby wanted to know how I had found out about Angie. When I told him that one of his friends had anonymously tipped me off about Angie, Baby explained they had been "just friends". I queried why he would address a friend the way he did in the email.

"I was just keeping my options open. You have nothing to worry about because Angie does not compare to you." Baby's words did not register in my mind. What I heard instead was that I was inadequate. After all I had done to show him my entire dedication to the relationship, I could not understand why Baby needed to keep his options open. I was hurt and inconsolable, and he decided to go mute. Communication and intimacy came to a complete halt in our home.

I could not believe that so soon after declaring publicly to our families and friends that I would love a man "till death do us part", I had developed so much resentment towards him and wanted nothing to do with him. My heart ached in a way I had never felt, I began to take painkillers for relief. Morris, who I had known for so long and trusted more than anyone in this world, the one who had never given me reason to think there was anyone and anything else for him but me, had the capacity to break my heart. "Sweetness" was a label I thought was reserved for me, the love of his life. How did he know how sweet Angie was anyway? The discovery of

Angie injured my soul, but it seemed I was not allowed to say "ouch!" In typical misogynistic fashion I had witnessed in Baba, a strong prohibition against being an angry woman was implied by Morris's silent treatment and withdrawal of intimacy. My reaction to this incident was an unintended attack to his ego, which further proved my inadequacy, and warranted further punishment from him. We had stumbled into a vicious cycle of toxicity.

Out of desperation for a more convincing answer, I thought Angie might be kind enough to explain to me what had been going on. I forwarded the emails to Angie, whose email address I took from the email chain, with a cover note politely requesting an explanation. A few exchanges followed. Angie said she was gobsmacked by my contact, then explained she was a friend of Morris at university. They had not communicated in a long time and she wanted to know why I was interested in knowing the nature of their relationship. I explained I was his wife and was engaged to him when he sent her the emails from Guildford, while he was visiting me. I queried the names they called each other and the general tone of the communication, which did not correspond with being "just friends". Angie suggested I speak to Morris about the matter, not her, and the only reason she had bothered to respond was that she too was married and empathised with me.

Oh, I thought! She too was married and must have been at least engaged to her husband when she was busy messing around with Morris. Being a naïve perfectionist, I found the situation completely unacceptable. I thought Angie's response, which led me nowhere, was cruel. In a fit of emotional turmoil, I sent her a final email, informing her that her friendship with Morris had messed up my relationship with him. I told her I was glad she was now married so she could keep her paws off other people's men. I thanked her for her empty responses then signed off with a bitter warning. "Pray I never find out who your husband is, because if I do, I will fuck him!"

I felt disoriented and desperately needed to speak to someone about my situation. I had not anticipated that my marriage would be over so soon after our wedding. I could not trust any of my aunts with the problem. Only one of them was still married, and most of them did not believe in marriage. I knew their likely advice would be to stay in the marriage and cheat on Baby to get revenge or leave. I was not prepared to try either option. The matter would have been dealt with publicly, with no respect to how I preferred my issues to stay private. The victim shaming by my family would have been relentless. In addition to all this, I was after all the perfect one, a role that had been assigned to me from my childhood. I was not allowed to be imperfect, and this implied that I had to sweep a lot of my problems under the carpet, even when encouraged to speak up. The few times I did speak up, my concerns were always dismissed as not serious enough. This was exactly how Tete Vimbai had found herself in a situation so hopeless and ended her own life. Nobody helped her, and all her suffering was eventually reduced to a mere family legend.

I thought of seeking counsel from Mhamha, as we had become closer. I had previously raised concerns with her, that I suspected Morris might have been gay. The reason for my concern was, as months progressed after we began cohabiting, intimacy had gradually declined between us. Morris had joined a local adult hockey team and one of the players, who he worked with at the manufacturing company, could not keep his hands off him. I could not understand whether it was normal for men to grab each other's testicles or give each other celebratory kisses on the lips when they got drunk after winning matches. The colleague in question also began giving Morris random gifts for no reason, including expensive organic artisan cheeses and wines. Mhamha had dismissed my overactive imagination, saying Morris would not have got me pregnant if he was gay. The after-sport rituals may have been normal laddish sporting behaviour in the UK; but my insecurity was deep-rooted in a disturbing incident that had happened when we were in high school.

Morris's friend Tanaka had been dating my best friend Fadzai at the time, and we naturally compared notes. She reported consistently that her relationship with Tanaka seriously lacked the emotion and intimacy that was apparent in mine and Baby's. During our sixth form, my brother Tizai had whistle-blown a worrying matter to me. Tanaka, who was a senior prefect in Tizai's boarding house, was regularly crawling into Tizai's bed at night, masturbating and ejaculating on him. I did not have to think twice that this was sexual abuse, so I encouraged Tizai to escalate the matter to my parents and schoolteachers immediately, which he did.

Perhaps it was due to extreme homophobia in Zimbabwe, but the school leadership could not get their heads around what had happened to my brother. The feedback I got from Tizai was the school governance team concluded that Tanaka must have had a crush on me; so he got relief from his frustrations by imagining Tizai as me, and performing his sexual rituals on my brother instead. Within a few days of the report, Tanaka was demoted from his prefect position and moved to another boarding house but was allowed to stay in the school to complete his A level exams.

When I told Baby about the issue at the time, he rubbished it, asserting Tanaka would never do such a thing. When I challenged Baby about why Tanaka had subsequently been demoted, he said there had been another reason, which he would not disclose to me. I was not convinced by Baby's response, and I found his aloofness on the matter disturbing. Despite never speaking about it again, the incident tormented my mind in frequent streams of consciousness. Although Mhamha was aware of what had happened to Tizai, I never told her that the perpetrator of the abuse was in fact a close friend of Baby, so the connection which would have tainted my marriage, remained missing.

Mhamha had stayed in Zimbabwe after the wedding, to recuperate. She decided to take a further month off sick to ensure that when she returned to the UK she would be fit enough to return to work. I could not trouble her with the email incident while she was healing; it would stress her out and delay her recovery. Baba had scheduled a three-week business trip to Johannesburg, so Mhamha decided to tag along to South Africa. She had decided to disregard Baba's advice and wanted to find Tizai, who had now been missing for nearly three years. While Baba was busy politicking during the day, Mhamha visited prisons and mortuaries on her own to check that Tizai had not been imprisoned or died and had not been identified. Her efforts were futile, and she returned to the UK very broken-hearted. Mhamha desperately wanted to find her son, who was undoubtedly her favourite. I often wondered if Mhamha had divulged her marriage problems with Baba to Tizai, the way she had started doing with me after Tizai went missing. I wondered if it had been too much for him, seeing Baba in action in Mhamha's absence, knowing how much Mhamha was hurting in the loveless relationship. I wondered if all the drama had become too much for him, when he decided to leave. I wondered if Tizai had simply become exhausted of being Baba's son. There were no answers.

When Mhamha returned to the UK in May, she immediately complained of pains in her abdomen that made her feel like the cancer was back. She returned to hospital for further investigations, which confirmed that Mhamha's cancer had spread to all her internal organs. Her prognosis was six months. No one was prepared for this untimely news. I certainly remained in denial and carried on with life as if I had not heard the news of Mhamha's looming death. Every weekend, Morris, Maya and I would travel to visit Mhamha in Surrey, mostly for moral support, but not because I thought she was dying.

In June that year, I interviewed for a property paralegal job at a regional law firm Moonlight Solicitors Ltd and was offered my first professional job. Mhamha was ecstatic that my struggling at university had finally paid off. This change in my life gave me a much-needed confidence boost, following the discovery of Morris's clandestine behaviour. Perhaps out of guilt, Morris encouraged me to buy a nearly new car on credit, that I would use to drive to my new job. I would have otherwise bought a banger, similar to the one he drove. I cashed Mhamha's cheque to pay the deposit, and we got the nearly new car, which gave me a further esteem boost. I felt nervous about driving, as I had not driven for nearly two years since Baby had taught me to drive in Zimbabwe.

As I was driving to work on my first day in the new job, I took a wrong turn onto a road restricted to buses and taxis only. A frantic Asian taxi driver got out of his car, shouting and waving at me to leave, "You can't be here! Look, up there, you're on camera! Police will be here to arrest you any minute now! Go! Go! Please!" Without catching my breath to figure out my bearings, I started my car too eager to escape, and without checking my mirrors I sped into a bus coming from my right-hand side, headed for the bus station up ahead.

When I got out of my car and made eye contact with passengers on the bus who stared at me through the window in disgust, I was engulfed with shock and shame. As the passengers dropped their jaws, I felt my eyes watering. The bus driver got out of the bus, stood in front of my car and dramatically clapped his hands, as if to say, "well done!" Luckily, no one was injured. I burst into tears and called my employer to tell them I had had an accident and would not come into work. After exchanging car insurance details with the bus driver, I locked my car and walked back home, then phoned Baby to tell him I would never drive again. Baby picked my car up from town and arranged to get it fixed. I did of course gain more confidence as I got used to driving to work thereafter.

Maya was seven months old and I hesitated to sign her up for nursery school. Mhamha, despite being unwell, volunteered to look after her for the first two weeks while I got used to the new work routine, so we left Maya in Surrey and saw her at weekends. Runako volunteered to look after

Maya for a week thereafter, then Baby took a week off work to look after her. I was grateful for the support from my family, but after a month, the childcare arrangements became tedious to me, and they carried the disadvantage of not seeing Maya daily, so I succumbed to signing her up for full-time nursery. I learned the new routine of getting up early to get ready for work, taking Maya to nursery school, then driving to Maidstone to a modern glass building, where I spent the day feeling like an alien.

No one, except me and the department head who was a partner had a university degree in the department I worked in. I therefore posed a threat to everyone, including the team leaders and managers. I had been interviewed by a partner of the firm during a graduate open day and he had offered me the job on the spot. It was obvious from my CV that I had no previous experience of working in a law firm, so I needed on-the-job practical training. The partner had assured me I would be trained, and if I worked hard enough, the firm would fund my professional qualifications. These promises, which I naively disclosed to my colleagues made them resent me more. I was the only black woman in the entire firm, which made me suspect I had been hired simply as a token to demonstrate diversity within the firm.

A few weeks into my new job, I found myself twiddling my fingers, with not much work to do. When I spoke to my team leader Melanie in one to ones, querying what I was meant to be doing, she casually responded that I needed to be proactive. When I researched what it meant to be proactive in the context of my profession, I identified a professional qualification that would bring me up to speed with my line of work and make me more confident. My manager Jack was not interested in sponsoring the conveyancing qualification I had identified because it was "too specialist in nature". He would have preferred to sponsor me if I had picked a more generic course. I decided to personally fund the long-distance course in staggered instalments, and I began learning how to do my job properly that way. I suggested changing the way my team delivered certain pieces of work and to improve processes to meet industry standards set by the professional body I had joined, but that made my colleagues feel even more threatened by me.

When I asked for help with new concepts, the responses from my team were always discouraging. One morning, when I had asked Melanie to give me some work, she handed me a pile of files and told me to add them to the case management system and send out client care letters to her clients. In the absence of training or written procedures, I had no idea how to complete the task. "Where do I find the case management system Mel?" I asked. A slow eye-roll was followed by a statement that shocked me out of my wits, "Oh for fucks' sake *Roovha*! You have a law degree! Figure it out yeah!" She said it out so loud, I felt embarrassed by her unprofessional conduct, yet no one in the office flinched.

"They don't teach case management systems at university Mel. They teach the theory behind the conveyancing transaction." This was my explanation that landed on deaf ears.

As time progressed, I did figure it out, mainly by secretly watching what other team members did, eavesdropping on conversations in other teams, and reading my professional notes. As I got better at my job, Melanie withdrew my projects and ensured I got less and less work, leaving me in the awkward predicament of trying to look busy at work. Another team leader in the same department, Sophie, would sometimes mentor me when she had spare time to do so. I returned the favour by doing some of her team's menial tasks.

In addition to being victimised for desperately wanting to progress and do better, my accent was made fun of in the office, so I became self-conscious and spoke less. I was not prepared to doctor the way I spoke, in order to sound the way other people expected me to sound. The stance fuelled my seclusion at work, coupled with comments that further ostracised me, "She never says anything." My colleagues progressed to speak about me in third person, as if I was not present, making small presumptuous decisions for me. "She doesn't usually come to the pub at lunch time as it's a bit pricey for her," and off they would go without me to socialise at lunchtime at a local pub. I sometimes spoke up when I did want to eat out; on days I had spare cash and had not been organised enough to make a sandwich or bring in leftover dinner from home. I was often made the subject of discussion at those lunches, with everyone marvelling at how my hair changed so much, from very short and kinky one minute, to long and chunky the next – how did I make my hair grow and change colours so quickly? I tried to explain the concept of hair extensions, to which my colleagues responded with inquisitions of how frequently I washed my hair, and that it must have been hard work. Being around my colleagues in and outside the office was hard work.

When I was not in the tough work environment, I was in a tough home environment where love had flown out of the window. When I was not at work or at home, I was visiting Mhamha who was dying of cancer. Around July that year, Mhamha was offered surgery to improve her kidney function, only to buy her a little extra time. She had not fully healed from the hysterectomy, so now had two surgeries to recover from.

Desperate for some positive communication, I got in touch with my friend Bridget. She had eventually migrated from Scotland to the US, married the love of her life who she used to visit in Nebraska, then they moved to North Carolina. They had had a baby girl who was a few months old and kept Bridget on her toes, so our communication had been intermittent. I sent Bridget an email, attaching my wedding photos and gave her false impressions of how wonderful my life was. All I wanted was for her to tell me I looked happy in my wedding pictures, so that I could convince myself I was in fact still truly happy. I needed to know I had not made a mistake marrying Baby. I hoped Morris's insinuation that I was inadequate for him was an illusion on my part. It was an aspersion that had left me deflated in the same way I had felt for a few years after the rape. A rape that had robbed me of my divine feminine strength. An energy that only Baby had managed to resuscitate but had now taken back from me. I desperately needed an answer, a sign, something; but I was looking for it in the wrong places.

Bridget must have been having a bad day when she got my email and responded with a one-liner, "Hahaaaa! Somebody finally made an honest person out of you!" I did not get the response I had desperately hoped for, so I failed to digest Bridget's reply, and without taking a moment to breathe and make sense of it first, I fired back a cup final. I told her I could not believe how jealous she was of my happy life, and that she ought to find someone else to take out her frustrations on if she could not be happy for me. I never responded to her apology email where she frantically explained that she had been at work when she got my email, and she had meant to respond fully later. Her quick response had meant to be a joke, she said, and she truly thought I looked beautiful and happy in the pictures.

Her apology was sincere. Of course it was, because I knew what the idiom she had used meant, but because I was not okay, the meaning of her statement went over my head and instead triggered me. I had worked so hard to shed off my family reputation of deceit and dishonesty, by getting married and changing my last name. That marriage, which had seemed so vital to cleanse my family reputation, had quickly turned sour and I was angry. Very angry in fact, because had the big white wedding not happened under duress, I may have found Morris and Angie's emails on time, and I would have quietly ended our secret marriage. Now that we were publicly married, I felt stuck with a man I could not forgive. In addition to all this, Bridget's choice of words made me think she had not vindicated me for dating her husband's married cousin, William. With that potpourri of negative thoughts, I took her words "made an honest person out of you" literally and blew up. It took me a long time to figure this out, but it was done, and I was extremely ashamed of my harsh cup final, so I did not respond to Bridget. I could not. I had no strength to explain to her what had been going on in my life. I was in a bad place and needed help. I continued to take painkillers and washed them down with plenty of wine.

During the summer of that year, Nigel, whom I had not heard from for a while, contacted me to check how I was doing. I was grateful for the contact, which allowed me to release all the tension and drama I had suffered in the past year or so to someone I knew would not judge me. I updated him that I had a daughter now and had married my high school sweetheart who he knew about. I told him about my wedding, and how I had found out about Angie in Morris's emails only two weeks after our wedding. I was heartbroken and did not know whether I was coming or going.

When I divulged Angie's name to Nigel, he said he knew her and had actually had an affair with her married friend. I found his confession disgusting. Nigel always had a lot of scandalous confessions to tell, but I had got used to them over the years. He told me the name of Angie's husband and assured me that Angie was nothing to worry about. He said I looked a million times better than Angie and Morris must have been crazy to be involved with her in the first place.

Nigel's comments awarded me some much-needed relief, but somewhere in my heart, I knew I would not rest until I had seen Angie with my own eyes. I sensed she may have contacted Baby after I contacted her, and he may have told her how to respond to my emails. Baby's explanations did not feel complete, so I became obsessed with investigating Angie. I searched her name online, but her face was never visible. This agitated me. Without any evidence at all, I managed to convince myself that she was still in contact with Baby, and I needed to inspect the competition. I began having nightmares about this evil person I had never seen. I despised every woman who shared her name. When I saw her first name written in any media – magazines, social media, or even on television, I would get an instant headache which only healed when I changed channels or skipped to other pages. My hatred towards an unsubstantiated threat from Angie was out of control. It was a strong loathing I should have directed to Morris but could not – because with him, I needed to focus on surviving our public marriage that looked perfect to the world. It was also easier to direct my anger to someone I did not know. I suggested couples' therapy to Morris, but he did not think it was necessary, so he refused it.

Nigel had introduced me to a female friend of his, Clara, a few years back, when she was still based in Zimbabwe. Clara was now living in the UK, was married and experiencing marital problems with her husband, Isaac. Nigel re-introduced us online, and I had a new friend I could vent to about life, without judgement. Nigel had decided he was tired of playing games and wanted to settle down too and get married. He was going to have a massive engagement party and invited Baby and I to attend.

When I told Baby about the invitation, he said he was not interested in attending the event, and he did not want me to attend it either. He announced then that he did not expect me to have any male friends. This ban came as a shock to me, because it reminded me of Tawanda who had been an overprotective, jealous boyfriend. The overprotectiveness that I had and still mistook for being wanted. Keen to do whatever it took to get my Baby back, I complied in anticipation for a brighter future. This marked the end of my friendship with Nigel, but this time, I explained to him that Baby did not trust me to have innocent friendships with people of the opposite sex. Nigel did not respond. My friendship with Clara strengthened. We emailed and text messaged each other a lot. We were kindred spirits with a lot in common. Her marriage lacked intimacy, like mine and her mother was also battling cancer.

At work, when I was pretending to look busy, I sent Mhamha emails of encouragement and links to websites that would help to boost her morale. Mhamha asked me to see if someone at my work could help her put a will in place. I said I would look into it but did not, because I was still in denial about her deteriorating health. Sorting out a will would have confirmed she was dying, and I was not prepared to deal with that eventuality.

I also used my time at work to communicate with many relatives across the globe who wanted to know how Mhamha was coping. Sekuru Tonderai was now based in South Africa completing a PHD in linguistics. He arranged prayers and group fasts and would often email to get me involved in the fasting, a concept I struggled with because I ate for comfort and was addicted to food. Sekuru Tonderai's wife, Mbuya Mavis, was based in New Zealand at the time and she would send me prayers and bible verses to pass on to Mhamha, as well as music recordings of her and her brother singing for Mhamha. Friends and relatives I had not heard from for a very long time also got in touch with me to wish our family well and express their hopes that Mhamha would heal.

Tsvakai who lived in the United States with Tete Mary, had now married a white American husband who was difficult to live with from the very first time they got together, Jacob. Tsvakai and I sent each other emails daily. When we were not talking about Mhamha's deteriorating health, we were comparing notes of our difficult husbands.

Chapter 18

As Mhamha's illness progressed, we continued to visit her every weekend. When we visited Mhamha, Baby and I slept in Runako's bedroom, which was usually unkempt, but we did not mind it too much. Following a night of steamy sex where Baby had ripped off my underwear and thrown it in the air, I was surprised to find replicas of my lingerie in a different size on the floor in the morning. I did not want to think it strange that Runako would own identical lingerie to mine. After all, I had habitually passed on clothes I no longer wore to her, so our dress sense at the time was similar. However, something made me venture into her drawers to check if the twin knickers on the floor were coincidental.

I was surprised to find that Runako had a drawerful of lingerie in the same colours and designs as mine. I decided this may have been a coincidence, because Runako sometimes shopped at the department stores where I bought my clothes. I then noticed a 100ml bottle of Chanel No5 perfume on top of her dresser, which was the perfume I had exclusively used for many years. That morning, I tried to convince myself that Runako might have maintained her childhood admiration for me as her older sister, but I felt a pang of doubt in my gut that would stay with me forever, like a faithful shadow.

In Surrey, I would still braid my clients' hair in between hospital visits or when Mhamha was at home to supplement my income. I had forged good relationships with my clientele, so I did not want to let them go. I found solace in leaving my usual problems and audience by escaping for a few hours into the world of my friendly clients. While I was out braiding hair, Tongai produced his beats and spent hours on end in a small reception room in Mhamha's house sampling and producing music. Beats were my brother's passion, and he was competent in producing them, but Baba who thought pursuing a music career was improvident, avidly discouraged the hobby. Mhamha spent a lot of time sleeping in her bedroom when she was not in hospital. She had developed a daily routine of waking up in the morning to have breakfast if she had the appetite, then watching the video recording of my wedding, and going to bed thereafter.

This meant Baby and Runako sat in the lounge for hours on end, developing a friendship that began to cross my boundaries. Runako, who loved to practice her dancing before she went night clubbing with her friends at night, would do so in front of the television, in front of Baby, who felt had "no choice but to sit and watch". They also watched films together and talked for hours; about topics I never knew. Sometimes, when we returned to our home, Baby would make comments on subjects he discussed with Runako, that made me slightly uncomfortable. Runako would also discuss in great detail Mhamha's illness and how she felt about it, and Baby had become her shoulder to cry on.

Runako had grown into a beautiful late adolescent self-assured extrovert. She did as she pleased and got away with it. Any attempts by my parents or anybody else to offer her guidance resulted in sharp riposte, which reminded me of her childhood tantrums, even when she had summoned the counsel herself. Because she seemed averse to constructive criticism and unable to accept anything other than positive feedback, I preferred to distance myself from her energy sapping battles.

One day, when I had returned to Mhamha's home from a full day of hair braiding, Runako announced that Baby would teach her to drive. Having received driving lessons from Baby, which I felt were a sentimental activity exclusive to our relationship, I was surprised that Baby had agreed to this. I had several reasons to feel insecure about the proposed arrangement.

Had the state of my relationship with Baby been healthy, and had he not become distant to me, I might have been okay with him spending intimate time with other women. However, our relationship was screaming for help, but nobody heard it. I felt that any of Baby's attention that went to other women should have been mine, and I challenged it in the hope for its redirection to me. In addition to this, Baby had proven a propensity to keep his options open, so my trust for him had flown out of the window. My experience with Alan did not help my thought processes either. The last thing I wanted was Baby unleashing his penis on my sister as Alan had done to me.

A part of me felt the belief that husbands stopped feeling attracted to their wives after they had given birth, was becoming a reality for me. Many single childless women seemed to believe this, as I had done before I was in the situation myself. I had witnessed some single women going to the extent of seducing married men whose wives had just given birth, in the hope they would topple the wife during her period of vulnerability. I had also seen some of my aunts engaging in this very behaviour during my childhood, so my fears felt very real.

Perhaps Baby's groans of pleasure and whimpers of delight during our toe-curling sex should have assured me that I was still delicious and esteemed, but in the absence of open communication there was no real intimacy, and I was paranoid of losing him.

When I asked Baby how the decision to offer Runako driving lessons had been reached, he explained that Runako had pressured him to give her the lessons and he had found it difficult to refuse. I told him I was uncomfortable with the arrangement, and that Tongai could teach her to drive, or she could work and pay for driving lessons herself. Baby suggested that I told Runako myself how I felt about the driving lessons. At this point, Runako seemed to appear on all of Baby's contact lists – mobile phone, email, Skype, WhatsApp. Unsure how to deal with the situation, I took Baby's advice and told Runako in an email that I was uncomfortable with the friendship that was developing between her and Baby, and given their age gap, their growing friendship did not make any sense to me. Runako rubbished my concerns, saying Baby was "just like an older brother" to her. As diplomatically as I could, I insisted she made alternative arrangements regarding her driving lessons, to which she obliged.

Around September that year, Runako began her degree in Sociology at Middlesex University. Baba came to visit Mhamha, whose health was deteriorating. Gogo had arrived a month before then to help look after Mhamha. When Mhamha was in hospital, Baba avoided going to visit her. If there was limited space in the cars available to drive to hospital, Baba would volunteer to stay behind to give others a chance to visit Mhamha. He spent all his free time in town instead, shopping for trinkets, perfumes and other small gifts for other women. When challenged why he was buying Oil of Olay anti-ageing facial products by Mhamha, he declared that he used them himself, which was why he looked so young.

Baba loved to gamble in betting shops and online when he was not watching pornography on the family computer. Baba also bought Viagra from varying online sources, using Mhamha's debit cards. The packages would arrive addressed to Mhamha for this reason, and this was how his activity was discovered. He failed to get to one of his packages before Mhamha, who opened it to find the shocking contents. When questioned why he needed Viagra, he explained to Mhamha that he sold it for huge profits to his political cronies. Baba seemed completely detached from the trauma we were going through, watching our mother's health deteriorating.

I was extremely annoyed with Baba for borrowing £300 from Runako who had been temping during the run up to her university course, to aid his shopping which had clearly got out of hand. Baba was to return the money in time for Runako's university preparations, but when my sister chased the debt, Baba directed her to Baby. Without considering the financial difficulty we were in, attributable to him, Baba rationalised that Baby was to pay the money to Runako and offset it against his *roora* debt to Baba.

"That boy has hardly given me anything for Ruva! He can pay you back your money, and we can deduct it from his *roora* debt!"

In addition to his shocking spending habits, Baba who we knew had sold one of his tractors for at least £15,000 in Zimbabwe, refused to contribute any money towards Runako's university fees. "There is no point in educating a girl child who might get married immediately after qualifying, before I get the chance to spend her money," he said.

We felt relieved when Baba returned to Zimbabwe, where his vileness and lack of empathy was diluted by distance. Throughout her illness, Mhamha repeatedly told us two things.

First, she wanted to be cremated when she died, but she knew Gogo would not allow that to happen. If she was not cremated, she did not want to be buried at our family graveyard in Chivi. She wanted to be buried next to her father, Khulu, with whom she had been very close. Khulu had died of liver cirrhosis in the mid-eighties, a few weeks before Tizai was born, leaving Gogo who was in her forties at the time, to raise her younger children on her own. I was around three years old when Khulu died, so I had no recollection of him. Khulu was buried in the community cemetery in Epworth.

Second, she did not want any of her pension and death in service money to be passed on to Baba. She wanted Runako's university fees to be paid off to ensure she completed her course with no complications. Mhamha remained bitter that she had been wrongfully accused of causing Babamunini Benjy's death, and although my aunts had begun liking Mhamha when she moved to the UK, they never apologised for the disgrace they had caused her. Mhamha was also deeply heartbroken by Baba who seemed to have completely lost interest in her. This, she repeated time after time to me, my siblings and Gogo.

In early October, Tongai had had enough of Baba's behaviour and sent him an email confronting his behaviour. He raised the issue of Baba's unfaithfulness to Mhamha, and how he had continued to disrespect her, despite the fact that I had confronted him two years earlier. Tongai expressed that Baba had been a bad example to him and that he was the sole cause of our mother's cancer. He copied and pasted an excerpt from the internet, explaining that women who had sex with men who had had many sexual partners, were susceptible to human papillomavirus infection, which was responsible for virtually all cases of cervical cancer. Tongai went on to name Baba as the cause of Tizai's disappearance.

A friend of Tizai had spoken to Tongai at my wedding and told him that Tizai had seen Baba with a young girl at a public function. Tizai had confronted Baba about the girl and Baba publicly told him off and humiliated him in front of a large audience, a spectacle that provided entertainment as a topic of interest for months thereafter in Masvingo. Tongai raised the issue that Baba had spent over £300 on Viagra during his last visit, when Runako was struggling with raising university tuition fees. Tongai pointed out that two of Baba's brothers had died of AIDS and queried whether he had not learnt anything from those experiences. He condemned Baba for being a selfish, self-centred man who never owned up to his faults, was never apologetic, and never changing his behaviours. Tongai ended the email by stating that Baba used to be a hero he looked up to, but he was left with no choice but to sever ties with him.

We continued to visit Mhamha in hospital. I had always hated hospitals, but more so now due to the numerous times we had to be in them. The undoubted presence of sickness evident in patients lying in beds, and on sad faces of their visiting relatives. The mundaneness of the white and grey walls, the artificial lighting, the antiseptic smell, staff pushing trolleys of medicine or patients being wheeled in and out of surgery. The slower than usual elevators. The strict visiting hours that were not always convenient. The extortionate car park charges. The only positive thing about hospitals was that they made sick people better, but in our case, they could not make Mhamha better, so I hated them more. I was tired of witnessing Mhamha squirming in pain, in a manner that resembled a woman having childbirth contractions. I felt helpless. If only her pain could be shared.

Baby and I were still enduring a modest hand to mouth existence, so the weekly trips to Surrey had a significant impact on our budget. The fuel to travel between Chatham and Surrey weekly, contributions to groceries when we arrived in Surrey, and the car breakdowns we began to experience due to overusing our car, all added up. I often felt bad during hospital visits when we found Mhamha surrounded by beautiful flowers and expensive fruit hampers from well-wishers, and we turned up with nothing. My selfish consolation was that she had stopped eating much because she could barely keep any food down due to chemotherapy, so the fruit hampers were eventually shared between her hospital visitors. I constantly wished I had enough money to do something big for Mhamha, perhaps better private healthcare, or a holiday experience somewhere special.

In mid-October, as Mhamha's health rapidly declined, peculiar things began to happen during some of our hospital visits. One of Mhamha's colleagues, a black South African lady, came to see Mhamha in hospital. Before she left, she offered to say a prayer. The prayer started off calm and dignified, then quickly graduated into a histrionic outburst that made me open my eyes to see how everyone else on Mhamha's bedside was reacting. Baby had already nudged me with his elbow several times, and I had avoided looking at him, to keep my laughter suppressed. I had coughed a few times to release some of the tension that had been building up in my core. As Mhamha's colleague paced up and down, speaking in tongues, breaking into song, removing her wig and shoving it into her handbag, shaking her body, all during the prayer, I caught Mhamha giggling quietly, and I felt less guilty for passing judgement.

On another occasion, Babamukuru Gilbert was in London on a business trip and he came to visit Mhamha in hospital. I had never seen him looking so sombre and humble. He did not stay very long, but as he was leaving, Babamukuru Gilbert kissed Mhamha on the lips, then he walked away without looking back. I had only ever seen Baba kissing Mhamha on the lips, so Babamukuru Gilbert's kiss was strange in a way that made me lose hope in Mhamha's recovery. It made me wonder if Maiguru Chiedza had asked her husband to kiss her sister goodbye, on her behalf.

I was glad Babamukuru did not stay long, because I was upset with him for causing Baby and me a massive inconvenience. Valerie had been managing the sale of our property in Zimbabwe and Babamukuru Gilbert had made an offer on it and begun the purchase transaction. Valerie had met Maiguru Chiedza in a local supermarket and gave her an update on the property transaction. It transpired that Babamukuru Gilbert had been buying the property for a *small house* and Maiguru Chiedza should not have known about it. Assuming it was an investment, Valerie, Baby and I had not questioned why Babamukuru Gilbert was buying the property. He ended up pulling out of the transaction and Maiguru Chiedza was furious at me for "facilitating her husband's shenanigans". Why Maiguru Chiedza chose to direct her anger at me for her husband's shortcomings remained a mystery to me. Baby and I returned our property to market and began to look for a new buyer.

In late October, Mhamha was discharged from hospital one more time. When I spoke to her mid-week, she told me the hospital was releasing her into palliative care with MacMillan Cancer charity. I did not find out what palliative care meant, and Mhamha knew this, because I responded to her news by saying, "Ah, they must have seen the progress you've made getting better lately. You will heal a lot quicker at home anyway." My denial of Mhamha's state of health was painfully obvious, but she probably preferred it that way. Mhamha would call or text me to tell me she had managed to walk to the end of her cul de sac, in a manner that showed pride in her achievement. I feigned my applause to her, because my mind remained in denial that she was signing out.

During the first week of November, we went to visit Mhamha over the weekend. She seemed better and more energetic than usual, which raised my hopes for her recovery. I drove into town with her, and I shopped for one set of lingerie with some of the little money I had made braiding hair that weekend. Mhamha went to close her bank account, and to pay some final bills and debts.

On our drive back home, Mhamha was in good spirits, and laughed at me for wasting time and money on pretty lingerie.

"Men don't care about such things, Ruva," she said then chuckled. "If they really want you, it doesn't matter whether you wear beautiful expensive lingerie, torn underwear, or nothing at all," she said.

I wanted to tell Mhamha how desperately I wanted to make things right in my marriage, and how I thought the sexy lingerie might bring back the spark that had once existed between Baby and me, but I could not.

When I parked the car, Mhamha looked more serious and spoke quietly about how she wanted me to take over some of her businesses in Zimbabwe. Her hair salon had the most sentimental value to her, and she knew Baba would sell it as soon as she died, then spend the money on other women. I did not want to have that conversation with Mhamha. I knew it was impossible for me to run her businesses from the UK, because I did not have the capacity to do so. I felt guilty to tell her upfront that I was not interested in running her businesses, so I did not respond to her request but broke into tears instead. Mhamha concluded the difficult conversation by begging me to forgive Baba.

"He will always be your father," she said, "You have to love him unconditionally despite all his faults."

I explained to Mhamha that we would not visit her the following weekend because Maya's birthday was approaching, and we needed to prepare for it. We agreed that Maya's first birthday party would be held at Mhamha house to avoid her travelling to Kent for it, so we would see her the weekend after the following one. When we were leaving, Mhamha hugged us for longer than usual, and she kissed us all, including Baby her *mukuwasha*. Culturally, it was unusual for such an intimate act to happen between in-laws. Baby, Maya and I returned to Kent on the Sunday evening, exhausted.

Chapter 19

Mhamha phoned me on Friday evening, asking how my week at work had been, how the party preparations for Maya's birthday were going, and other usual things a mother would ask a busy daughter. At the end of the call, Mhamha asked me to look after the family and told me she loved me.

The conversation felt extremely unusual and I felt a deep sadness after the call. Mhamha had lately got into the habit of saying things like "that would be too late", or "I won't be here by then", when anyone tried to make plans for the near future, like Christmas the following month. I was emotionally exhausted from worrying and I yearned for Mhamha's wellness, and normalcy.

On Saturday evening, Morris who had been working excessively was home from a double day shift and would be going back to work the next day, so needed to sleep soon. For the first time in weeks, he was trying to lure me into sex on the sofa, and I simply was not interested. I was depressed by life in general, I had got tired of waiting for him to want me, I was frustrated by Mhamha's illness and worried she might die. I was physically exhausted from commuting to and from work, looking after Maya on my own and cooking meals for a man who would eat the food and vanish. He was never there. After an unsuccessful lazy attempt to have intercourse, Morris left me on my own in the lounge and went to bed, where Maya was already asleep in her cot bed.

As I sat on my own in silence, I replayed my last conversation with Mhamha. Her last words mirrored those she had said to me when she had attempted suicide when I was seven. As I tried to confront my fear of abandonment, chills of agitation made me grab a knitted throw from the other end of the sofa and cover myself up with it. As I was contemplating retiring on the sofa for the night, my mobile phone rang. It was Tongai.

"Mhamha is not breathing, so I've called an ambulance and they have taken her away."

I asked Tongai several probing questions to seek clarification, but he remained subtle, until he inadvertently stated Mhamha's body had been carried out in a bag. Despite knowing what that meant, I still did not want to believe Mhamha was gone.

I woke Morris up frantically and asked him to drive me to Surrey immediately. It was late and he had to work the next day, so he suggested waiting until we heard further news. By the time he finished trying to resist going to Surrey, I had finished packing our bags and was ready to go. Morris drove, and I cried all the way to Mhamha's house. Upon arrival, I found Gogo wailing and throwing herself everywhere because her baby was dead. I felt numb and did not want to believe what my eyes were seeing and what my ears were hearing.

Baba, who I had not spoken to since he left the UK in September called on my mobile phone to say he was sorry for my loss.

A few days earlier, Baba had finally caught wind, through his sisters who I had told how disgusted I was with him, that I had seen his pornographic photographs that Mhamha showed me. He had subsequently sent me a text message which read, "Read *Genesis 9 vs 22 – 25*. You are cursed!" to which I did not respond.

Earlier that day, Mhamha had been very relaxed, talking to Gogo and Tongai. She had reiterated her last wishes. Her palliative care team had been to visit, and Mhamha had been very prescriptive on the medical drugs they administered to her. She had asked for a particularly large dosage of

Morphine, to which her palliative care team obliged. She had appeared weaker and weaker as the day progressed, then when Gogo was nodding off on the sofa and Tongai was making his beats, Mhamha slipped away to the toilet, where she left the door unlocked, sat on the toilet seat and took her last breath. Tongai and Gogo noticed that Mhamha was missing from her usual seat, but they thought she may have gone up to her bedroom for a change of scenery. It was only when Gogo went to use the toilet that she found Mhamha looking lifeless. When Gogo called Tongai, he called the ambulance then tried unsuccessfully to resuscitate her.

I waited for Monday to excuse myself from work and stayed with Baby and Maya in Surrey. On Monday morning, Baby, Tongai, Runako and I were invited to view Mhamha's body at the local mortuary. I was not sure how I felt about going to see my dead mother, but I went anyway. On arrival at the mortuary, we were asked to sit in a waiting area while Mhamha's body was prepared for viewing in a private room. As we waited, I was worried I might not cope with what I was about to see and have an emotional breakdown. When it was time, we slowly walked into the room, which was filled with serene energy. Mhamha looked very peaceful, with a slight smile on her face. I touched her forehead, to make sure she was indeed gone. She was stone cold. I squeezed her hand and kissed her forehead and hoped to see her react, but she truly was not there anymore. I felt solace in knowing she was finally at peace. Mhamha had escaped, for good, and was no longer suffering from cancer and from her marriage. I suddenly felt happy for her, but I knew I would miss her terribly. Viewing Mhamha's body helped me come to terms with the reality of our loss.

Mhamha's house was flooded with family, friends and well-wishers from all over the UK. As was customary, a lot of Zimbabwean well-wishers gifted us *chema*, a Shona burial custom where well-wishers gifted money to a bereaved family to help with funeral costs. When we began to make Mhamha's funeral arrangements, Baba said he wanted to be present and began preparing to fly to the UK. Gogo decided that her daughter would not be cremated, so she would be buried at Epworth Mission in Zimbabwe, in accordance with her last wishes. It was therefore unnecessary for Baba to travel to the UK; instead we encouraged him to stay in Zimbabwe to begin preparing for the funeral. In the UK, we began preparing for the repatriation of my Mhamha's body. Using our savings and the *chema* generously donated by well-wishers, we were able to arrange the repatriation of Mhamha's body and pay for flights for Gogo, Tongai, Runako, Baby, Maya and me. We arranged for a memorial service at Mhamha's local Methodist church in Surrey, which was held on Maya's first birthday, the day before we flew out to Zimbabwe.

While we waited for the UK memorial service, a debate about where in Zimbabwe Mhamha would be buried ensued. As was customary, Baba and his family expected

Mhamha to be buried at our rural homestead in Chivi. Gogo, my siblings and I stood up to Baba and told him Mhamha's final wishes, to which he responded by launching an attack. First, he intimated how disappointed he was that my siblings and I were not taking his side, then he began reaching out to us individually to weaken us with his evil offence.

"You're a liar! My wife loved me and would never make wishes designed to embarrass me and my family!" Baba fired in a text.

I explained that Mhamha's wishes had nothing to do with him and his ego. He went on to call me a *mhunzamusha*, because I had tried to wreck his marriage before, and now I was splitting up the family with my controversial lies.

"*Takakutengesa iwe! Siyana nenyaya dzemhuri yedu!* We sold you off! So, stay out of our family affairs!" Baba struck again, then simultaneously launched an attack on Baby's phone.

"Keep that wife of yours on a tight leash. She is now your property and is no longer allowed to stray back into our family matters."

"We do not expect her to make any decisions or participate in our family debates. She is after all just a woman, and her strengths are limited by the confines of her kitchen. Man up and ensure she keeps her focus on cooking!"

"Man up, spineless boy, and ensure Ruva focuses on kitchen and bedroom tasks!"

The barrage of poisonous messages from Baba to Baby's phone was relentless. Baby sat quietly taking it all in, drinking his beer and passing on his phone to me to read the messages as and when they came in. We stopped responding to Baba.

Baba's behaviour not only broke my heart, but it confirmed to me what I had always fearfully suspected; that within a dysfunctional set up, traditional marriage symbolised the exiling of a "bad girl", to shut her up once and for all. I was very disappointed in Baba, whose behaviours revealed to Baby that I did not have paternal support. Baba made me incredibly vulnerable to Baby who was already not himself. Baby could do anything to me now because I had nowhere to run to.

Baba also attacked Tongai.

"Stay away from grown up discussions, boy! You're just my sperm after all!"

Tongai was furious.

Runako who had not offended Baba was spared the attacks.

The emotional abuse was intense, to the point that we almost forgot Mhamha was gone. All discussions with Baba were centred around changing Gogo's mind about where Mhamha would be buried. Baba's friends based in the UK would arrive at Mhamha's house, take us to the side and try to convince us that going against cultural expectations was the worst thing we could ever do, and the spirits of our ancestors would perpetually punish us for making such a bad move. The threats forced us into the uncomfortable position of divulging to his messengers, Baba's attitude and emotional abuse towards Mhamha in the last few years. We were meant to forgive him and do as we were told, the messengers said. At that point, we stopped communicating with anyone attempting to change our minds in Baba's favour.

At some point during the week, Baby and I drove back to Kent to pack our luggage for the trip to Zimbabwe. I was able to collect two birthday cakes I had specially ordered for Maya and Baby's birthdays and took them back to Surrey. Upon arrival, Gogo asked Runako, Mainini Portia, Mainini Joy and me to pack all of Mhamha's clothes, so that they would be distributed after her funeral. *Kugova nhumbi*, sharing of the deceased's clothes was a customary ceremony held a day to a month after the funeral to distribute clothing and other belongings to the deceased's family and friends. On Thursday, I went shopping in Aldershot, for black clothes, for myself and Maya; and found the retail therapy soothing.

On Friday, Mhamha's memorial service was held in Aldershot. There was a huge turnout of people who truly loved her. Belinda and my other friends from Canterbury turned up to join the service, which was expertly coordinated by the church. Even Raviro who I had not seen since she left my shared house in Canterbury was present. I was grateful for the support of my friends. The funeral parlour had embalmed and dressed Mhamha, who never wore make-up when she was alive. It was therefore very strange to see her face with make up on, especially the dark burgundy shade of lipstick which made her unrecognisable. I rationalised that the body in front of us was no longer Mhamha, so it did not matter what it looked like.

The memorial service went well and incorporated English and Shona hymns and readings. A buffet lunch was served at the church after the ceremony. Belinda came to speak to me before she left, "Call me when you get back Ruva. You have a very difficult situation ahead of you, and you will need all the support you can get when you return from Zim." I thanked Belinda for coming and promised to keep in touch. When most attendees had left, we returned to Mhamha's house with close relatives and friends who had stayed behind. We had drinks to celebrate Mhamha's life, then we sang "happy birthday" to celebrate Maya's first birthday and shared her cake with everyone present.

On Saturday afternoon, we made our way to Gatwick airport where we would board our flight to Zimbabwe with Mhamha's body in the cargo section of the aeroplane. Several relatives drove our family to the airport. Alan was part of the convoy that drove to Gatwick. Although Moira had divorced him and moved on, he acted like a loyal *mukuwasha,* as was customary, running errands with vigour and his usual grin displayed for all to see. I avoided eye contact with Alan, as always, because I was afraid of what he might do if our eyes met. All I saw was a man who was not ashamed to unleash his penis onto unsuspecting young female relatives of his ex-wife, and I could not stand him.

After checking-in our luggage, we sang "happy birthday" to Baby and shared his birthday cake. When we had bid farewell to our UK well-wishers, we hoarded a variety of alcoholic spirits in the Duty-Free shopping area to see us through the next few days. We desperately needed to calm down our nerves, because we had no idea what awaited us in Zimbabwe. There had been so much fighting between Baba and Mhamha's families, and we had been thrown in the middle of the feud, so we did not look forward to what was coming. We drank until we passed out on the flight.

Chapter
20

On arrival in Zimbabwe, we found a huge turnout of family and friends waiting for us at the Harare International Airport. People who were not aware of the drama regarding where Mhamha would be buried came freely to hug us and pass their condolences. Baba and his sisters walked towards us hesitantly and we were unsure what would happen next, but we did not care. Baba shook my hand, and Tongai's, then threw himself onto Runako and burst into tears. I felt my eyes rolling then looked away. The tension was tangible, and the dramatics were cringey. Tete Gwinyai shrieked the loudest, while Tete Gertrude and Tete Primrose offered more dignified whimpers. Our tearful paternal aunts hugged us and whispered words of comfort. I could not help thinking they were the very people who had offended my mother, resulting in the kerfuffle we faced ahead. They seemed to be filled with guilt, but still took no responsibility for what they had done.

Maiguru Chiedza, Mainini Rosey and many relatives of Mhamha, including Gogo's brothers and sisters were also at the airport. Maiguru Chiedza was evidently still angry about my trying to sell a property to her husband for a *small house*, because she kept her distance from me.

There was a lot of singing of sad funeral songs at the airport, as we waited for Mhamha's body to be cleared by customs and handed to a local funeral parlour. While we were waiting for the body to be released, I noticed I was being talked about and being pointed at by many people. I was being identified as the defiant daughter of Baba who was causing a lot of stress by lying that Mhamha did not want to be buried in Chivi. I paid no attention to the tittle-tattle and focussed on getting the job done. Baby's family was at the airport, and once the body was released, they managed to whisk us away to Valerie's home, where I got some relief from our family drama.

The following day, a body viewing session was running at the funeral parlour, for family and friends who wanted to view Mhamha's body. Baba had calmed down by then, and probably thought if he was a bit pleasant to me, I might change my mind and help him to win the battle over Mhamha's body. As we stood outside the funeral parlour waiting for a signal to proceed, Baba could not help himself but offend me. Out of nowhere, he began referring to me as "the chief mourner", when introducing me to people or having a conversation with me. He also managed to crack a few jokes about crocodile tears at funerals, and how professional mourning was now a booming career. A few people caught the bug of his contagious laugh and giggled away with him.

I maintained my expressionless face and avoided eye contact with him. He was definitely at it again, making subtle jokes to discredit my purpose, making me doubt my reality by devaluing the emotions I felt about Mhamha's death. For whatever reason, he was projecting his own lack of empathy on me. I had after all been brainwashed by his family to distance myself from Mhamha, so perhaps he genuinely did not believe I was sincerely hurting. What Baba failed to grasp was that Mhamha and I had miraculously managed to salvage the painful sabotage of our relationship and had become great friends.

When we eventually got into the funeral parlour, the body viewing took place, with singing and bible readings carrying on in the background. I felt time was running out. Mhamha's body would soon be six feet under, and I would never see her again, so I wanted to kiss her. As I lowered my face to the body, I was stopped suddenly by the manager of the parlour.

"It's not allowed!" she screamed.

I asked her why, which shocked her, then she mumbled something about the toxicity of embalming fluid, and how it would make me sick if I got in contact with it.

As I pondered the unfairness of her deterrence, I felt I was truly back in Zimbabwe, where a restrictive culture prevailed, always. It was a place where people were addicted to controlling those who were addicted to being controlled. I had no appetite to argue, as the debate would undoubtedly lapse into the meeting of cultural expectations and avoiding upsetting ancestral spirits.

While I was considering the issue of control, Babamukuru Gilbert decided Mhamha's coffin was not good enough, so he wanted to buy her a more expensive casket. Babamukuru Gilbert was a grandiose larger than life being who certainly had a fear of being ordinary. A lot of people disliked him for this reason. His whole life was centred around trying to prove he was better than everyone else. His offer to buy an expensive casket for Mhamha emasculated Baba for a moment, which I found amusing.

I told Babamukuru Gilbert that Mhamha did not need a new casket, so she would remain where she was. From there, Babamukuru Gilbert announced his financial and food donations towards the funeral and stated continuously how fond he was of Mhamha. After the body viewing session ended, we all proceeded to Epworth, where whispers ensued about whether Baba and Babamukuru Gilbert might have shared a *small house*. Their resentment towards each other was tangible and the reasons for their animosity provided a lot of gossip content. Baba, who felt uneasy at Gogo's home in Epworth, randomly made declarations that he had not caused Mhamha's death.

"It's not AIDS, please, it's cancer that killed her. I didn't give her AIDS!" No one responded to his announcements, which I thought were completely unnecessary.

Mhamha would be buried in two days' time. Baba's family who had given up on fighting to have Mhamha buried at our rural homestead asked if she could be buried in Masvingo town somewhere near my childhood home instead. That way, she would not be laid to rest in the same soil as the family who had offended her. The patriarchy of Mhamha's family who now dominated the debate alongside Gogo refused. Baba's family, who were by now desperate, begged for Mhamha's body to go and lie in state overnight at our childhood home, so that family friends and relatives who could not attend the funeral could pay their last respects. My aunts pleaded for my help.

"It would be very embarrassing to our family if Mhamha's body does not at least go to Masvingo for show, even for only a few hours. What will our neighbours and Baba's constituents think?" they negotiated tirelessly. I could not help them and their egos. What was happening was a direct consequence of their own actions. Acceptance of the situation was their only option.

Drama continued to dominate the atmosphere in the run up to Mhamha's funeral. *Varoora* of Mhamha's family who thought we were loaded with foreign currency recurrently demanded cash or alcohol, a cultural practice called *kushonongorwa;* otherwise they would discontinue cooking for the masses. Distant uncles from Mhamha's family who seemed addicted to consulting men of God for everything, occasionally turned up with the latest narratives of what they had been told by prophets at Domboramwari,

"Your father is following your mother in six months' time because our ancestors are very unhappy."

"A prophet says your mother had a cell phone; the gadget must be given to a male relative of hers when her possessions are distributed next week," and the list went on.

I hardly saw Baby who was running errands and bonding with his brothers and cousins. Amongst his errands, Baby had to find a cow to feed the masses; a tradition we never knew existed until we arrived in Zimbabwe for Mhamha's funeral. The economic situation in Zimbabwe made it impossible to find a cow within such a short space of time, so Baby ended up buying several goats instead. Mhaiyo, Valerie and Baby's other female relatives were more visible. They ran easier errands on Baby's behalf, including buying a shroud to wrap around Mhamha's coffin; a custom believed to keep her warm as she journeyed out of this world.

The day before Mhamha's funeral, before her body was released, we attended a short church service in the chapel at the funeral parlour. Methodist hymn three was sung, then a sermon about David's son's death in *2 Samuel 12* followed. Our family was encouraged to resume normal life, as David did when he realised he had done all he could before his son died. Any actions after his son's death would not bring him back, because God had made His irreversible decision. After the service, there was more singing of familiar hymns, and Mhamha's body was transported in a simple pick-up van to Epworth. Funeral parlours in Zimbabwe did not have luxury cars to transport the dead at the time. That night, Mhamha's body lay in state in Gogo's lounge. We sang and danced continuously all night, until our throats and feet hurt. It was truly a celebration of Mhamha's life, and for the first time since her passing on, my heart momentarily forgot to ache.

On the morning of Mhamha's funeral, I woke up immersed in a pool of sadness. The gravity that came with losing someone you could not imagine life without dragged me down, and I was drowning. A short ritual took place, where Tongai and Runako presented shrouds they had bought for Mhamha's coffin to "keep her warm". Baby's blanket, which was bigger than the others, was placed on top of Tongai and Runako's blankets. I felt a deep heartache knowing I would never see Mhamha again. I felt sorry that she had had to suffer terribly in order to escape her challenging life. My failure to control the concoction of bad memories in the run up to Mhamha's death debilitated me.

I dreaded witnessing Mhamha's body being lowered into the ground only a few hours later to be covered in soil forever; a familiar ritual confirming the finality of death. I felt too drained to move, and I desperately wanted to pause time. I could not eat or drink, so my energy was depleting.

Gogo who was in her mid-70s whimpered continuously, and I imagined how painful it must be to bury your own child, even at old age. Mhamha was Gogo's first adult child to die. She had had another male child who died of malaria at the age of 10 in the early 1960s. Immediately before Mhamha was diagnosed with cancer, she had dreamt of her late little brother, Sekuru John. In the dream, Sekuru John rode an elephant, which slowly approached Mhamha, then stretching out his hand he pointed to her and said, "You are next, and I will be waiting for you on the other side."

Gogo was a beautiful self-assured modern woman who had worked first as a nurse, then as a primary school teacher until her late 60s. Khulu had been a headmaster, and together they had relocated several times to rural schools where they had both taught. Gogo had ended her teaching career in Epworth, long after Khulu had died. When she retired from teaching, she volunteered at the Girl Guides headquarters in Harare, where she drove three times a week to spend the day serving others. Babamukuru Gilbert ensured Gogo always drove a Mercedes.

Throughout my childhood, I admired Gogo's dress sense, especially the leather loafers and kitten heels she wore to work and church, and the beautiful leather handbags she carried around. She wore wigs, but never needed to wear make-up. Her glowing skin was spotless, and her full set of white teeth remained intact. Gogo maintained a beauty regime of cleansing, toning and moisturising her face twice daily for as long as I could remember, and she did not have a single wrinkle on her face.

Gogo had a melodious voice which I found therapeutic, and her offspring seemed to speak like her too. I never got tired of listening to her beautiful healing voice. Mhamha's whole family loved to sing and often did as a choir at weddings and funerals. Baba's family often made fun of the way Mhamha's family spoke, because they had never heard anyone speaking so slowly, rhythmically and eloquently. Gogo was a classy woman who loved her mature single-malt whisky and maintained her cool most times. She appeared very gentle as long as she was not provoked.

We did not spend as many holidays visiting Gogo as we did Mbuya, but the times we went to visit her were always memorable. Gogo had a special gift of making whoever was in her company feel special in that moment. I loved going to Epworth, a high-density settlement established by the Methodist church, where Gogo lived. There was an opportunity to hang out with the poor, and egos did not seem to exist, so I felt authentic and was never self-conscious when I was there. We were allowed to be imperfect children, focusing on playing in the dirt and occasionally running to the shops to buy *freezits, maputi,* or sweets when Gogo gave us pocket money. Around Gogo's yard she had strategically built small residences which generated her retirement income, so she was never broke.

When times were hard, Gogo's lodgers sometimes struggled to pay their rent on time, and Gogo was usually very forgiving. Gogo did, however, have the discernment to recognise men who tried to take advantage of her feminine gentleness by proving difficult to pay rent nearly every month. Such lodgers could afford to attend the beer halls daily but only paid rent after significant harassment. When the need arose, Gogo started her evening on lagers, then graduated to single malt whisky. She always had a steady supply of nothing younger than 12 years, from her in-laws and grandchildren who lived abroad. When she was ready for some confrontation, she would ask one of the young boys to go and call the lodger in question. When they arrived, Gogo kickstarted the conversation by asking for her money gently. She would by then have intel that the lodger had been paid and was seen in various places spending their money. When the predictable excuses came, Gogo rose to her feet and turned into a vicious lioness who had had enough. She grabbed them by the collar if necessary, tightening her grip gradually until her rental money magically appeared. We laughed about the incidents in hindsight, and in those moments Gogo took a trip down memory lane, telling us how vicious she used to be back in the day. When any of her sons in law disrespected her daughters or broke their hearts, she had driven to their offices and beat them up in front of their subordinates. Gogo, a woman who was raised in an evangelical family and married into one, had zero tolerance for men who disrespected her and her daughters.

At Mhamha's funeral, Gogo appeared like a defeated soul. Sekuru Tonderai had travelled from Cape Town for Mhamha's funeral. Maiguru Chiedza and Mainini Rosey were also present and broken. The final service was held in Epworth Methodist church where my parents had got married in the early 1980s. Gogo had been the treasurer of the choir in that church, where she sang alto. On that day, I barely heard Gogo's voice. The service was more of the same – singing, bible readings, speeches and testimonials. I was unprepared to deliver a speech, but in my disorientation, I rose and said a few words, which probably meant nothing to most people. Several friends and family from Masvingo, Mhamha's old friends from her church, faces I had not seen in a long time, were present to pay their last respects to Mhamha. Mainini Gemma came too and looked visibly ill and weaker than she had been earlier in the year at my wedding. A political colleague of Baba's gave a politically themed speech which made me want to tell him the funeral was not about him. An old friend of Mhamha's, Sister Doris, a nurse she had worked with gave a touching testimony of Mhamha's life and read the nurse's creed in her honour.

A touching speech was made by Mhamha's uncle, Sekuru Robert, who had been like a father to her. He started by saying *"Mwana arere apo igamba muzviito.* That child lying there is a hero indeed." He went on to explain that his daughter, Gamu, had requested to be buried next to her father, an unusual request by a married woman. He therefore wanted to thank Baba's family for honouring her request with love. "Let's give them a round of applause!" he said to end his speech. If it was possible to infringe the hearts and minds of Baba's family who appeared aloof during the speech, we might have seen a blazing inferno ravaging their egos from the inside out.

There was a final viewing of the body before Mhamha was laid to rest. As mourners walked past Mhamha's body to pay their last respects, the older generation danced and waved as they walked past her. Some women curtseyed and some men stopped to bow and salute her. Before her coffin was sealed permanently, I howled my guts out with an effort I had not exerted before, genuinely hoping that my desperate cry might change Mhamha's mind and make her come back, but she was steadfast in her coldness. We had so much unfinished business, so much making-up for lost time, so much mother-daughtering to do, so much forgiving our pasts and moving on. I needed a mother to mentor me through my mothering journey. How could I possibly do it on my own?

A huge turnout of people, family and friends we had not seen in many years, Mhamha's former colleagues, workers and church family from Masvingo, all walked slowly to the graveside after the church service. Baba, who never wore his wedding ring, had it on, and as my siblings and I placed Arum lilies on top of Mhamha's coffin, Baba dramatically took off his wedding ring and placed it next to our flowers. As Mhamha's coffin was lowered into the ground slowly, I felt my energy depleting rapidly. I needed someone to hold onto, but there was no one. Where was Morris? I needed him now, more than ever. I ached at the realisation that the journey of losing Mhamha was unique to me and would be very lonely indeed. No one, not even one who had lost their own mother, would make me heal from losing Mhamha.

Following Mhamha's funeral, her possessions from the UK were distributed to her relatives. Mhamha had loved to buy gemstone embellished gold jewellery from catalogues, and she had given my siblings and I some of her favourite pieces while she was still alive. Her rings were disformed because Mhamha had been squeezing them into oblong shapes to prevent them from falling off her fingers that had shrunk during her battle with cancer. When we were packing her clothes in Surrey, Gogo had allowed us to pick a few of her clothes we wanted to keep. I chose the outfits she had worn to my wedding and my graduation, amongst a few other items.

Mainini Rosey was nominated as *sara pavana*, guardian of the deceased's children. This was a Shona traditional role where an individual was given the mandate to look after children of the deceased without venturing into their marital bed. For us, this function was perfunctory because my siblings and I lived in the UK independently, and the emotional support Mainini Rosey may have been able to provide would be limited by distance. The practical implications of the mandate would have been for my siblings and I to support our aunt financially, as most people living in the diaspora supported their parents in Zimbabwe, but we chose to not burden ourselves with the responsibility.

We spent minimal time with Baba and his siblings because they could not help but incessantly cause offence to us. On one occasion, we gathered at a local restaurant for lunch in Harare and Tete Gwinyai felt the need to justify Baba's estrangement from Mhamha during the last few years of her life.

"*Chete vaigodiniko bhudhi Davis, mai venyu dzakanga dzangova mvura dzoga dzoga?* What was our brother to do, your mum's vagina had lost elasticity and she had become useless in bed?"

I was not sure how anyone might have been expected to respond to such a comment about their mother, so I looked at Tete Gwinyai with an eye that clapped her across the face, then pretended I had not heard her. If my mind had quickly registered that she was no longer young and feisty enough to retaliate violence, I might have pounced on Tete Gwinyai to deliver a torrent of fists.

Baba, who had softened a bit after the funeral, wanted to know more details of Mhamha's last wishes. When we restated that Mhamha's pension and death in service money had to pay for Runako's university fees and Baba was to stay away from it, he declared he was making a lot of money in Zimbabwe and had no interest in Mhamha's benefit money. Baba apologised to Tongai, Runako and me for having behaved out of character and stated he had been shocked and emotionally shaken by Mhamha's illness and death. He wanted to make amends with us, and he promised to be a better father going forward. We welcomed Baba's sentiments and bought into his oratory.

A few days after Mhamha's funeral, we travelled to Masvingo where a memorial service had been arranged. Mhamha's relatives, including Maiguru Chiedza and Mainini Rosey attended the service with many other relatives of Mhamha who had hitched a ride in Maiguru Chiedza's haulage truck; the one she had volunteered to transport provisions for my wedding only seven months ago. Mhamha's friends from her church, ex-colleagues, business associates and other well-wishers all attended the beautiful service that had been arranged for her. As was her funeral, there was singing, prayer and heartfelt speeches, but this time more light-hearted and positive. It felt like a true celebration of Mhamha's life, at her home where she had dedicated her life glorifying Baba and raising her children, in a town she had served the community first as a nurse, and later as a hospice counsellor.

The next day, Maiguru Chiedza announced that Mhamha's belongings would be removed from our house, then she instructed Mhamha's relatives to fill up her truck. It felt like a bad dream to watch all the rooms in our childhood home being stripped of items I had never thought of as Mhamha's, but ours. Furniture, bedding, curtains, her clothes, wall hangings, kitchen utensils and cutlery – they took it all.

"It's for the best Ruva," Maiguru Chiedza pacified me, when she noticed my subtle wince to resist a teary blink.

"Another woman will eventually live here, and it is not good for that woman to use my sister's belongings. We need to remove as much energy of your mother's from this house, to make it easier for the next woman who moves in." Maiguru Chiedza's words chopped my heart into pieces and did not make it easier for me to accept what was going on. When they began dismantling Baba's bed where Mhamha had also slept, Baba desperately negotiated with Mhamha's tribe, explaining that Tongai could inherit the bed, and they agreed. For the first time in a long while, I felt sorry for Baba. When Mhamha's relatives had taken all they could, they left our home for Harare at dusk. I wondered silently whether their ice-cold vigilance in hoarding our belongings was enough to avenge Mhamha's suffering. Tears began streaming down my face uncontrollably, despite making an effort to stop them. Everything in that moment felt so final.

As Maiguru Chiedza's truck drove off slowly, full of things that had made our childhood home feel like a home, I stood in our driveway and watched the end of an era disappearing into the horizon.

A few days later, we were packing our luggage in preparation for our return to the UK. Maya and I had been sleeping in Tizai's bedroom and I found myself inspecting his drawers. I was looking for evidence of why Tizai may have decided to leave and not come back. I still found it difficult to process that Tizai had missed Mhamha's funeral, my wedding, the birth of Maya. Life was carrying on as if he had never existed, except that I silently thought of him every day. We all did. But why had Baba been so nonchalant about his own son's disappearance? As my stream of consciousness ran wild, I opened one more drawer, and there it was.

I carefully pulled out the piece of paper from the drawer and took my time to appreciate it. A relief painting that spoke the pain of a lack of nurturing, the lack of boundaries, hypocrisy, lies, double standards, self-centredness, lack of privacy, jealousy, control, criticism, abuse, victim blaming and shaming; some of the hallmarks of the mire we had grown up in. I had found Tizai's artwork, the Mirage!

When we returned to Harare, I spent as much time as I could visiting Mhamha's final resting place. The visits were never private. An army of comforters always escorted me to Mhamha's grave, and when we got there, I was never allowed to mourn in peace.

"Don't cry! Look, you're the eldest, yet you're crying louder than the younger ones."

"Who will they look up to if you're crying like this?"

"You're now their mother, so you really need to bow to fate."

On my final afternoon in Zimbabwe, during my last visit to Mhamha's grave, my patience had completely worn off to the graveside instructions by Mhamha's people.

"Kneel and clap before you speak. Show her some respect!"

"Tell VaNyemba it is you, her daughter Ruva speaking, and that you have brought her more flowers."

"Promise her you will look after the others."

"Stop crying. How can she rest in peace if you're crying like this?"

"Let her go so she may rest in peace."

"Suck it up!" That was the last straw! I took a deep breath first, then let out the loudest roar of anguish before delivering a cup final.

"None of you get to tell me what to do at my mother's grave! Why should I kneel for her now when I never knelt for her when she was alive? Why should I call her VaNyemba now, when I never used that name when she was alive? Show her some respect, you say? How many of you here kneel for each other but do not actually respect each other? I don't do acting. I respected Mhamha when she was alive, and I always will, and I do that in my own way. I will speak to Mhamha however I want! I will cry as loud as I like! You're a bunch of control freaks! Leave me alone! *Moda kuti ndiseke mai vangu vafa? Kure!* You want me to laugh when my mother has just died? Get away!" The patriarchy murmured quiet disapproval, but I did not care.

The reality that I would not be able to visit Mhamha as much as I would have liked to was weighing on me and I could not bear the thought. It was going to be yet another long-distance relationship between us; one I never imagined would be imposed on us so soon after our five-year reunion in the UK, where our relationship had begun in Dagenham.

A few hours later, my family and I left Zimbabwe and returned to the UK for a cold, sombre Christmas.

Painting a mirage – Who's who

1. Ruva – the narrator
2. Mhamha – Gamuchirai, or Gamu, Ruva's mother
3. Baba – Davis, Ruva's father
4. Morris – also intimately known as Baby, Ruva's high school sweetheart, then husband. Usually referred to as Morris by the narrator when she is upset with him
5. Maya – Ruva and Morris's daughter
6. Tizai – Ruva's first younger brother
7. Tongai – Ruva's second younger brother
8. Runako - Ruva's younger sister
9. Mbuya – Ruva's paternal grandmother
10. Sekuru – Ruva's paternal grandfather
11. Gogo – Ruva's maternal grandmother
12. Khulu – Ruva's maternal grandfather
13. Tete Gwinyai – Ruva's paternal aunt, Baba's first younger sister
14. Tete Gertrude - Ruva's paternal aunt, Baba's second younger sister
15. Tete Primrose - Ruva's paternal aunt, Baba's third younger sister
16. Babamukuru Francis - Tete Primrose's husband
17. Tete Vimbai - Ruva's paternal aunt, Baba's forth younger sister
18. Babamukuru Batanai – Tete Vimbai's husband

19. James – Tete Vimbai's son

20. Tete Mary - Ruva's paternal aunt, Baba's fifth younger sister

21. Babamunini Tafara - Ruva's paternal uncle, Baba's first younger brother

22. Mainini Gemma – Babamunini Tafara's wife

23. Nyarai - Babamunini Tafara's daughter

24. Kudzai - Babamunini Tafara's son

25. Matthew - Babamunini Tafara's son

26. Babamunini Farai - Ruva's paternal uncle, Baba's second younger brother

27. Babamunini Benjy - Ruva's paternal uncle, Baba's third younger brother

28. Maiguru Chiedza – Ruva's maternal aunt, Mhamha's older sister

29. Babamukuru Gilbert – Maiguru Chiedza's husband

30. Mainini Rosey - Ruva's maternal aunt, Mhamha's first younger sister

31. Babamunini Tom – Mainini Rosey's husband

32. Mainini Portia - Ruva's maternal aunt, Mhamha's second younger sister

33. George - Mainini Portia's husband

34. Mainini Joy - Ruva's maternal aunt, Mhamha's third younger sister

35. Sekuru Tonderai - Ruva's maternal uncle, Mhamha's younger brother

36. Mbuya Mavis – Sekuru Tonderai's wife

37. Sekuru John - Ruva's late maternal uncle, Mhamha's younger brother
38. Sisi Fungai – Ruva's childhood housegirl
39. Mukoma Lameck – Tete Gwinyai's driver
40. Gogaz – Tete Gwinyai's housegirl
41. Oliver – Ruva's childhood boyfriend
42. Peter – Ruva's childhood boyfriend
43. Geoff – Ruva's suitor
44. Thomas – Ruva's suitor
45. Brian – Ruva's short-term boyfriend
46. William – Ruva's short-term boyfriend
47. Tawanda – Ruva's long-term boyfriend
48. Nicholas – Ruva's distant paternal cousin, a friend of Peter's
49. Mai Godo – Babamunini Batanai's mother
50. VaGodo - Babamunini Batanai's father
51. VaJongwe – Friend in common to Baba and Bambo, brother-in-law to Babamunini Tafara
52. Mai Jongwe – VaJongwe's wife, older sister to Mainini Gemma
53. Bambo - Morris's father
54. Mhaiyo – Morris's mother
55. Daniel – Morris's older brother
56. Memory – Daniel's wife
57. Valerie – Morris's older sister
58. Calvin – Valerie's husband
59. Maynard – Morris's paternal cousin, Tete Miriam's

son

60. June – Maynard's wife

61. Noel – Morris's paternal cousin, Tete Miriam's son

62. Nigel – Ruva's friend from university

63. Karen – Nigel's university girlfriend

64. Rudo – Ruva's childhood friend and maid of honour

65. Tete Miriam – Bambo's sister, mother to Maynard and Noel

66. John – Ruva's paternal cousin, Tete Gwinyai's son

67. Imogen - Ruva's paternal cousin, Tete Gwinyai's daughter

68. Tsvakai – Ruva's paternal cousin, Tete Gertrude's daughter

69. Tarisai - Ruva's paternal cousin, Tete Gertrude's daughter

70. Jacob – Tsvakai's husband

71. Vatete Guvudzai – Ruva's great aunt, Sekuru's first cousin

72. Babamukuru Pukunyani – Vatete Guvudzai's husband

73. Melanie – Ruva's work colleague

74. Sophie - Ruva's work colleague

75. Jack - Ruva's work colleague

76. Mr. Khan – Mhamha's landlord

77. Belinda – Ruva's friend

78. Bridget – Ruva's friend who she inherited from Tete

Mary

79. Chipiwa - Ruva's high school friend
80. Raviro - Ruva's high school friend
81. Melody - Ruva's high school friend
82. Janet – Sister to Babamunini Farai's ex-girlfriend
83. Jean - Sister to Babamunini Farai's ex-girlfriend
84. Stembile – Sister to Babamunini Farai's ex-girlfriend
85. Chenai - Ruva's maternal cousin, Mainini Rosey's daughter
86. Moira – Ruva's maternal cousin, Maiguru Chiedza's daughter
87. Richard - Ruva's maternal cousin, Maiguru Chiedza's son
88. Angie – Morris's ex-side chick
89. Thandi - Morris's ex-girlfriend
90. Clara – A friend to Ruva
91. Isaac – Clara's husband
92. Alan – Moira's first husband
93. Tendai – Moira's second husband
94. Tanaka - Morris's friend
95. Precious – School prefect at Ruva's boarding house
96. Loveness – a hairdresser friend who Ruva meets through Tete Mary
97. Reem – Ruva's first friend in the UK
98. Michael - A friend to Janet and Jean
99. Fadzai – Ruva's high school friend
100. Nancy – Ruva's hairdresser friend

101. Mai Zorodzai – A family friend who helps to organise Ruva's wedding
102. Mai Zawiza – Ruva's boarding school mistress
103. Kumbirai – Baby's friend and groomsmen
104. Kundai – Baby's friend and civil ceremony witness
105. Beauty – Babamunini Farai's daughter
106. Dorothy – Hairdresser at Mhamha's hair salon
107. Patience – Former worker of Mhamha's
108. Mbuya Shuro – The old woman who "finds" and takes Ruva back to Mbuya
109. Doctor Mbeva – Ruva's childhood family doctor

Ingram Content Group UK Ltd.
Milton Keynes UK
UKHW012321140323
418546UK00004B/89